Praise for **WH** **JOE**

"So good that you never actually notice just how good because you are far too busy turning the pages." *Sunday Telegraph*

"An ice-cold thriller about identity, pain and veracity." *Daily Telegraph*

Praise for **ALM ST TRUE**

"Certainly a book about big questions...
Perhaps Keren David's biggest achievement, however, is that these issues play second fiddle to the psychological authenticity of her troubled hero, and the longing she rouses in the reader for Ty's ultimate redemption."
Books for Keeps

"A thrilling adventure... an emotional roller coaster."
Julia Eccleshare *Lovereading.co.uk*

"Not a single page is wasted. A truly excellent sequel from this talented author. Highly recommended."
Write Away

"Another powerful, utterly compelling novel.
For me, it is really a novel of our time and of our culture. Keren David is a master of suspenseful, contemporary writing."

For I[...]r

First published in Great Britain and the USA in 2012 by
Frances Lincoln Children's Books, 4 Torriano Mews,
Torriano Avenue, London NW5 2RZ
www.franceslincoln.com

A catalogue record for this book is available from the British Library.

ISBN 978-1-84780-286-6

Set in Palatino

Printed and bound by CPI Group (UK) Ltd, Croydon, CR0 4YY
in July 2012

9 8 7 6 5 4 3 2 1

ANOTHER LIFE

Keren David

F

FRANCES LINCOLN
CHILDREN'S BOOKS

CHAPTER 1
Plan A

There's a matchbox of weed sitting on the headmaster's desk – good quality Dutch skunk. I can smell it, sweet and strong, from my uncomfortably low chair, which has been carefully positioned so I am looking up Father Roderick's flared nostrils.

He knows and I know that it came from my bedside locker drawer.

I'm not admitting it, though. I'm not the son of two top lawyers for nothing.

'Just tell me how you got the drugs into the school,' says Father Roderick in his smoothest, most sympathetic voice. 'I need to know the full facts, Archie, before we decide what action to take. You may need help; this may not even be your doing.'

I don't want him to think I'm innocent. That would

scupper my chance of getting expelled. But I'm certainly not admitting anything. I'm staying in the grey area of silence.

I shrug. He sighs.

'I have contacted your parents. It appears your mother is abroad, but your father is on his way.' He looks at his watch – a plain, brown leather strap, a simple black and white face. I'd so hate being a monk. I bet he wears really scratchy underwear.

'He said he'd be here by three. I suggest you sit here and have a good think about your options, while we wait for him.'

That's three hours – three hours of no lunch, nothing to drink, nothing to do. God, it's so boring just thinking. Father Roderick gets on with his work – loads of rustling papers and clicking at his keyboard. I wonder if he's looking at porn. I wonder if his computer's got a whole history of busty blondes and Asian babes. If he's dim enough to leave the room without logging out – he has to get some lunch, surely – maybe I could run round to the other side of the desk and infect his screen with some tasty pop-ups. I imagine Father Roderick's horrified face, his round, blue, innocent eyes widening in horror. I turn a laugh into a cough.

'I'm glad you find this amusing, because I don't,' he says. 'Ahh, thank you, Miss Johnson.'

Miss Johnson is his secretary and she's just brought him a massive sandwich – chicken on granary with mayo and lettuce. We never get food like that. We get watery mashed snotballs, chewy donkey-arse stew and fried incontinence pads. This place is like something on a boring TV documentary about the third world. Father Roderick tucks into his sandwich noisily. I ignore him.

I'm sure he's actually not allowed to starve me like this. It's virtually torture. I bet the European Court of Human Rights would have something to say about the way I'm being treated. When my dad arrives, I'll get him to look up the UN declaration on the rights of children on his iPhone.

My dad. He's not going to be very pleased with me. He really disapproves of drugs and rule-breaking and getting expelled. On the other hand, I don't think he was all that happy when Mum cooked up this idea of sending me to a super-strict Catholic boys' school ('We succeed with the boys that other schools fail').

'I should have been consulted, not presented with a fait accompli. You know my feelings about faith schools,' he said, when I was packing to go off to Allingham Priory. And then he said a load more. I was really hopeful that they'd call the whole thing off, but Mum just rolled her eyes and said, 'Look, it wasn't so easy finding anywhere that would take him, after he got chucked out of Hadley House – and don't think we've forgotten how naughty that was, Archie, because we haven't – and you weren't exactly around to go looking at schools.'

'Well, nor were you,' Dad pointed out. 'We were both abroad. You got your secretary to ring around. What did you tell her? "Can you find somewhere traditional where monks will make sure Archie is steeped in his Catholic heritage?"'

'Not at all. I just asked Christina to find somewhere with high academic standards that could take on a challenge – a challenge who'd just been expelled for booking a strippergram for his housemaster's birthday. We were lucky to find him somewhere so quickly. I'm sure it's just what he needs. Discipline. High standards. It'll be fine, won't it, Archie?'

'No,' I said, 'it won't. I really, really don't want to go. Can't I stay at home and go to a day school? Please?'

Then Dad went all grumpy and said, 'I don't think we can trust you at home when we're away so much,' and Mum said, 'Don't be silly. You'd be lonely all by yourself at home. You're much better off at school surrounded by friends and with loads of things to do.'

I tried again during the summer holidays, but they were both busy at work and they'd booked me into tennis camp and when I came home there was no one to whinge to except Veselina the cleaner, who only speaks Albanian or whatever.

So I went round to my friend Oscar, who lives virtually next door, and we started plotting my escape. Plan A, provided by Oscar's older brother Marcus (without his knowledge, obviously), is in a matchbox on Father Roderick's desk.

The bell rings for the end of lunch. Father Roderick stands up.

'Miss Johnson,' he calls, 'can you come and sit with Archie Stone, please? I have to go and teach.'

Miss Johnson bustles in. She's about fifty and the general consensus is that she's got the hots for Father Roderick and stays in her job in the hope that one day he will see the error of his monkish ways, renounce celibacy and take her ancient virginity on the hearthrug. Maybe he has already. It looks quite well-worn. She's always been really nice to me before,

5

but she's obviously been tipped off about the hidden stash of weed, because she's stony-faced as she takes Father Roderick's chair and sits down.

I wait until he's plodded off in the direction of the sixth form extension. Then I sigh and wipe my brow. No response. I try again, a little louder.

She can't resist my best victim face.

'What is it, Archie? Anything to tell me?'

'I'm hungry, miss. I'm starving. I get low blood sugar if I don't eat and I think I might faint.' I lift up my hand, let it tremble a little. 'Look, I'm shaking.'

Naturally, I've stolen all this from my Nana Bertha, who is eighty-five, borderline diabetic and a total drama queen. Whenever we see her – every Christmas – she pretends to be at death's door. It drives my dad crazy, because he has to play along.

Miss Johnson falls for it.

'Oh dear . . . I can't leave you. Do you feel bad? You'd better have a biscuit.' And she opens Father Roderick's special cupboard.

By the time my dad arrives at 3.35, I've eaten an entire packet of chocolate HobNobs, she's made me a cup of tea, I'm sitting on Father Roderick's sofa-for-prospective-parents and we're having a boring but friendly chat about her hobby, which is breeding Abyssinian guinea pigs. One of my many skills is the ability to talk to anyone. It's an undervalued asset. I could marry into the royal family any time and fit right in.

One of the sixth-formers brings Dad to the study. I have a bit of a shock when he arrives. His eyes are a bit baggier than usual, and the way he's hunched his shoulders – well, I'm kind of used to my dad being older than everyone else's but I don't like to see him looking like an old man.

Then he snaps, 'Hello Archie, I thought you were in deep trouble, but it appears I was wrong,' and I remember that he's actually only fifty-five and last year the *Financial Times* called him 'Possibly the most energetic and aggressive corporate lawyer currently operating in the City of London. Definitely someone you want on your side.'

Miss Johnson jumps up guiltily, and tells the sixth-former to go and get Father Roderick.

'Archie, you'd better come and sit over here again,' she says.

I brush the biscuit crumbs onto the Rug of Desire, and think about whether I should hug my dad or not. But he's too busy handing his coat to Miss Johnson. She goes off to hang it up and he hisses at me, 'I hope you haven't said anything to give them reason to call in the police.'

'I haven't said anything,' I say, and he nods, face set and unsmiling.

'Good.'

Father Roderick runs through the school's procedure when drugs are found on the premises – calling in the police, suspension and/or expulsion.

'Of course we greatly regret involving the police, but possession of drugs is a criminal offence.'

'I can see a small amount of drugs on your desk,' says my dad, cool and calm, 'but nothing at all to link my son with them. It would appear that you currently possess these drugs, and therefore you are the one who will need to speak to the police.'

Father Roderick turns purple.

'My son is only fourteen years old, and I would prefer him not to spend any more time in an educational institution where drugs are so readily available,' says my dad, looking at his Rolex. He only wears it when he's away from the office. At work he has a much plainer watch so his clients won't feel they're being ripped off.

'These drugs were found amongst Archie's things,' says Father Roderick.

'Then you should have called the police immediately and left the evidence in situ. I shall be taking Archie away with me today, and my assistant will be sending you an agreement to sign which makes it clear that we have removed him from school and you will not be giving him a bad report when we approach other schools, or accusing him of anything to do with drugs. Is that acceptable? Or shall we discuss the laws of libel?'

Woo! Go Dad! I'm hoping that he'll actually believe someone planted the drugs in my stuff, and then I won't get into any trouble at all.

And there's no way they can send me to another boarding school after this.

Dad turns to me. 'Archie,' he says, 'I want you packed and ready to leave in thirty minutes. I'll meet you in the front hall.'

'Err. . .' I say, wondering how I'm going to achieve that when I have absolutely no idea where they put our cases after we unpack on the first day of term. Miss Johnson will have to tell me.

And that's it. No need for goodbyes, no need for supper (chilli con concrete and apple puke), last glimpse of Father Roderick, spitting mad and virtually foaming at the mouth. Ha! Even better than I'd hoped!

I heave my case (there's a storeroom, it turns out, by the sixth form studies) into the back of the Prius (bought to impress clients with Dad's caring attitude towards the environment – he says that as soon as he retires he's getting a BMW).

I do up my seat belt. I sigh with relief as the car glides through the school gates.

I'm ready for Dad's lecture, ready to be told off. Whatever he says, it was well worth it. I'm smug in the knowledge that any risks I took weren't just for me.

The thing is, I made a promise – a promise that I'd be somewhere at a certain time. The time is next Tuesday, and the place is a courtroom in north London.

I'm going to be there for my cousin Ty.

CHAPTER 2
Judgement

Ty isn't a bad person. He's a bit violent, maybe, but nothing excessive. Mostly he's just really unlucky in being in the wrong place at the wrong time with the wrong people, saying and doing the wrong things.

He's got this thing called post-traumatic stress disorder, which basically means that exciting but potentially scary things like wars and murders send you round the twist. When we googled it, there was a list of millions of symptoms and Ty had nearly all of them.

Ty didn't go to war but he did see a murder, and one of the people who did the murdering came from this big criminal family and they decided to shut Ty up so he couldn't tell what he'd seen.

That was a year and a half ago and they've been trying to shut him up ever since. Even though they're mostly all in prison now, he's still in hiding, just in case.

Anyway, that's not his biggest problem today. Today's all about what the judge thinks is a suitable punishment for two counts of carrying an offensive weapon.

Grandpa picked me up this morning, which was really nice of him because it was a bit of a detour. I recruited his help when Dad was unbelievably resistant to me going to the court. Grandpa's normally a bit grumpy, and he totally wasn't impressed by the Freedom Matchbox stunt, but he phoned up my mum and told her he'd take me.

'Do him good, Penelope, to see how justice works,' he told her, 'find that actions have consequences. Archie can be moral support for Tyler as well.'

Dad didn't give up the fight – he thinks Ty's a bad influence, and I'm not sure he's that keen on Grandpa, either. But Mum pursed her lips and said, 'Look, Ty's a member of the family.' And Dad humphed a bit, muttering, 'Oh well, there's no arguing with The Family,' making us sound like the Mafia.

I think he's a bit jealous, because there are loads of us Tylers and when we sort of discovered Ty last year, that made another one. Dad's only got Nana

Bertha and she's in sheltered accommodation in Essex and he sees her about once a year. He says he can just take small doses of her toxic personality, although she always fusses over me and gives me After Eights.

Mum and Dad have been arguing a lot, anyway, about me and the matchbox, and what school I might be going to. Both my parents are professional arguers, and they practise a lot at home.

Anyway, it's only after we get to the court building and everyone's standing around outside, smoking and/or making awkward polite conversation, that Grandpa tells me that I'm not going to be allowed to go in to see what happens.

'But that's totally *unfair*!' I protest.

Ty's leaning against the courtroom wall, looking a bit pale and nibbling his thumbnail. He still manages a half smile.

'I'm happy to swap. Why not? Go ahead, Arch, you do it instead of me.'

I pretend to consider the offer.

'I'm sure I'd be able to persuade the judge to let you off. I'll just treat him to some classic one-liners—'

'No, I think I'd better go in myself,' he says quickly. 'You'd probably get me a life sentence.'

I laugh, and Ty's gran shoots me an evil glare.

'This isn't a joke,' she says. 'Doesn't give a good impression, does it, you two larking around. Stand up straight, Tyler, for goodness sake.'

I can't really see what difference it's going to make, but Ty stops leaning on the wall and tightens the knot of his tie. He's unnaturally smart in dark trousers, a white shirt and a blue nylon tie – school uniform, I should think. His eyes look even bigger than normal, gleaming, pale khaki against his tan. His nails are bitten so far down that they're virtually bleeding stumps.

What's unfortunate is that he's been working out all summer, and his bulging upper-body muscles kind of show despite the smart clothes. I'm jealous as hell, of course, and feel really puny and soft in comparison, but anyone can see that this isn't a good look when you're on trial for violent offences.

'It'll be OK,' I tell him. 'It's just two counts of carrying a knife. You'll probably just have to do community service, like cleaning graffiti or picking up litter.'

I'm trying to sound like I know everything there is to know about the legal system, but actually I'm just spouting what Grandpa said in the car. He's distracting Ty's gran by asking her how her other daughters are doing. They've both skipped the country, and who can blame them, because since Ty told the police about the murder he witnessed, the whole family has been numero uno target of some massive mob of gangsters.

Ty's parents are chatting to some a guy who's his lawyer, and they seem to be having an argument. This isn't totally surprising. Ty's mum is the most explosive woman in the world, and his dad is kind of unpredictable.

'That is totally *unfair*.'

I jump, because for one minute I think that there's some weird psychic time warp going on, but then I realise that it's my uncle Danny speaking.

'How come they only let one parent go in? And why does it have to be you?'

'Obviously it's going to be me,' says Ty's mum, and he just shuts right up. Anyone would. Although she looks completely gorgeous, and soft and gentle as well, there's something about Nicki (that's what Ty calls her, so I do too) that means you just don't argue with her unless it's totally necessary, e.g. if a gunman is about to shoot her and she hasn't noticed and is refusing to move.

That's the kind of scenario I think up sometimes,

and how I'd have to leap on her to get her out of the way, and how grateful she'd be when she realised what danger I'd saved her from and. . .

I know it's wrong to perv after my aunt. But a) she's not a blood relation and b) she's not really like an aunt at all, because I never knew Nicki and Ty at all before last year. There was some huge family row years ago and they never got in contact with us. I only got to know them because Ty had to stay with our grandparents after some boyfriend of his mum's got shot by the people hunting after Ty.

He's had a really exciting life compared to me, stuck in a stupid boarding school.

'It'll be fine,' I say to Ty, and he rolls his eyes and says, 'Yeah, right, Archie, I believe you.'

'It will. I'll send special telepathic messages to the judge and get him to let you off completely. After all, it's only the two offences, and the one in the park doesn't really count, does it, because your friend Arron didn't make a complaint about you.'

'Yeah, but I admitted that one.'

'And then the other one doesn't really count either, does it, because you just took the knife after you were mugged on that bus?'

'I don't know if they believe that.' His breathing's

a bit jittery. 'The CCTV wasn't working on the bus. They say there's no proof. And when the police tried to search me, I ran away and they don't like that either.'

He's not only always in the wrong place at the wrong time. Ty also makes some pretty crap decisions.

'Oh well. It's not much, is it?'

'No, but there's a third one now.'

'A third one?'

'Ashley – she was my girlfriend. She went to the police and told them I had a knife.'

'What a cow!'

He shakes his head and I'm going to ask him more – who's this Ashley, anyway? – when they call his name, his witness protection name. I don't even realise until he's turning away to follow his mum and his lawyer.

'Good luck!' I call after him, and he glances back over his shoulder and does that half-smile again.

'Bloody hell,' says Danny, tugging at his tie. I've never seen him look so smart. I'm betting the suit is Armani, and the violet tie is awesome. Usually he's all ripped jeans and leather jacket, wild hair and stubble, but today he's smooth, sleek and tidy.

I never really knew him when I was growing up because he was too busy being a rock star (great music too, better than Muse or Linkin Park, I swear) and taking drugs, avoiding his family and just generally being the coolest dude ever.

Ty didn't even know him, and Ty's his son.

He's stopped being a rock star now and stopped taking drugs. He's a photographer to the stars, and one of my ambitions is to work for him and entertain his clients with my banter.

We go into the court building and sit in a row – Danny and Ty's gran and Grandpa and me. Ty's gran is trying to entertain his little baby sister Alyssa by waving toys at her, but you can see the baby's not interested and just wants to slobber and cry. In the end, Ty's gran sticks her in the buggy and takes her for a walk to try and get her to sleep.

Grandpa and Danny just sit there in silence, until Danny bursts out with, 'It really isn't fair! She just blocks me out as much as she can! And the system lets her get away with it.'

'It's difficult for you, I understand,' says Grandpa.

'I'm trying to be there for him. I'm doing my best. I even cancelled a shoot with Cheryl Cole to be here today. . .'

Grandpa's silent. I bet he's wondering who Cheryl Cole is. Then he heaves a big sigh and says, 'Patience is the most important part of parenthood; that's what I've learnt over the last forty-odd years.'

This is all a bit heavy, and it doesn't seem to have cheered up Danny at all, so I interrupt.

'What are we going to do to celebrate when it's over?'

'Maybe a curry,' Danny says vaguely, but Grandpa snaps, 'I think we'll need to get Ty out of London as quickly as possible. It's not exactly the safest place for him,' and quite soon afterwards Danny goes outside to have a cigarette.

How long can it take to decide what to do with someone for carrying a knife? This is mad. In some places (the Australian outback, for example, or bits of America) it's totally normal to have a knife on you, just in case you need to skin a rabbit or something. I've seen it on films. Why should London be any different? There are loads of squirrels and foxes and pigeons. Actually, in America it's your right to arm yourself all the time. If I were American I'd probably carry a pistol, just in case. Why is England so stupid?

'They're taking ages. What are they doing?'

'They'll be considering the factors that the judge

19

has to take into account when sentencing,' says Grandpa. 'I should think there will be a report by a social worker. Heaven knows, there are plenty of mitigating factors. He was only fourteen, for a start. I'm sure we've got nothing to worry about.'

'Oh right.'

Then we just sit there and pretend not to be worrying together. It's really boring.

Danny comes back and so does Ty's gran and they start talking about the baby (thank God she is asleep) and how funny and clever and amazing she is, just because she's learned to clap her hands or something equally basic.

I can't believe that all the excitement is happening behind closed doors, when I'm stuck out here. Plus I can't help feeling that if I were there, I could somehow help Ty. . . I'm not sure how, but I feel like I've failed him, abandoned him, let him down. . .

A door opens. Nicki comes striding out of the courtroom, followed by the lawyer. Her face is pink. Her mouth is slightly open. Danny leaps to his feet.

'What happened? Where's Ty?'

Her mouth opens and closes, like a goldfish. No sound comes out.

'I'm sorry,' says the lawyer.

'What . . . you mean—'

Danny's looking frantically about him. 'They can't have, not for that – not right away—'

'Nicki!' says Ty's gran. 'Tell us! What happened?'

Nicki's mouth is moving, but the words still don't come. Then she makes a noise like she's going to be sick and covers her mouth with both hands. The words are muffled as they flood out.

'They said . . . she said, the judge . . . she said he was very young . . . and he hadn't been in trouble before. And he hadn't . . . he was a good boy. Tell them, Mum, he was always a good boy. . . But then, then she . . . she said three times was a lot . . . like a habit . . . and she said . . . too many kids were carrying knives. . .'

'How long?' said Grandpa, and I don't think I've ever heard him sound so grim. That's when I realise what everyone else seems to know.

'Twelve weeks,' says Nicki. 'I didn't even get to say goodbye.'

CHAPTER 3
Losers

'How was he?' asks Grandpa, and Nicki gulps a bit and says, 'Just blank. He was in shock – never even looked at me.'

The lawyer coughs, and Nicki and Danny go off with him down the corridor. Their conversation starts in whispers, but it doesn't take long for the volume to go up. He makes his escape quite quickly.

'He's going to lodge an appeal against the sentence,' says Danny, striding back to us. 'Jesus. Talk about useless.'

'When can we see him, Nicki, did you ask?' says Ty's gran. Nicki is white-faced, dry-eyed.

'I told him,' she said, and her voice is almost a growl. 'I told him never to get into trouble. "I won't come and see you in prison," I said. I told him.'

'It'll only be six weeks,' says Grandpa, 'assuming he behaves himself.'

'Six weeks,' wails Ty's gran, 'it's a disaster, a disaster.'

Nicki snaps, 'Stop crying, Mum, it's not going to help anyone. It's OK. It's only six weeks. At least we'll know he's safe.'

And then everyone realises all at once that a Young Offender Institution is a really unsafe place for Ty to be.

Danny and I run after the lawyer. We catch up with him on the street. Danny grabs his arm.

'Ty – he's got enemies, kids in custody. What if they put him in with some of them? What's going to happen then?'

'They know his background,' says the lawyer, in a smooth, get-your-hands-off-me kind of voice. 'They know they need to be careful about his security.'

'They'd better,' says Danny.

They won't, I think. I know Ty's opinion of police protection, and it's not high.

We go and sit in a greasy spoon, opposite the court, just like the end of *The Apprentice*. I could point this out, but I'm not sure if they even watch it and they all seem too gloomy to be cheered up by being compared to a bunch of losers.

They order tea and coffee. I get egg and beans on

toast, chips, a diet coke and an iced bun. Nicki wrinkles her nose when my food arrives. Danny says to her, 'What about a sandwich or something?' She shakes her head. I douse my chips in vinegar, ketchup and a splash of mayo.

'What the hell did they think they were doing,' says Danny, 'putting him in prison, for that . . . for nothing? For carrying a knife. Jesus.'

Nicki's staring into her coffee. 'Oh come on,' she says. 'Why wouldn't they? We all know what happens when young lads run around with knives. People get killed. Ty's bright enough to know he was doing wrong. I've warned him, all his life I've warned him. "Don't get into trouble," I told him. "Don't get in with the bad boys. Keep your head down, keep out of trouble, work hard at school." Don't blame *me* for this. It's not *my* fault.'

'No one says it's your fault,' says Grandpa, 'least of all Ty. I'm sure he knows very well that this is all his own mess. But to put him in prison – I mean, what do they expect to achieve? The most likely thing is that it'll set him off on a life of crime. Those Young Offender Institutions, they're like academies of crime. Community service, surely, would've been more appropriate.'

'Thanks a lot, Dad,' says Danny, glaring furiously across the table.

'I'm going to ring your mother,' says Grandpa, completely oblivious. 'She'll want to know what's happened.'

He can't get a signal on his mobile in the café, so he goes outside. Danny puts his arm around Nicki.

'It'll be OK,' he murmurs into her hair. 'Six weeks he'll serve, just six weeks. It'll be OK.'

Ty's gran is shovelling mashed banana into the baby's gaping mouth. Her face is candle-pale and little drops of sweat bead her forehead.

The baby spits and dribbles the banana, and in the end Ty's gran gives up and hands her a biscuit.

'How's your mum, Archie love, how are the family?' she asks – she used to be my mum's nanny back in the olden days – but when I start telling her about everyone, tears streak down her face again and she disappears into her tissue.

'What's going to become of him?' she wails. 'Poor Ty – he's been doing so well . . . really settled down . . . running again . . . working hard for his GCSEs. . .'

I look over the other side of the table for help, but Danny and Nicki are having a long, intense, whispered conversation, heads together, his arm round her.

Grandpa's still outside. It's my job to try and cheer her up.

'Umm . . . I'm sure he'll be OK,' I say. 'I read somewhere that Young Offender Institutions are actually really good places. You get PlayStation and everything – television in your cell. It's actually meant to be more like a holiday camp nowadays. That's what this man said in my dad's newspaper.'

'Oh,' she says faintly. Her breathing's a bit rattly. 'A holiday camp? Really?'

'Actually it sounded better than my boarding school,' I say, savouring another loaded forkful of egg and chips. 'We only got television for two hours on a Saturday evening. And we had to pray all the time. I bet they don't make them pray at all in a Young Offender Institution.'

Oh-oh. I forgot Ty's gran is a holy roller bible-thumper. She gasps and puts her hand on her chest like I've punched her.

'A priest. . .' she says, and then falls silent, apart from her noisy breathing. Maybe she's asthmatic.

Nicki breaks off her heart-to-heart. I'm gazing at her. I can't help it. So is every man there. She's got shiny dark red hair and huge blue eyes, and you can quite clearly see a hint of white lace bra under her silky blouse when she leans over towards me – as she's doing now. Jesus.

Sometimes there are moments when you have to keep your mind off things . . . you know . . . and I find the London Underground very useful. The Bakerloo line is particularly calming. Elephant and Castle. Lambeth North.

Nicki pokes me in the chest, quite painfully, and says, 'Look, Archie, can't you see she's upset? Don't make things worse, for heavens' sake.'

'I'm not making things worse at all,' I say, thrilled that she's touched me, and then Danny shrugs and says, 'Hard to see how things could be worse. The lawyer said Ty might be able to ring tonight. Let's hope that's soon.'

'There you are,' I say. 'They didn't let us phone home for two solid weeks when we got to school. Meant to be unsettling. It does sound like they have it easier than us.'

Ty's probably making friends and looking around, playing PlayStation or watching telly and can't be bothered to phone home and get shouted at for something that wasn't his fault at all, i.e. getting sent to prison when he ought to have got community service instead.

Ty's gran gasps again, and now the sweat is trickling down her forehead. It's a bit embarrassing. Nicki sniffs and looks away and Danny rolls his eyes. I don't know why. I've just been reassuring them.

Grandpa comes striding back into the café, and straight away he says, 'Good God! Are you all right? Someone call an ambulance!'

And I'm just wondering who the hell he's talking to, when Ty's gran groans and slumps forward, face down, splat into the mashed banana.

CHAPTER 4
Home Sweet Home

I try to talk to the people at the court, but no one listens to me. They put me in a cell – white-walled, smelling of bleach and piss – and say, 'Tell it to the officers when you get there.'

I try to talk to the security guards who put me in the van. 'I'm in witness protection,' I say, 'and the thing is—'

They don't want to know either. 'Shut up,' says one, 'and put your hands out in front of you.' He pulls out some cuffs, locks me into them. The metal bites my wrists and makes me feel – I don't know – like a slave, subhuman, expelled from normal life.

In the back of the van there are compartments – long, tall, thin compartments, like a cross between a coffin and a Portaloo. There's a little shelf to sit on, and that's it. There's no seatbelt or anything, and it's incredibly hot and I can feel my breath bunching in my throat.

'What if I need to pee?' I ask the guy, and he laughs and says, 'That's your problem.'

And then we drive and drive and drive, and I can hear one guy retching, which makes me feel sick, and I'm boiling hot and sweating in floods and hurting all over and just trying to focus on breathing – breathing and enduring – as though I was running, except with none of the joy and freedom.

And I try not to think about who might be waiting for me at this prison.

Arron, who I put away for murder.

Or Jukes, who's already tried to kill me once.

Or even Mikey, because my evidence got him put away as well.

I told the truth. It's nearly killed me four times already. It's put me in constant danger.

Was it worth it?

I don't know how many Young Offender Institutions there are in London. I've only heard of one or two. I'm trying to remember which one Arron was in – I can't – but what if there are only two or three in the whole country? What will I do if they're all there waiting for me?

That can't be true. It can't be. Politicians are always banging on about locking people up. They've got to have loads of places to put them. It's probably really incredibly unlikely that anyone ever ends up with anyone they know.

Probably.

I've known this could happen ever since they charged me. I've done really well at blocking it, all these months. I've been running and studying and babysitting. But I can't block it any more.

The only good thing is that worrying about what might happen when I get there stops me thinking about Mum and Gran and Alyssa and everything else I left behind.

The van stops, and I wonder if it's a service station or whether we've arrived. Then the guard comes round and opens the doors and tells me to get out. I'm a bit dizzy and I stumble as I hit the ground. He shoves me back into place.

'No funny business,' he growls.

And then they take me inside and take off the cuffs and hand me over to a uniformed officer.

'Luke Smith,' he says.

'Yes, but, you see I'm. . . '

He glances at me. 'You're what?'

'I'm . . . errr. . .'

What if the gangsters have got their own guys on the staff of this prison? It's possible, isn't it? After all, that's how they found out where we were living before. They paid some girl who was working in the witness protection office. What if they're paying this man?

'I need to pee,' I say, and he says, 'That'll have to wait.'

The room they take me into is quite large, and there are a few other guys there. They're mostly older than me – eighteen, nineteen, maybe. Some look nervous. Some look bored.

'You new?' says one, in a Liverpool accent, and I nod warily, because obviously I'm new, and he says, 'I mean, this is your first time?'

'Yeah.'

'How'd you like the sweatbox?'

'The what?'

'Sweatbox. Van.' He glances at my wet hair and shirt. 'Hot, eh? Even in November.'

'Yeah, it was.'

'What're you in for?'

'Carrying a knife,' I say and he whistles and says, 'Unlucky. You'd normally get off with a bit of community service for that. I did six months of cleaning graffiti last year. Mind you, it was a right pain, had to get up when it was still dark. And I don't like them electronic tags, they bring out my eczema.'

'What're you in for?' I ask. He seems OK. Friendly, even.

'Burglary,' he says. 'Cops caught me climbing out of a bathroom window.'

One by one the guys are being called to a desk. They have a short conversation with an officer there, and then they're sent through a door. No one comes back.

'What happens through there?' I ask him.

He grins. 'Don't you know? You're going to get a surprise.'

'What?'

'Nah, not telling. Wait and see.' His smile isn't so friendly. He's laughing at me.

I can't believe I'm here, can't believe this is real. But I look at my wrists. They're bleeding where the cuffs rubbed my skin. This is happening right now, and it's happening to me. And there's absolutely nothing I can do about it.

They call my name – my Luke Smith false name

– and I go forward to the desk. The guy consults his paperwork and asks if I'm OK.

'You're one of the youngest here,' he says. 'I should tell you that it's a frightening experience at first, but there are people here to support you. It is not an adult prison. We recognise that you are a minor.'

I almost tell him. I almost lean forward and tell him that I'm in witness protection and I'm shit scared that the prison will be packed with the people I'm hiding from. He seems nice. He actually smiles at me.

But that's just what he'd do if he was spying for the gangsters.

And then he says, 'Go through that door and take off all your clothes. Put them in the box provided. Then walk through the second door and someone will meet you there.'

I think I've misheard. 'You mean everything except underwear, yeah?'

He shakes his head. 'We need to search you. You'll be given everything you need afterwards.'

If the cuffs made me feel like a slave, then getting naked and having men looking at me – touching me – makes me feel like a piece of meat. Except that a piece of meat doesn't feel anything. And I do.

When the judge said I was being sentenced to

twelve weeks in custody, she never said one word about having someone put on rubber gloves and stick a finger up my bum.

I swear, that's what they do. They should tell you. They should say, 'We're going to lock you away, but first we'll assault you.' I bet there'd be an outcry. I bet MPs would get up in parliament and talk about human rights and stuff.

Who am I kidding? They'd probably say it should happen more often.

I look around for my box of clothes afterwards, but they hand me a pile of stuff and say, 'Get dressed.' And that's when I realise that I'm going to have to wear boxers and socks that some other guy was in last week. It's disgusting. I'm grateful to be covering myself up, but the thought of it makes me want to heave. I mean, I'm used to wearing second-hand stuff – Mum got a lot of my clothes from Help the Aged – but never *underwear*.

I retch when I'm putting it on, but nothing comes out, and I take a deep breath and try and think of something else. Nothing comes to mind, though. Normality doesn't exist any more.

The T-shirt is bright orange and the trackie bottoms are grey – not a great combination. There are jeans and a blue shirt as well, grey socks, white trainers, which smell new and cheap and pinch my heels.

'We're going to take your photo now,' says an officer, and he takes me into a corner, lines me up against a wall. I remember all those times I'd been told to smile for the camera. Birthdays. School photos. First communion. Photos are for happy times, aren't they? Photos are there to remind you that you're growing and doing good and achieving stuff. Who knew they'd want a photo when you're hardly feeling human any more?

There's only one way to deal with this. It's not me that they're looking at. It's some stupid, stupid guy called Luke who didn't have the brains to realise that putting a knife in your pocket could lead to handcuffs and rubber gloves and having to wear minging boxers which must've been worn by hundreds of other people.

They let me use the loo, and then I have to talk to another person – a big guy, with a beard. Mr Wilde, he's called.

'I'm your key worker,' he says. 'I'll be sorting out your education programme, and keeping an eye on you generally. If you've got a problem, you need to talk to me about it.'

This is my moment. But I'm so tired that I don't think I could get any words in the right order, even if I thought it was safe to talk about what's bothering me.

'Do you want to call home?' he asks.

I suppose I'd better. I don't really want to hear what my mum has to say. But when I call, the phone rings and rings and no one answers. Maybe she's turned it off. Maybe she doesn't want to hear from me.

He's reading through my file.

'Ah. I see. We've got a problem, haven't we?'

I freeze. What does it say?

'You've been in witness protection. You must be nervous about coming in here.'

Someone knows! I'm half relieved, half terrified. I nod, watch his hands as they flick through the papers.

'We'll need to review your security, double check that this will be a safe environment for you,' he says.

I nod again.

'Don't worry, though. You'll be in a single room, because of your age. You'll be known as Luke Smith, which I'm assuming is not your real name. You're a long way from London, which I gather is where you started out.'

I can't think of one thing to say.

'Don't draw attention to yourself, and we'll discuss your situation with the Metropolitan Police, see if we need to move you,' he says. 'You'll spend most of your time in the classroom or your room. I see you're taking some GCSEs.'

His plan for making sure I'm safe seems to be to plonk me down in the middle of a prison full of potential killers and make a phone call to the police in London to see if they think I'll survive. Given that I nearly got shot twice under their care, I don't think I'm going to have much time to work towards external examinations.

'It'll be OK,' he says. 'Right, let's show you where you're going to be.'

As we walk through the prison, through echoing corridors, past rows of closed doors, he explains a few things. I'll get supper in my room – there's usually a choice, but tonight I'll have to eat what I'm given. I'll get woken up between 7.30 and 8 am, and breakfast around 8 am. Education starts at 8.45 am. I'll be meeting with someone to see which classes I fit into. They only teach a few GCSEs – 'There are lots of vocational courses too, might be interesting for you. Woodwork and gardening and mechanics. Some of our older trainees have jobs, but for you younger ones it's a real chance to improve your qualifications.'

Woodwork means drills and saws. Mechanics means screwdrivers and jacks. They've kitted out a whole prison so people can kill me.

He opens a door. 'Here you go. Home sweet home.'

It could be worse, I suppose. There's a bed and a cupboard and a TV on the wall. I look around for the remote, and he says, 'The TV won't work at first. You have to earn it. Good behaviour. You can earn points towards a radio, then a TV, then even a PlayStation.'

'Oh, right.' I wonder how long it takes to earn the right to watch sodding *EastEnders*. Will I be here long enough? How much do I care?

There's a loo and a sink and a towel. It's not the cosiest bedroom ever, but at least there's no one sharing it with me.

'OK, lad,' he says. 'They'll bring your food quite soon. You must be hungry, eh? Normally you'd have association now, or you'd be using the gym, but you can do that tomorrow. Lights go out at 11. You'll be woken up at 7.30.'

I wish he'd just go. I'm overloaded with information.

'Your door will be locked at 8.30 pm, but there is a panic button here – see it? – for use in emergencies. OK? See you tomorrow.'

When he's gone the room suddenly seems smaller and the quiet presses down on me, like a pillow over my head. I'm not sure I can breathe in here.

I sit and stare at the sink, wonder if there's a way of cleaning away the dirty feeling that's creeping over my skin. There isn't, I'm sure of it.

I'm trying to avoid thinking about people that I care about. I don't want Alyssa, Gran, Mum anywhere near my head at the moment. But I can't keep Claire out. She's my . . . my best friend, my love. She's clean and honest and there's no hiding from her.

I can't bear it. They've put me down in the dirt where I'm too low to even think about Claire.

There's a rattling noise. My door is opening.

'Supper,' says a voice.

I look up. I see a trolley laden with trays. I see a sandwich, an apple, a packet of crisps.

And the person handing them to me, I see him too. I see his long legs, his dirty nails, his short blond hair.

I see his brown eyes, the scar running from eye

to chin, the tattoo on his neck. 'Tanya,' it reads, 'forever.'

I know those eyes. I know those legs. I remember that tattoo.

Jesus. I was there when it was done.

CHAPTER 5
Lily and Oscar

I'm lying on a huge springy double bed with Lily – the girl of my dreams, ever since I started having dreams with girls in them.

She's sixteen – an older woman – she's got long legs and skinny shoulders, springy blonde fusilli curls and freckles splattered over her little stubby nose. She's one of those girls who kind of exudes gorgeousness, so that it doesn't matter what she looks like, although, actually, she looks great.

And this isn't a dream, it's the bed in Oscar's parents' bedroom. Lily and I are lying on a slippery green bedcover, surrounded by little brown cushions – like a field full of cowpats done in satin – and Oscar's sitting at his mum's dressing table, straightening his hair.

Even though both of us are completely fully-clothed,

it's still exciting enough to be lying this close to Lily that I have to focus on the chandelier light fitting – all white and tinkly and a bit cobwebby – try not to breathe in her spicy smell, and occasionally travel the Bakerloo line.

Things have been slightly difficult. Mum and Dad are completely fixated on the whole drug find thing, which is one big joke considering it was all a set-up. I get non-stop anti-drug lectures when they're home, which isn't all that often. And they're always arguing about what school to send me to. It's a bit boring.

In the end, to shut them up, I offered to go to the local comprehensive.

'You'd get murdered on day one,' said my dad, and Mum added, 'Have you seen the results? Only thirty per cent pass five GCSEs. It's a scandal.'

'I'll definitely pass more than five GCSEs,' I said. I'm not boasting, it's just that I find school quite easy. It's like Ty being good at running – just a natural talent. 'I could improve their statistics.'

'Don't talk nonsense, Archie,' Dad grunted. So now they're looking into really expensive tutorial colleges in central London – yes! – or small, caring boarding schools.

It's a bummer that Ty's in prison and not allowed

a mobile. I can't even ring him for a chat. Luckily I've got Oscar's house just down the road to escape to. It's so nice to see my friends again, especially as they're both incredibly cool and a year older than me and if I get to stay in London, they'll give me a massive leg-up in the popularity stakes.

'It's so good to see you!' says Lily, patting my leg. Tingles run up and down my thigh. I close my eyes.

Elephant and Castle. Lambeth North.

It doesn't matter that I've known Lily since we all went to Baby Mozart classes together. She used to be this scrawny, fighty girl who, luckily, adored me on sight. She fought my battles for me at prep school – Scary Lily, people called her – and at the weekends we'd go over to Oscar's house and watch television, play computer games and hang out.

Then I turned thirteen and went away to boarding school (it took eighteen months to engineer getting expelled – I tried everything, including bedwetting) and the first time I came home for the holidays, Lily had evolved into a sex goddess, like a tadpole turns into a frog, only with breasts.

'I don't know how long I'm here, ' I say gloomily. 'They might send me away again.'

'It was you who wanted to go to boarding school in the first place,' points out Oscar – a bit unnecessarily, in my opinion.

'I didn't realise what it would be like. They should've known I wouldn't like it.'

'What did you think it'd be like?' says Lily. 'I've always thought it would be awful. Curfew . . . shared showers . . . hockey . . . getting up at 6 am. . .'

I'm not going to tell them that I thought it'd be kind of fun to have midnight feasts and stuff, plus I kept on hearing from Oscar how hard you had to work at day schools.

'I don't know, I just thought it'd be different.' I certainly wasn't expecting to feel so stripped of everything that made me myself, and kind of worried about Mum and Dad when I wasn't there to keep an eye on them.

'He thought he was getting on the Hogwarts Express,' says Oscar. 'What happened, Arch, did the sorting hat put you in Hufflepuff with all the other thickies?'

I throw a cushion at him, and he bats it away with the straighteners.

'I was in Slytherin,' I say, 'obviously. But they

couldn't contain my talent for the dark arts, so they threw me out.'

'And now Mummy and Daddy want to get rid of you again?'

He didn't need to put it like that.

'They think I'm lonely in London because I haven't got any brothers and sisters,' I explain.

Mum and Dad both grew up with loads of brothers and sisters. Even though Dad never talks to his, he still agrees with Mum that it's freakishly odd to be an only child. I think they'd have had a few more if it hadn't been for Mum's wonky womb (I don't want to know the details) and lucrative career.

'And anyway,' I add, 'they're both away on business a lot.'

Lily snorts. 'My mum's away all the time. I'm OK with Maria. Why are your folks so bothered?'

Maria is their au pair. She's from Portugal and she's here for a year before going to university in Lisbon to study mathematics. She's actually from an island called Madeira and she finds London so terrifying that she never leaves their flat. Lily's offered to take her clubbing and shopping and stuff, but she just scuttles off to her room to Skype her boyfriend. 'The perfect au pair,' according to Lily's mum.

'My mum says she won't have another au pair. Not since Paola from Padua's psychotic episode.'

'Oh well, fair enough.'

Oscar laughs. 'You can come and live here. Have my brother and sister. I'll swap with you any time. Marcus is a total grumpy git and Eliza's a chav.'

'Marcus is a misunderstood genius, and Eliza's not a real chav,' says Lily, 'she's just needs some style advice. I'll take her in hand, Oscar. Lose the false eyelashes and the Fake Bake and halve the jewellery.'

Eliza's only twelve. Last time I saw her, she had pigtails and she told me all about how she was taking Grade Two on the oboe.

'Misunderstood genius, my arse,' says Oscar. 'He's too lazy to do A levels, so he's pretending he's a great poet slash songwriter. Actually he's only interested in getting stoned and sleeping.'

I'd hate to be part of a big family. I think that being an only child gets an unfairly bad press. You never have to share. You never have to fight for attention. I read an article once about China where they have a very sensible policy of only allowing families one child – good for the planet, good for China, good for the kid. 'Little emperors', they're called. Who wouldn't want to be a little emperor?

'When are you finally coming out of the closet, Oscar?' says Lily, watching Oscar comb his fringe forwards. 'Archie and me, we'll throw you a party.'

Oscar raises a well-plucked eyebrow. 'Lily, darling, I'd have thought you'd know a metrosexual man when you saw one. . .'

She's laughing at him. 'Oscar, if you're going to be that beautiful, you need to prove your manliness somehow.'

'Be patient,' he says. 'All in good time. Let's go into my room. I've just had a new delivery, perfect for welcoming Archie back to civilisation.'

Ooh. Wow. What could this mean?

We roll off Oscar's parents' bed – Oscar smooths the cover and carefully rearranges the cowpats – and decamp to Oscar's lair, which is upstairs in the converted loft. Moaning noises leak from Eliza's room – she's still playing the oboe, then – and Oscar shuts her door and then latches his.

Lily leaps onto Oscar's bed, I think about joining her, but it's only a single – might look a bit harassing. So I collapse onto a silver bean bag, and Oscar straddles his one and only chair.

And then he pulls open a drawer and scrabbles

in the back of it, and there's a plastic bag full of . . . yes, it is. Weed, a lot of it.

'Won't Marcus notice that you've got all that?' I ask, and Oscar pulls a packet of Rizlas out of the drawer as well and says, 'Things have moved on, Archie-boy. I've got my own source now – some guy from east London. Marcus introduced me.'

OK, the drawback with being an only child is that you don't have a cool big brother to sort you out with a dealer.

'This is it, Big A,' says Lil. 'Your first ever joint.'

'Don't call me that,' I say automatically. That was my nickname when I was a freakily undersized seven-year-old. Now I'm completely normally proportioned in every way – not that Lily would know, unfortunately.

She pulls out her phone. 'We should record the occasion.'

Oscar's expertly packing the Rizla. 'I don't think so, Lil. In your room, maybe.'

'Next time!' says Lily. 'Are you ready, Archie?'

'It's not actually my first time,' I say, accepting the roach and Oscar's lighter. I'm trying to look cool and like I've been doing this for years. I'm glad that Lily and Oscar introduced me to normal smoking some time ago.

I'm trying to look like this is no big deal, nothing special, nothing new.

But it feels like it might be.

CHAPTER 6
Funeral

I'm feeling kind of bubbly inside and completely starving. There wasn't any food at Oscar's without getting past his mum, who was crying at the kitchen table, so I came home.

In Oscar's room the main effect of the weed was feeling as though my skeleton had hardened to iron inside me, with my flesh waving in the wind like clothes on a line – which was funny, obviously, so I laughed a lot and showed Oscar and Lily how I could make my skin wobble around. They thought it was hilarious too.

We hung out for a while and then we heard Marcus come into the house (you couldn't miss it, his mum was shouting so loud) and Lily went downstairs to see if he'd written any new songs. Oscar says she's trying to get noticed so she can join Marcus's band as lead singer.

Oscar and I watched *Phineas and Ferb* in his room. It's actually very funny if you're stoned.

And that was four hours ago, so by now I'm almost totally back to normal, except I'm very hungry and I can still feel that flesh-wobble.

I grab some peanut butter and pile it onto a piece of bread, before I even notice that my mum's sitting at the kitchen table next to a box of tissues. She's still in her gym stuff, and her face is a bit red.

'Whassup?' I say, mouth full of crunchy goodness. Is this what mothers do in London? Sit and cry in their brand new customised kitchens?

She sniffs. 'Archie, darling . . . some bad news. . . Julie . . . she died. . .'

Who the hell is Julie? 'Oh, sad,' I say, randomly, slapping two more slices of bread into the toaster.

Mum grabs a tissue and says, 'I can't believe it. So young.'

Some young girl called Julie has died. . . Hmmm . . . maybe that was the cleaner's name?

'Will they ship her back to Albania?' I say, trying not to laugh. I can see it's inappropriate and a bit sick, but somehow the idea of a corpse having to fly back home . . . in a wheelchair, maybe . . . being X-rayed at security . . . leading a zombie takeover of the cockpit. . .

My mouth is so full of toast that I don't think she hears me splutter.

'Poor Ty, poor Nicki. . .' says Mum, sniffling into her tissue.

Oh my God. That's who Julie is – Ty's gran. He's going to be really upset. I feel like someone's poured a huge bucket of ice-cold water on my head.

'I thought she was all right . . . in hospital but getting better.'

'She was, but last night she had another massive heart attack. There was nothing they could do. She was only fifty-four, Archie. She used to look after us, me and my sisters, when we were little. She was like a big sister, poor Julie. She's had such a hard time.'

God, Ty's gran was actually younger than my dad. I hope he's not going to go splat into a plate of banana any time soon. Luckily he's superfit and runs the London marathon every year. He's been nagging me to come cycling with him, thinks we could do triathlons together. I've been waiting to find the right time to tell him that's not going to happen – ideally after he's ruled out boarding schools.

'Was her heart . . . you know . . . kind of worn out?'

'She smoked,' says Mum, switching to lecture mode, 'and you know that's really bad for you, Archie.'

She can't possibly smell any fumes on me from over here by the toaster. Why don't they keep more bread in this house?

'Yeah, but that's lung cancer.'

'Heart disease too. It blocks the arteries. And of course she'd been under terrible stress. Try the freezer if you want more sliced bread, darling.'

Seems to me the human body is really badly designed if it can't cope with a few cigarettes and a tiny bit of stress without self-destructing well before its sell-by date. I mean, Ty's gran didn't even look that old. You could totally see where his mum got her looks from.

I'd have almost fancied her if she wasn't actually a grandmother. You have to draw the line somewhere.

• • •

The next time I see Julie she's looking pretty good, really – apart from being dead, that is – because she's lying there in her coffin for everyone to see at the funeral.

I'm transfixed. She's looking a load healthier than the last time I saw her, and they've obviously cleaned off all the banana. She's got pink lipstick. It's the first time I've ever seen a real live dead body.

I'm trying, really, really trying, to feel solemn and sad and respectful, like you should at a funeral. I've never been to a funeral before. But the problem is that I didn't really know Ty's gran at all, so I don't actually feel sad, and I'm not a solemn person.

My natural instinct would be to cheer people up with a bit of banter, but just before we came in my dad turned to me and said, 'None of your nonsense, do me a favour, Archie.'

Mum had been wiping her eyes with a hankie all the way from Fulham – driving here only took thirty minutes because it's incredibly early in the morning. London without traffic is strange – it's like time has been sped up. Normally it'd take about four hours.

I spent most of the journey staring out of the window, gazing at locked-up shops armoured with security shutters. As we got further east, there were more people on the street – Muslim men in white robes spilling out of a mosque, Orthodox Jewish men, with black hats and beards charging along the pavement, ringlets flying at the side of their faces. They mixed together, like a surreal game of chess.

In Fulham, where we live, it's all delis and brasseries, designer shops for babies and Scandinavian interior designers. Here in Hackney it's halal butchers and Turkish kebabs, *Polski skleps* and a tattoo parlour painted black on the outside.

I had a hundred questions, but a glance at my dad told me that this wasn't the time. He was too busy swearing at the satnav, 'No, you silly cow, I am not turning right. That street's never been two-way.'

Mum was fussing about how dangerous it was that the funeral was going to be at Ty's gran's old church in Hackney. Maybe they shouldn't have brought me.

'What if some gunman turns up?'

'A 6 am massacre at St Michael's?' scoffed my dad. 'Don't worry, they've got all the bad guys under lock and key. And these old school gangsters, they respect a funeral. Mind you, I think they should've done it somewhere else, but there you go. People are sentimental.'

I didn't know whether to hope a gunman would turn up – I could be a hero, shielding Nicki from the flying bullets – or not. Ideally not, on reflection.

'She loved that church,' said my mum, wiping away a tear. 'And then they'll bury her next to Mick. She loved him so much, and he died so young . . . oh, poor Julie. . .'

She was off again.

'Come on, Pen,' said Dad. 'Pull yourself together.

You're not family. Can't have you wailing louder than the mourners.'

She sniffed, blew her nose, and said, 'Thanks a lot, David, for your sympathy. I'm crying now so I won't have to once we get there.'

'Good to hear it. I hadn't realised tears were a limited resource.'

'Well, mine are, actually. I wouldn't dream of making an exhibition of myself at the funeral. But it's not just me. My sisters are just as upset.'

'She was only your nanny,' he said, turning a corner – without indicating, I noticed. A car beeped at us.

'Oh, you wouldn't understand.'

'No, true, I wasn't brought up knee-deep in loyal retainers.'

'No, well, we can't all grow up in the East End slums and battle our way out single-handed.'

'No, we can't,' said Dad smugly.

Honestly, one downside of not being at boarding school is listening to them arguing all the time. Luckily they both work really long hours and go away a lot.

Then the satnav said, 'You have reached your destination,' and my dad sighed and said, 'Here we go.' We parked in a side road, a terrace of red-brick houses, not unlike our road in Fulham, actually, except there was more rubbish in the street, and peeling paint on doors and windows, and there was no noise from builders digging out basements or converting lofts.

The church is crammed in between a Cypriot bakery and something called a Private Shop. There's an armed policeman on the doorstep and he quizzes us about who we are and why we're here. Mum explains and he lets us in. It's like trying to get into a top nightclub.

Inside, about twenty people are scattered among the pews, someone's playing gloomy tunes on the organ, and there are two more armed policemen.

'An open coffin? Is that normal?' whispers Dad, looking around as Mum crosses herself, and she nods and says, 'Julie was always very traditional. That's how they do it back in Ireland.'

'Jesus,' says Dad, and Mum gives him a killer glare.

There are only about twenty people at the funeral, and more of them are related to me than are part of Ty's other family. I feel a bit sorry for his gran – her coffin looks lonely. Her daughters are there, obviously, and Danny, sitting behind them, next to some guy with a tangerine tan, a pink shirt and blinding white teeth.

Nicki looks gorgeous, as per usual, in a tight black suit which hugs her curves – *Lambeth North* – high heels and a shimmery white blouse, through which I can see . . . *Elephant and Castle*. Stop it, Archie. This is a funeral.

Her sister Emma isn't bad, either – a bit plump, which isn't a bad thing, with super-straight blonde hair. Then there's the older one, Louise, who's a teacher at an international school somewhere weird. She looks a bit grim. I've met her before and I don't think I've ever seen her smile. She gives me a piercing stare, and I can see her thoughts as though she had a speech bubble over her head.

Not at school? she's thinking. *Bet he's been expelled again*.

There's no sign of Ty.

'Is he here?' asks my mum, and Louise says, 'They're keeping him in a side room. They'll just bring him in for the service. He's had a bit of time to say goodbye –' she jerks her head towards the corpse, '– and he's going to be allowed to help carry the coffin. That's what Mum would've expected.'

'Isn't it very risky?' says my mum, and Dad interrupts and says, 'The place is crawling with armed police, Pen, I'm sure everything's under control.

Louise, this must be incredibly difficult for you. When do you go back to Tashkent? Tomorrow? Good thinking.'

They start walking past the coffin, but I stay put.

'How's Ty?' I ask. 'Can I see him? After, maybe?'

Louise stares at me, a really searching look. Then she says, 'They're taking him away as soon as we're done. This is your only chance. Come with me, quickly. I think he'd like to see you.'

She clip-clops to the front of the church – every sound echoes in the emptiness – and opens a door.

'Can we come in?' she asks. 'It's only Archie.'

Ty's sitting on a kitchen chair at a wooden table, gazing into space. He looks really zombified. He reminds me of Oscar's brother Marcus when he's really stoned and away with the fairies.

I wonder how Ty's got hold of weed, banged up in prison?

'Yo, Ty,' I say. 'I'm sorry about your gran.'

He narrows his eyes, tries to focus. 'Archie?'

'Yeah. How are you?'

He shrugs. I wish the guy standing guard – a prison officer, I guess – would go away.

'Do they have PlayStation? What's the food like? Have you made friends?'

'Umm . . . yes they do. You have to earn it, though. Good behaviour.'

'Have you earned it?'

'Takes ages. I earned a radio.'

'Oh, cool. You can listen to *Gardeners' Question Time*.'

He gives me a half-smile.

'What's the food like?'

'School dinners. All the time. And you can't just have what you want, when you want it.'

'Have you made friends there?'

'Friends?' He almost laughs. 'Not really friends. Allies. Comrades. People who'll watch my back.'

That doesn't sound too bad. 'It's only for a few weeks,' I say.

'Yeah. As long as I behave myself.'

'That's kind of funny, ' I say, 'because I got out of boarding school by not behaving myself.'

'You are such a tosser,' he says, but his eyes aren't all spacey any more and there's a glimmer of a smile on his face.

Then the organ tune changes and I get up to go.

'Archie – can you . . . can you talk to Claire?' he says.

'Um, yeah, but what do you want me to say?'

Claire is Ty's supposed girlfriend, except they

never get to see each other, her parents think he's the devil and his mum's not all that keen on Claire, either. They're kind of obsessed with each other. Zoe – Claire's really hot friend, who I'm sort of seeing in a casual, long-distance, Skypey way – says it'll end in tears.

'Will you just tell her about . . . about everything? I haven't . . . I can't. . .'

'Yeah, sure, leave it to the Archmeister.'

I have not one clue in my head about how that conversation's going to go, when I'm going to have it, or why he's picked on me.

Actually, I've been avoiding talking to Zoe ever since Ty got sent to the Young Offender Institution because he got a bit upset one time when I only told her he'd been charged. Zoe's dad is a policeman, so I thought she'd know a bit about how Ty might get off. But he acted as if I'd broadcast it on the ten o'clock news. Talk about oversensitive. Now he's asking me to tell Claire everything. Some people just aren't consistent.

Then the organ starts playing really loud and the prison officer says, 'Here we go,' and I have to find my parents, and five minutes later Ty's sitting next to his auntie Emma in the front pew.

Funerals are pretty awful, really. Apparently some people choose good music and stuff (I'd have something upbeat, like Chipmunk's 'Until You Were Gone' and maybe some guardsmen playing trumpets), but this time it's all really depressing hymns and prayers and then the priest going on and on about Julie – about how she was a good daughter, and she worked hard all her life, and she was a devoted wife and a loving mother and a wonderful grandmother and she touched the lives of all who knew her. Yawn.

It makes me think about what people might say at my funeral, which obviously (well, hopefully) won't be for another sixty years at least. They'll all be talking about what an amazing guy I was, and all my wisecracks and how I was a rich and famous television presenter or rock star or actor, maybe. And there'll be a queue of beautiful women throwing red roses as they file out of the church, and maybe there'll be a Union Jack over my coffin, because I'll have died being a big hero, and it'll be televised and the entire nation will be wearing black and leaving flowers outside my mansion.

'Julie's whole life was her family,' says the priest. 'She would do anything for them. She'll be watching over them from heaven.'

Ty's head is bowed and his auntie Emma has her arm around him. This must be horrible for him, although, on the other hand, it's a day out of prison and a chance to see his aunts, which doesn't happen often, as one lives in Spain and the other's in wherever Tashkent is – Turkey? Iran? Azerbaijan?

I wonder what Ty's funeral will be like. I imagine myself getting up to give a speech.

'Ty didn't mean to be a criminal,' I'd say. 'He just made a few mistakes and that set him off on a life of violence and dishonesty.'

I shiver. That wasn't funny, even said privately to myself. Ty isn't going to be a criminal all his life. I try and rethink the speech.

My cousin Tyler was a great athlete, I think, *and he learned to speak eighty-three languages fluently. He was married to Claire for seventy years and they have thirty-five great-grandchildren.*

I'm not really concentrating, and Dad has to prod me to get up. We've got to drive to the cemetery. I look for Ty – maybe he can come in our car – but I can't see him, and I guess he's with the prison guys, anyway.

Dad ducks into the car and lets out a sigh.

'Get me out of here,' he says.

Mum's adjusting the satnav.

'Why don't you ever come back, Dad? Don't you still have relatives here?'

He laughs. 'Your nana Bertha once a year at Christmas is all the relatives I need, thanks a lot, Archie. It's been my life's mission to escape from this place.'

'Why?'

'I've got nothing in common with them,' he says, 'and that's enough questions. Penny, forget the satnav, I'm following the cortège.'

It's raining when we get to the cemetery, and I'm glad it's not me that has to shoulder the coffin – all closed up now – and carry it to the hole in the ground. Ty's got that job, and although I don't envy him, still . . . it's a real sign of being a man, isn't it? Ty seems to be the only male relative, but there are guys there from the undertakers to help him. His knuckles are white where they're gripping the coffin. It's a good thing he did all that weight-training this summer.

As we watch, my grandpa Patrick leans over to me.

'You'll be doing that for me, one of these days,' he says, quite cheerfully, 'you and Ty. We'll try and wait for the twins to grow up a bit, eh?'

I have a sudden flashforward of me and Ty,

proper grown-up men (pinstripe suits, designer stubble) and our twin cousins Ludo and Atticus, who are now only about seven. We're carrying a really, really long coffin (our grandpa's pretty tall).

How can he be smiling?

I nod and say, 'OK, I suppose so,' and he says, 'Excellent. It's good to have these things arranged.'

Then the coffin's in the ground and the priest is saying some stuff about punishment and sins and mercy and resurrection. They're shovelling earth on top of it and I'm thinking about Ty's gran's face when she heard he was going to prison. It's a shame that she couldn't die happy, it really is, and I feel a little bit sad.

There's a quick meet-up afterwards. Emma kisses my mum and introduces her boyfriend, Carlos, the shiny-toothed Tango man.

'We can't do a wake, we're so sorry,' she says, and my grandma pats her on the shoulder and says, 'Everyone understands, Emma. We're all so sorry.'

It's 7 am and we're all yawning. Ty nods goodbye to everyone, glances over to me. He hugs his aunts, Grandpa slaps him on the back and Danny and Nicki walk with him to the prison van. They don't hug, I notice. Ty turns away and gets into the van without looking back, as though he can't wait to get back to his cell, his mates and his radio.

In the car, going home, no one talks except the satnav. I sit and wonder whether Ty's gran really is in heaven, and if so, whether she's feeling better. Maybe they have a whole stress-reduction package for new arrivals – like the yoga retreat Mum went to last year on Lesbos. She had to ban Dad and me from making inappropriate jokes.

I watch the streets of Hackney turn into Islington, and then the Euston Road – now crawling with traffic – and I wonder what I would be like if I'd grown up where Ty did, where my dad did.

Would I be like Ty, getting into trouble from being in the wrong place at the wrong time, or like my dad, getting everything right and escaping to fame and fortune (in the *Financial Times*)?

I don't know, and it bothers me. How can I find out?

CHAPTER 7
Anger management

'Who d'you think you're looking at? Fancy me, do you?'

He's yelling in my face, spitting. His fist is waving near my head.

'Stop looking at me, you poof. . .'

He's swearing, getting louder and louder. A roomful of lads are watching us. Someone laughs. They're waiting to see what I'll do next.

We're in a classroom – grey chairs, grey tables. We're all wearing grey trackies. It's hot and airless. We're not allowed to open the windows. And his voice is banging in my ears.

He's about my height, sweating like a pig, pink-faced and flabby. Dion, his mates call him. He's got quite a few mates. I've not got any. I don't care. I can look after myself.

I could take him out, no question – a punch to the head, chop to his neck, knee to the balls. I could push him over and run. I'm breathing hard, considering my options.

He pokes me in the chest.

'What're you looking at, pretty boy?'

I take a deep breath. I count . . . one, two, three.

I say, 'Not looking at nothing, mate. Sorry.'

I put my hands up, show him there's no weapon, step backwards.

He growls, 'Keep outta my way,' and I say, 'Yeah, OK.'

I don't like saying it. A sharp, sick taste burns my throat. But I stumble backwards, head down, no eye contact.

'Well done, excellent,' says Mr Thomas. 'Very good. Who wants to have a go next?'

The group murmurs. I don't care what they're saying. I sit down quickly on my plastic chair. Then another victim is picked and Dion starts raving at him. I put my mind into neutral and let the shouting wash over me.

Attending the anger management programme is compulsory if they think it will help you, and that applies to 100 per cent of people in here.

Mr Wilde told me I had to do it.

'I think you'll find it very useful,' he said. 'You'll learn to reflect on your behaviour, practise strategies for coping in conflict situations. The aim is to minimise the risk of reoffending. Let's see how you go on.'

And I shrugged and looked away and he said, 'This needn't be a totally negative experience for you if you put your mind to it.'

Of all the stuff we have to do in here, anger management is the worst. I hate it. It makes me feel weak and vulnerable. I want to tear my flesh afterwards, to get rid of the fury that's going nowhere. Instead I go to the gym, run on the machine – no one else dares to use it when I'm there – until I feel pain in my legs, my feet, my bursting heart.

No one else thinks I'm weak. I'm getting a reputation as a hard man.

Luke's body tells its own story. People see the muscles, they see the scars and they work out something that frightens them.

It's as though the more scared I am, the more I scare other people.

And I am pretty scared now, because any day, any second of the day, Mikey could work out who I am.

He was never that bright, Mikey, and he didn't

really know me. I was just Arron's friend, the tag-along. Back then I was short and podgy and I had short hair and a school blazer.

I suppose I must look very different now.

There was not even a flicker in his eyes as he handed me my food that first night, and I must have managed to keep my face really blank, because he didn't say anything to make me think he knows who I am.

I've not said anything, either – not to anyone. I haven't seen him again, but that doesn't mean he isn't here.

He's never in the classroom and he's never in the gym and he's never come near my room again. Sometimes I even wonder if it was really him at all.

Every day I chuck my food down the toilet uneaten in case he's done something to it. I only eat the sealed stuff – yoghurt, crisps, that kind of thing.

I'm getting thinner, which is good because when he knew me I was fat.

Watching for Mikey, feeling hungry all the time, well, it takes the edge off everything else. I'm choked inside, thinking about Gran, about how no one even told me she was ill. They didn't let me see her.

I could have saved her. Last year, when she was in a coma, I said a Hail Mary and she woke up and it was a miracle, like she always believed could happen.

Why couldn't I try for another miracle this time?

I hate the people who kept it from me – the prison officers worse, but also Mum and my aunts and my dad. They all knew. They didn't tell me.

I scare myself with how much I hate them.

So I've put Ty away in a box somewhere inside me, and when he starts hating, I slam the lid down and think cold, hard, blank Luke thoughts until Ty shuts up.

Which leaves Claire. I can't need her without being Ty. I'll just have to hope that Archie – shit, that fool Archie, of all people – can sort of put her on hold for a bit, that she'll understand.

Stupid Ty's stupid hope, his memories of what it felt like to be with Claire – that goes in the box as well.

It's a week after the funeral and I'm just about OK, when the guy in charge of the gym, Mr Jones, he's called, says he's been watching me.

They've all been watching me. They know about Gran and they know about witness protection and they're waiting for something to kick off. I'm not giving them the satisfaction.

'You what?' I forget to be polite.

'You. You can run, can't you?'

'Yeah, right,' I say.

'Ever been to a running club? Ever tried to make anything of yourself?'

He's clearly expecting the answer to be no. He's got the same look in his eye that the education guy got when he discovered I could do Maths.

Two kinds of people work in here – the ones who've written us off already, who just want to keep us quiet until we get out of here and become someone else's problem.

That's most of them.

Then there are the few who want to Make a Difference, put us on the Right Path, find something to transform us from feral criminals into pillars of the community.

There are only about three like that and they're a pain.

'I have been to a running club,' I say. Big mistake. He wants all the details, all the races I've won. Times, dates, distances.

'I could get you a community order, get you out of here to train once a week, maybe even compete.'

'Nah,' I say, although my whole body's aching for

a proper run, a run outside, and it'd feel so good if there were people to run against, people that I could crush and humiliate and stomp all over just by running much faster than they do.

'Are you sure?' he says. 'You've not got long here, have you? Wouldn't it make the time go quicker if you could achieve something while you're here? Get out somehow?'

I'm shocked. I thought that prison meant prison. I thought that all I had to do was keep my head down, keep alive, survive for six weeks. Now he's telling me I can have little trips to the outside world. I can run races. He's messing with my mind.

Is he the one? Is he working for them? Is he trying to get me out of here for a reason?

'Nah,' I say, again, but my voice is weak and wavery and he can see – anyone can see – that I don't really mean it.

'I'll make enquiries,' he says.

And that was a week ago and he's sorted it so I can go and train twice a week at a running club, and he's got a list of competitions too.

Driving out of the prison, it's like my body's been wrapped in chains, and someone opens the padlocks and they all drop off. My legs feel longer, looser, my arms swing free. My lungs expand. The throbbing headache that I've had on and off for the last two weeks eases a little.

I must have made a noise, sighed or something, because Mr Jones asks me if I'm OK.

'Yeah.'

'Happy to be out?'

I'm not sure that happy is actually a word that will ever apply to me again.

'Sorry about your gran. Getting on a bit, was she?'

I wish he'd just shut up. I don't say anything and he turns the car into a side road and parks.

'No tricks now,' he says. 'I'm trusting you to behave. No trying to give me the slip.'

I don't bother to reply to that one.

'You realise that if you do one thing wrong you'll lose all your privileges?'

I nod. It'd actually kill me to lose that radio. Music helps to drown out the words in your head.

'You'll be serving the whole sentence.'

'Yeah, all right.'

'You can talk!' he says. 'I was wondering. Here we go.'

We go into the club and through to the track. I'm already changed, I just peel off my tracksuit. I'm not sure how well I can perform in these crap trainers.

Then I see the other runners – normal kids, free, kids who sleep in their own beds at night, kids who see their families every day.

I hate them. And from the way they're staring, they're not that keen on me, either.

'This is Luke,' says Mr Jones. 'Why don't you warm up, Luke?' and he starts chatting to the trainer. Neither of them takes their eyes off me. The other kids are warming up too. I jog, stretch, jog a bit more. Christ, it feels good. The headache's gone. I'm drunk on fresh air.

The trainer lines us up for the 1500 metres – four of us. Two big, tall black guys. A redhead with a freckle-splattered face. Me.

Beating them is so easy that they might as well not have bothered to run.

'Told you,' says Mr Jones to the trainer. He shows me my time. 'Outstanding.'

'I can do better,' I say, 'if I get to train properly – every day.'

'I'll talk to the governor,' he says. 'I'm not sure what will be possible. I'll do my best.'

'Thanks,' I say, and for one blessed minute the hate and rage inside me die down and I don't feel less than human any more and I'm looking at him like we're both from the same species.

'That's better,' he says, and I think he's going to pat me on the back. I step backwards.

'If – and it's a big if – I can organise better training for you, and if the governor agrees, then there's an athletics meet in Northampton next month,' he says. 'You interested?'

Am I interested?

On the one hand it's crazy to do anything at all that could draw attention to myself.

On the other – a day out of prison a chance to compete, to beat, to triumph.

And all in Northampton. Approximately seven miles from Claire's home

I could write to her. She could be there.

'I'm interested,' I say.

CHAPTER 8
Claire

I thought for a long time about the best way to tell Claire all Ty's bad news and in the end I sent her a message on Facebook.

Yes, I did.

No, actually, I don't think that was stupid and insensitive.

I didn't write it on her wall, I sent her a private message. I sent her my phone number so she could call me. I think that I handled it very well. I sent it on Friday and today is Sunday, so she's had all weekend to call me.

So what the hell is she doing standing on our doorstep, talking to my mum?

'Go and get dressed, Archie,' says Mum, not even bothering to check whether I am dressed or not – fair enough, really, because it's only 10.30 am and I was at a party (Lily's cousin Maia in Notting Hill) until 2 am.

By the time I'm ready (my new hairstyle takes ages, I have to pull it all forward and then tousle – Oscar showed me how) Mum's got her in the interrogation chamber, i.e. the conservatory, has disarmed her with coffee and croissants and is metaphorically shining a light into her eyes.

'Claire's come all the way from Northamptonshire!' she says, a note of triumph in her voice.

Claire looks as fierce as you can when you're the height and build of a twelve year old, you have short blonde hair, big blue eyes and a soft sweet voice. She's not my type at all – I prefer Real Women with real breasts – but I can see how she and Ty look cool together in a world's-least-suited-couple way. Not really Beauty and the Beast, more like a straight version of Batman and Robin, or Tom and Jerry – assuming (as I do) they were gay couples.

'Err . . . hey, Claire,' I say, dead casual. 'What brings you here?'

I'm still a bit wasted from the party last night. My head is throbbing and my eyes are sore. The last thing I need is some hideous tearful scene, and, let's face it, whenever I've seen Claire, she's usually turned on the waterworks sooner or later.

'I need to ask you some questions,' says Claire, like she's Inspector Morse and I've murdered a professor.

Mum's nose twitches, and I say, 'Oh right . . . maybe we should go out.'

'Fresh croissants!' says Mum. 'I'll froth some milk for your latte!'

But Claire's already out of her chair and saying, 'Yes, let's. Thanks for the coffee, Mrs Stone.'

'Oh, call me Penny,' says Mum, who's actually never changed her name to Stone and insists on being called Ms Penelope Tyler. I think it's a bit sexist when women don't change their names when they get married. It's like she thinks she's better than Dad and me.

'Thanks, Penny, come on, Archie.'

There's a café around the corner and I suggest going there, but Claire wants to take the Tube into town. I agree – I'm waiting for the emotional storm to burst and I'm certainly not risking arguing with her.

But she doesn't mention Ty or his gran or prison or Facebook. Instead she starts asking me questions.

Why aren't I at boarding school any more? How do I feel about that? What school will I go to now? She seems really interested, and she listens carefully to my answers and then follows up the questions with more. Why do I want to stay in London? Why are my parents away a lot? Which school would I really like to go to?

We talk all the way to Temple station, and then she leaps up and says, 'Let's get out here.'

So we cross over the Thames and we're wandering along the South Bank and I'm almost forgetting that we're here to talk about my jailbird cousin, because there's a second-hand book stall and I find out she's recently got into manga and has been trying to draw some, which is kind of amazing, because I'm the only person I know who does that.

I mean, for all I know everyone at Allingham Priory was secretly creating manga masterpieces, but it's not something we'd ever have found out about each other, because we were too busy being forced to play rugby.

When we get to the National Theatre she says, 'Wow . . . I wish we could get tickets for something.'

'Do you? Like what? It's not musicals and stuff in there, it's, y'know, Shakespeare etc.'

I've been there quite often. My mum and dad believe in taking me to cultural things. I mostly enjoy them, actually, but I don't want her to think I'm some sort of goody-goody intellectual.

'I think I might want to be an actress,' she says.

'Really?'

I can't imagine Claire up on stage. She's so quiet and small.

'I like it,' she says. 'It's like you can be someone else completely. It's fascinating.'

'I'd like to see you act,' I say, and she grins and says, 'Maybe you can one day. I'll tell Zoe next time I'm in something.'

Oh yes, Zoe. My long-distance girlfriend, Zoe. I'd kind of forgotten about her.

'Maybe we can get tickets,' I say. 'I've got some cash and they might have cut-price tickets just before the performance.'

She looks wistful, but says, 'No, I need to be on the 5 pm train, or I'll be in trouble.'

'Does anyone know you're here?'

'Not my family. I told Zoe – I needed to get your address. She'll cover for me if I'm late back. But it's better if I'm not. And, anyway, we need to talk.'

We end up walking towards the London Eye. She's looking at it, impressed – all non-Londoners are – so I say, 'Shall we go and queue up? It's not so bad this time of year, we shouldn't have to wait too long,' as though I'm working for the London Tourist Office.

She smiles – and right there and then I truly get what Ty sees in Claire. Her smile is something else. When someone's expression is naturally serious, to see their eyes widen, their face change shape . . . it's like getting into a warm car on an icy day. I swear, you feel like you'd do anything to see that smile again.

She doesn't mention Ty until we're high in the sky, until I've told her a bit about the only thing I really enjoyed at my first boarding school, which was taking part in a Gilbert and Sullivan opera, all dressed up in a Japanese kimono. I liked it all, the singing and being on stage and everything about it, actually. It's completely naff – I know, sad.

Oscar and Lily would have laughed at me, never let me forget it, God knows what Ty would've said, but Claire nods solemnly and says, 'If it was fun, why didn't you want to stay at that school?'

'Oh, you know. Because I didn't want to be there.'

'I'd quite like to go to boarding school,' says Claire, gazing out over London. 'I can't wait to leave home. Where's the bit where you live?'

I locate some landmarks . . . Tower Bridge due east . . . and then point to the west.

'Look, Fulham, over there.'

'And where does Ty come from?'

'That way . . . over there.'

And I gesture past Tower Bridge, over to St Pauls, up and east to the grubby streets of the East End. Seen from so high up, London is vast and never-ending, a huge nest of ants, all scurrying around, busy and biting and not realising how small they are, how easily crushed. The Thames gleams and twists like a snake in the mud. There's a yellow-brown haze in the air.

London is one of the biggest cities in the world. It started out small and it grew and grew, eating little villages, swallowing fields and farms, hills and valleys. It doesn't really believe in itself as a city. It still thinks it's just a load of bits stuck together.

'He was a long way from you,' says Claire. 'Did you see him much when you both lived in London?'

Ty was a long way from me. He was poor, I was rich. He was east, I was west. He knew people in gangs, people who mugged and fought and killed. I worried about getting mugged.

'I never saw him at all. I never even knew I had a cousin. Actually, I think Grandma might have mentioned him sometimes, but I didn't realise what she was on about. He was like a family secret.'

'Why?'

'It's like, you know, those things that happen when you're a baby and no one ever bothers to explain.'

'Oh yeah,' she said, 'like my sister's accident. I was only about eight and I thought it was all my fault because I asked her to show me her gymnastics routine and then she fell off the beam. They only bothered to tell me last year that actually the equipment was faulty. All those years I thought it was my fault she was in a wheelchair.'

'Wow,' I say. 'It must have been good to find out that wasn't true.'

'It was, but I was angry that no one told me before. Turned out they all thought I knew.'

'Exactly,' I say, and she grins at me.

'Ty's having a hard time,' she says.

'A really hard time,' I agree, 'but he seemed OK, Claire, at the funeral. He asked me to tell you about everything.' I swallow nervously. 'Maybe Facebook wasn't the best way, but I thought. . .'

'Epic fail, Archie,' says Claire, but she doesn't seem angry.

'Anyway, he's OK and we can write to him and they said he'd only serve six weeks. . .'

'Archie,' she says, 'you're probably wondering what I'm doing here.'

'Umm . . . well. . .'

'The thing is that when I met Ty, he was someone else completely.'

'Oh I know about that,' I say. 'He was Joe, wasn't he – the false identity because of witness protection?'

'Yes. He was Joe. He was, like, the most popular, best-looking, most impressive, amazing person in our school.'

I think about the Ty I know. OK, I can just about imagine that.

'Really?'

'Yes, really. And then . . . he noticed me. I was . . . I wasn't a very happy person then, Archie. For me, just talking to someone like Joe – I know it sounds crazy – but it made me feel. . .'

Her voice trails off. She's blushing.

I've always been confident. I've always assumed that people basically like me, find me interesting, entertaining. I'm struggling to put myself in her position here.

'That must have been nice.'

'It was . . . much more than nice.' She's smiling at the memory. 'It was overwhelming. Have you ever been in love, Archie?'

Oh God. Is she here to interrogate me for Zoe?

'Well . . . you know. . .'

'It made me feel like I was a newer, better, braver version of myself,' she says. 'I felt like I could do all the things that had felt impossible before. And I completely, utterly, absolutely believed that Joe was a good person.'

'OK . . . right. . .'

'And then I started having doubts,' she says, 'because he sent me this email which said he'd hurt someone. And he's never really explained it. And I want everything to be all right, Archie, I really do, but now he's in prison and I'm thinking, who is this person I'm in love with? I think I love him, but do I know him? Am I making a colossal error?'

I summon up all my loyalty to my cousin – even though I hardly know him myself.

'I'm certain Ty really loves you too,' I say, which sounds good, but isn't really an answer.

The London Eye glides to a halt. We're back down on earth.

Claire looks at me. 'Archie, I've come to you because you're the best friend Ty's got. You're family.'

I like Claire. I really do. If she wasn't going out with my cousin and I wasn't sort of long-distance-Skypingly involved with her best friend, then I think I might really like her a lot.

'Right, OK,' I say. 'I'll keep you up to date on how he's doing.'

'I need to ask you to do something for me,' she says.

What the hell?

'Sure, anything,' I say.

'It might be a bit dangerous,' she says, looking worried.

To be completely honest, I'm in severe danger here already.

'Don't worry about that,' I say. 'What can I do for you?'

'I want you to tell Ty that I need a break. I'm not sure I'm the right person to support him through this. I don't know if we've got a future any more.'

CHAPTER 9
Danny

My mum is a connoisseur of other people's feelings. She's very kind and caring and all that, but you can see from the shine in her eyes that when things get heavy and emotional, she's really quite enjoying it.

My dad says she should have been a therapist or a tabloid journalist – not a lawyer. I personally would never dream of telling her any secrets. It's not that she wouldn't be helpful, it's just that with such an appreciative audience, I might never stop.

Her brother obviously never learned this when he was growing up. When I get back from seeing Claire off at Euston station, Danny's sitting at the kitchen table, cradling a large glass of wine, muttering and mumbling into his chest.

Mum looks up as I come in, and jerks her head

very briefly to indicate that I need to scoot. But I'm just as nosy as she is. I back out of the room as silently as possible, but as soon as she turns her back I drop down on my hands and knees and crawl past them to the conservatory, where I curl up behind some large, green, leafy thing. I can hear everything that's going on, and, in my opinion, what I can hear is a grown man crying.

'I've got another bottle in the fridge,' says Mum, 'if you're sure you're OK with alcohol. I'm not nagging, but you've done so well. Oh, OK . . . just this once. . .'

Sniff, gulp, a kind of hiccupping sound. Sniff. Groan. And then glug, glug, glug – she's pouring him another glass.

Gulp. And then, 'Thanks, Pen. Jesus. I'm sorry. I didn't mean to . . . I ought to be going.'

'You're not going anywhere,' says Mum, predictably. 'Stay here for supper and you can sleep in the spare room, if necessary. I'm worried about you, Danny.'

'Don't worry about me. It's Ty you need to worry about.'

There's another choking, gulping, sniffing pause. Mum's voice is almost supernaturally inviting.

'Why don't you get it all off your chest? I'm sure you'll feel better.'

'I can't talk to anyone else,' he says. 'All my friends – I mean, most of them haven't even got children yet, or they have babies, but it's all so much simpler, I mean, no one else I know of my age has to deal with all of this . . . has a teenager. . .'

'I know, I know,' says Mum. She's loads more tactful than Dad. He would've said, 'Well you should have thought of that when you had a baby when you were in the sixth form.'

'I don't feel old enough – I sit there in that Young Offender Institution, trying to talk to him, but I hardly know him and I'm thinking, look, I can't do this. I'm not grown-up enough. . .'

'How's Nicki coping?' says Mum. 'She must be grateful to have you there – to have your support.'

'Terrible,' he says. 'Terrible. She won't even see him. I'm so worried.'

'Have a tissue.'

'Thanks.'

Loud nose-blowing noise.

'I called Emma last night – asked if Nicki and the baby could go and stay with her in Spain. It's too much for me to deal with. I can't do it, Pen.'

'I know, you're right,' she says, which doesn't strike me as wildly supportive.

'And Ty . . . Ty, he's. . .'

Mum's phone rings. Damn. She goes into a long, loud, boring conversation about something at work, and I can hardly hear him sniffing and gulping and glugging more wine into his glass.

When she finally finishes the call, she fusses around finding him some chicken and salad and ciabatta. She never thinks about feeding me, I notice. Good thing Claire and I shared a pizza before she got the train.

He says, 'I can't eat a thing. I don't know what to do.'

'Maybe. . .' she pauses. 'Maybe you should take someone along with you next time. You said they're allowing him extra visits because of the circumstances – Julie and all that. How about taking . . . I know you won't like it, but—'

'I am not taking Pa with me, if that's what you mean.'

I bet it was, but she rallies quickly.

'No, Danny, how about taking Archie? He and Ty are quite close now. Maybe it'd be good for them to see each other.'

Ah. I'm not sure this is a great idea. I'm not happy at all about the job Claire's given me. I think I'd better wait until Ty's out and free.

On the other hand, what if he tries to see her, goes berserk? Would it be my fault? Maybe he's better off knowing about it when he's nice and safe in prison, and everyone else is nice and safe outside.

I'd like to spend time with Danny and persuade him that he needs me as an assistant in the studio to entertain celebrity clients. From the way he's acting now, he's not going to be up to the job.

Danny's voice is muffled. He must've decided to try the ciabatta, after all.

'He'll just be a pain.'

'No he won't. He'll cheer Ty up. And Danny, maybe you can talk to him a bit about . . . you know . . . about why drugs aren't a great idea. I'm worried about him. We've always tried to keep him away from that London party lifestyle, but now he seems to have plunged in at the deep end. And I told you what they found in his room at Allingham Priory.'

'Pen, I'm not really the person for health education lectures.'

'But Danny, you are. Really. You've had the experience, you see, and that's what the kids listen to. Honestly. He's much more likely to listen to you than to me or David.'

'Don't sell yourself short, Pen. And as for David,

I'm sure there are loads of stories he could tell. . .'

'Yes, but that's not a great idea, is it? We've always kept Archie away from . . . well. . . And I never got involved in anything at all.'

'Yeah, right, big sister,' he says and suddenly they're both actually giggling, and I have no idea why. Mind you, it is laughable, the idea that my mum would ever do anything even vaguely illegal.

'How's . . . what's her name . . . Tess?' says Mum, in her best I'm-not-very-interested voice.

'Oh, we don't really . . . I'm not so. . .'

'Good. I thought she was a bit hard-faced.'

'Oh, thanks Pen, nice of you to say so.'

'Is there anyone else?'

'Nothing serious.'

'Nicki?'

'Just a friend. It's best that way.'

'I'm sorry, Danny.'

'Don't be.'

Argh! I've got cramp! I writhe around silently, but then I crash into a massive cactus, which topples over, spraying me with dirt and spiking my chest. I yelp in agony.

'Archie?' says Mum. 'What are you doing there? What have you done to Bertha?'

'Who the hell is Bertha?' asks Danny.

'It's my name for the cactus. It reminds me of my mother-in-law – large and prickly. What were you doing in there, anyway?'

'Oh um, nothing. . .' I say, painfully disengaging from the vicious plant.

'Maybe he came in through the cat flap,' says Danny.

Huh. I'll do the sarcasm around here . . . or actually, that's my dad's speciality.

'We don't even have a cat,' says Mum.

'I'm starving! When are you going to feed me?'

She flicks a tea towel at me. 'Now, but you're naughty to spy on people. Too much time on your hands, that's your problem.'

'That's not my fault,' I point out, before I remember that actually it is.

'Well, you'll be busy from next week. You're going to start at Butler's.' I must have looked blank, because she says, 'The tutorial college that Lily might go to. Her mum's thinking of transferring her. Costs an arm and a leg, but you'll get through your GCSEs very quickly with intensive teaching in small groups.'

The cramp disappears instantly, I forget Bertha's prickles. I'm leaping around with excitement.

'Woo! Thanks Ma! You mean I can stay here? Woo!'
I give her a big hug and a kiss on the cheek.

'Sweet,' says Danny gloomily, helping himself to
another glass of wine.

Mum looks really pleased and she's already
forgotten that I was spying on them.

'You'll have to work hard,' she says.

'I will! I promise!'

'If Dad and I are both away at the same time then
you'll have to stay with Marina or Elizabeth.'

I like my aunts, but I know what I'd prefer.

'Umm Danny, couldn't I stay with you
sometimes?'

He looks startled. 'What? I don't think so, Archie.
I can't even stay in my flat at the moment – since Ty was
attacked there the police think it might be dangerous.
I'm kipping at my studio – it's not that big.'

'I'd really like to come and see it, anyway.'

He raises an eyebrow – just like my grandpa does –
and says, 'Maybe. One day.'

'When Ty's out, we can come together.'

He sighs. 'It's not going to be that easy for Ty.'

'But I thought everything was OK now. The
criminals are all locked up and once he gets out of . . .
you know . . . he'll have a normal life.'

Danny puts his head in his hands. 'I don't know,' he says – at least, I think that's what he says, it's a bit of a muffled mumble.

'Are you staying here, Danny?' asks Mum, and he says no, he'll get a cab.

I go upstairs and I think about Skyping Zoe. I feel bad. She is meant to be my girlfriend.

But I don't do it. Instead I think about Claire and what I'm going to tell Ty and how nice it was to talk to Claire, and how I'm going to be in London and free to go where I want and see who I want to see, and do what I want.

Life is full of possibilities.

How lucky am I?

CHAPTER 10
Like You Used To

Butler's Tutorial College isn't like any other school I've ever heard of. It's not like a school at all.

There's no uniform, no real classrooms, hardly any rules and not that many pupils. I'm doing English GCSE in a group of five, Maths in a group of four, History with just two others. You can actually talk to the teacher properly during the lessons, ask questions and discuss things and stuff.

There are advantages to having parents who are loaded, besides the obvious electronic goods.

'We aim to get you through the curriculum in a year,' says Richard, who's my supposed 'base tutor' – that's what they call form masters here – although all that means is that I can go to him with any general questions I've got, or problems and stuff. He's the only person in the place who's wearing a tie, although even so he manages to look pretty cool, with his slicked-back dark hair and cool steel-rimmed glasses. 'It's hard work, but hopefully you'll find it interesting.'

I don't think any teacher has ever cared if I find the work interesting before. This is great.

I've done a week at Butler's and so far, I'd say it's like heaven on earth, assuming you have to do GCSEs in heaven. It's going to be a breeze. I'll even have loads of free time to do whatever I want.

Today I've got English for the first time. My teacher loads me up with booklists – *Romeo and Juliet, Of Mice and Men, An Inspector Calls.* He's set me a creative writing assignment – imagine you're an American soldier in Iraq – which shouldn't take too long to polish off. Bang, bang, bang, look at all the corpses, look at the sand, why the hell are we here? Whoosh! I'm dead, sort of thing.

Then it's the student lounge to wait for thirty minutes before a session with the Maths guy. I tell you, they don't sweat it here.

I've bought a coke from the machine and I'm texting Claire from my iPhone – just seeing if she's OK – and I'm admiring the female talent on display.

The girls here are gorgeous, sure, but lots of them are kind of older-looking and a bit sneery. There are all sorts here, kids from all over the world. Some have got in on scholarships. So it's a lot more mixed than any other school I've ever been to. You never know who you're going to be talking to.

Lily advised me to stay a little bit separate, not talk too much, keep the girls wondering. It's not my natural way, but it seems to work. In English, a girl called Sophie (blonde, long legs in skinny jeans) smiled at me and asked my name, and although I can't see her in the lounge right now, maybe she'll come and chat later.

Right in front of me are two girls talking about some club they went to last night, and one of them catches my eye and asks if I've been there.

'Nah,' I say, not liking to admit that I'm way too young to confidently blag my way into clubs. 'I've not been in London much. Only just come back.'

And then a guy sitting opposite me looks up. He's staring at me. I try and ignore him, and carry on talking to the girls. They're called Georgia and Paige, they live in Chelsea and Holland Park, and they left their old school after an epidemic of anorexia.

'My parents thought this would be a better

environment,' says Georgia. Paige laughs. 'Little did they know.'

They ask me which groups I'm in, will they see me at lunchtime, am I on Facebook? We whip out our iPhones.

'I'm having a party, Saturday. Want to come?' says Paige.

And then they wander off to their Biology class.

He hasn't stopped staring. Creepy. As soon as they've gone, he leans towards me. He's a tall, spotty guy, long, gangly legs and arms, head slightly too small for his body. Hollister jeans, Superdry hoodie, black Converses. It's what passes for a uniform in this place.

'Hey,' he says.

'Hey,' I reply.

'I know you, don't I?'

I don't recognise him, but that means nothing. Since Lily styled my profile picture on Facebook (a great pose, mid-air on a skateboard, I look supercool) I've been getting loads of friend requests. I've gone from an embarrassing 220 friends to a respectable 740. I know the whole of west London (the independent school bit, anyway). I just wouldn't necessarily recognise them in the street.

So I say, 'Oh yeah, hi mate.'

'From school – you were at my old school,' he says. I don't remember him at all. He must've been at prep school – maybe in the year above. I shrug.

'Yeah, from school,' I say.

'So – how are you?' He seems a bit nervous.

'Uh. Fine.'

'Did it all . . . you know . . . sort itself out, when you were out of London?'

Maybe he was at boarding school number one and remembers me getting expelled. I scan my memory, but it's a bit blurred. I've been having loads of late nights, plus getting stoned maybe three times a week. I'm going to have to timetable in a bit more sleep in the mornings.

'Yeah,' I say. 'Well, I'm here now and it seems great. Just started last week.'

'It is great here,' he says. 'What a contrast, eh? And everyone here's a bit different. But it's pricey, isn't it?'

'Yeah, I suppose.'

'So that's why . . . I was a bit surprised. . .'

I raise an eyebrow. He doesn't finish his sentence. It's all a bit awkward. I take a swig of coke and stand up.

'Nice to see you again,' I say. 'Umm, sorry, I'm not sure I remember your name.'

'Kenny,' he says, 'Kenny Pritchard.'

'Oh right,' I say. I'm pretty sure I'd remember if someone called Kenny had friended me on Facebook. It's not exactly a normal name.

'Archie,' I say. 'Archie Stone.'

His face flickers a look of doubt and then he says, 'Oh right. I've heard about that kind of thing. OK, right. Archie. Archie Stone.'

OK, this Kenny guy is a weirdo. I'm going to have to make an exit. I start putting my stuff in my bag.

'So . . . we're all right then, *Archie*? No hard feelings?'

Is that some kind of euphemism? Is he coming on to me? I'm going to have to ask Oscar about this kind of thing. It must happen to him all the time.

'Absolutely none at all, whatsoever,' I say warily.

'It was my parents . . . my mum, really. She said I should do it,' he says in a rush.

'I really don't know what you're talking about.'

'Oh. Oh right. OK, *Archie*. Fair enough.'

'Err . . . I've got to go to Maths.'

'I'm sorry, you know, if I caused you any trouble.'

'You haven't caused me any trouble.' Better humour

him. I have no idea what he's on about.

'We're OK, then?' he says, looking delighted.

'Err . . . yeah.'

'And your friend?'

What friend? Does he mean Paige? Sophie?

'Don't worry about it,' I say, vague as possible, and make my escape. What a nutter! What's he on?

I'm out of the student lounge, standing in the corridor consulting my map of the college when he catches up with me. He puts his head close to mine. I jerk away, startled.

His voice is little more than a whisper. 'I was just wondering. Do you still have your contacts?'

'Contacts?'

'Can you get me some stuff?'

'Stuff?'

'You know. Like you used to. You and your friend.'

I've had enough. 'Look, you've got it wrong. I don't know who you think I am, but I'm not him. My name is Archie Stone and I can't help you.'

He steps away. 'Oh right. Sorry.' He taps the side of his nose. 'Sorry,' he says again.

On the way to Maths, I bump into Paige again. Nice girl. Her dad works in the music business and she can get free tickets to gigs. She tells me more about the party, and I ask if I can bring some friends.

'Your girlfriend?'

'Nah, just some friends.'

'Good,' she says and winks. This girl likes me. Excellent.

We arrange to meet for a coffee after Maths. It's good, really, that I'm building a social life that doesn't involve people from Northamptonshire. It's so far away, and so different from London – another world, really. And it'd be so awkward to break up with Zoe (even though I hardly ever talk to her) and then start anything with Claire – even if she was interested. Not to mention the Ty dimension.

My mum's delighted that I'm making lots of new friends. Apparently she was a bit socially-challenged as a teenager, way back in the olden days, and nothing makes her happier than my awesome popularity.

'Have a lovely time,' she trills, as I set out for Paige's party on Saturday night, looking fine in my new Superdry shirt.

Paige lives in a big house and it's a major party. There must be fifty kids milling around. Some are drinking, some are dancing, the air is heavy with smoke, the floor scattered with empty cider and beer cans. There's no sign of her parents, but she's got bouncers on the door.

Paige waves at me from across the room, but she doesn't come over or anything and Georgia and Sophie are nowhere to be seen. I asked Lily and Oscar to come, but they were already double-booked. I can feel my confidence shrivelling. I've wanted this life for ages, but now I'm wondering if I'm really ready for it.

I grab myself a drink – coke with some vodka to spice it up – and lean against the wall, surveying the scene, trying to look cool, trying not to look like a sad loser.

'Hey.'

Jesus. It's Kenny Weirdo again. I drain my glass.

'Hi.'

'This is a bit different for you, isn't it?' he says.

'You what?' On the one hand he's mad. On the other, it's better to be talking to someone than looking lonely and awkward.

'A bit different from what you're used to.'

OK, he must mean boarding school. But that's none of his business. Does he think that I don't fit in or something?

'What do you mean by that?' I ask.

He backs off slightly. 'Nothing, mate. Sorry.'

He actually seems a bit scared of me. Excellent. I finish my drink, reach for a can of cider. The music's louder. He's mouthing something, but I can't hear what it is.

'What?'

'You got any. . .' His words are lost. Paige is pushing though the crowd towards me, I notice.

I shrug, roll my eyes, tap my ear. He leans in closer.

Go away. Paige is nearly here.

'Got any gear?' he says.

'Sorry,' I say, and move towards her smiling face.

He looks disappointed. 'Can you get me some? Like you used to.'

Like I used to?

'I'll pay. Good money.'

'Errr . . . I don't think so,' I say.

'Hi Archie!' says Paige. She's wearing a dress that just barely skims her buttocks. I'm trying not to stare.

'Never mind, mate, another time,' says Kenny Pritchard and he disappears into the crowd.

My mind is buzzing with vodka and cider and Paige. We're dancing and laughing and this party is suddenly the best I've ever been to. Paige is great. We even have a bit of a snog in the back garden, and the feel of her warm body pressing against me means I hardly notice that it's freezing cold.

It's not until 2 am, when I'm waiting for the night bus that his words come back to me.

'Like you used to.'

'Get me some gear.'

Someone used to supply him with drugs – someone who looked a lot like me, someone at his last school.

I'm actually standing outside a school. It's a real old London school, forbidding building, grey schoolyard, black railings. The noticeboard tells me its name. St Saviour's, it says. Catholic. Secondary. Boys.

Ty went to St Saviour's – all the way across London, east to west, every day to come to this school. So did his friend Arron. Ty's dad came here, sixteen years ago – all the way from Highgate in north London. It's that kind of school, apparently. Parents really like it. Tradition. High standards. Catholic values. My mum and dad were arguing about whether I should go there. That's when I came up with my mad plan to go to Hogwarts, I mean boarding school.

Anyway, I'm willing to bet that Kenny Pritchard came here.

And Kenny thought that I looked like someone he'd been at school with. The only person I look like is Ty.

And that means that my cousin Ty was Kenny Pritchard's dealer.

CHAPTER 11
Record-breaker

What a mistake. I am stupid, stupid, stupid. All I thought about was winning a race, and Claire – seeing Claire and winning.

I should have realised there'd be hundreds of people and I'd be flanked by Mr Jones and a security guard at all times, which makes people stare – a lot.

I can't see Claire anywhere, and even if I did, how would we get to speak to each other with these guys at my side?

Anyone in the crowd could have a gun or a knife or anything. Any one of them could be on their mobile, reporting in, telling someone where I am, what name I'm running under. . .

'I've changed my mind,' I say to Mr Jones as we walk towards the registration table.

'Come on, Luke, we're here now. Don't want to

make the trip for nothing, do we?'

'Do people . . . does anyone know?'

I can see people glancing at the uniformed heavy at my side. What do they think? I'm pretty sure they're not assuming he's a bodyguard.

'Well, of course the organisers had to be told. But I'm sure they'll show every discretion, as long as you behave yourself. Nothing stupid, mind.'

'I can't do it,' I say.

It's just occurred to me that if it's easy for Claire to get here, that goes for anyone at my old school. And as it's an academy with a sports specialism then there's going to be a squad here, possibly Mr Henderson, my favourite teacher ever, last seen (by me) covered in vomit (mine). A load of people who think my name is Joe, not Luke.

What if I win? They'll complain to the organisers, tell them I'm competing under a false identity. And then . . . and then. . .

Mr Jones is not smiling.

'I've put my head on the block for you, Luke Smith,' he says. 'Don't make me look stupid now. I want to go back and tell the governor and all of them that you've won your race. Glory of the old school and all that.'

He's raving mad – thinks he's teaching at some

posh private school, not a sodding prison. I open my mouth to argue, but he carries on.

'Ever think about what it's like to be me, spending my time trying to help kids who've thrown their chances away? It's a bloody thankless task, that's what it is. Most of them are too lazy to get off their arses. But you . . . you're different. You've got what it takes. I'm going to have my little bit of credit for helping you and you're going to be a good example for others to follow. You and me, we're creating a precedent here. It's not fair to pull out now.'

I couldn't care less about him, and I almost tell him so. But we're at the registration table.

And, you know what, it's not fair. Why shouldn't I compete? My life is shit, and it couldn't be shittier and I'm probably going to die young. I'm going to take this chance. I may not get another one.

Plus, if I compete, then Claire will see me. That's if she's even here.

I wrote to her. I had to be careful what I wrote, because I'm sure they spy on our letters, but I told her I was running and I told her I might be racing, and I said that maybe there might be some races near her and that'd be odd, wouldn't it?

On the back, in tiny letters, I wrote today's date and

a capital 'N'. You'd have to look really carefully to see it. It's kind of scrunched up in a corner and it might look like a heart or it might just look like a scribble. Maybe the letter checkers would miss it, I thought. They wouldn't realise I was setting up a meeting.

Maybe Claire missed it too.

I didn't put love or I'm missing you or anything like that, because I was worried that someone in the prison would read it and work out that Claire was important to me and call up the gangsters and. . .

Maybe they did already. They'd tell me, wouldn't they, if Claire was dead?

I haven't been sleeping well or eating much. I hope I can actually run a race.

Mr Jones registers me, gets a number to pin on my shirt, talks me through the day's timetable. Then he leaves me with Steve, the security guy, while he talks to the organisers. Steve's huge and bald and his neck and arms are mottled with tattoos. I used to work as a cleaner in a tattoo parlour – that's how I saw Mikey getting his done – and in my professional opinion, Steve's tattoos were done by a blind man in the dark. I'd ask him, but he was moaning on to Mr Jones about how it wasn't his job to give toerags like me a day out, so I don't think he's going to be friendly.

Then I have to warm up, stretch, check out the opposition. They're a different calibre from the boys at the running club. These are more focussed, stronger, intent on winning. I can't see anyone I recognise, which is a relief.

They look at me with unfriendly eyes. I stare right back. You don't just beat your opponent on the track. You beat them with your belief that you can't fail to crush them. Believe it in your heart, and it'll seep into theirs.

The qualifier is a breeze. I leave them all behind.

'You didn't even break sweat,' says Mr Jones, as I saunter back. 'Well done. Well done. How did it feel?'

'Good,' I say, and I'm even smiling, I'm even feeling happy, when I see her.

Claire.

She's wearing a dark pink beret, and she's wrapped up in a grey fluffy scarf and the tip of her nose has gone a bit pink. She's all by herself in the stands. She's staring around, looking for someone.

Looking for me.

There's a warm, happy feeling in my stomach, spreading through my body. My toes tingle, my teeth ache. All I want to do is smile and smile and smile.

How am I going to speak to her? How can I give

114

Mr Jones the slip? Is there any way I can get her to the start point . . . or the finish? I can't imagine we'll get any time together, but just to touch her hand. . .

I pull myself together. I can't start blubbing like a baby here and now – not with tattoo Steve watching my every move.

Mr Jones is trying to get my attention. I come to, dazed like I've been hit on the head.

'Fantastic performance,' he's saying. 'I tell you, you've got a real talent. I'm amazed no one's ever spotted it before.'

'They have,' I say, annoyed on Mr Henderson's behalf, but he goes on.

'When you get out, I'm going to give you a list of good clubs and coaches.'

'Hmm, yeah,' I say. Claire's turning her head, looking this way. . .

'This is a perfect way to escape your life of crime.'

'Yeah. . .' Mr Jones's voice is loud and I'm praying no one will hear.

'Let's get you some lunch now, don't want you getting cramp for the final.'

'Oh, OK.'

'This way.'

And I have to walk away from her because

apparently prisoners don't get lunch in a café with normal people. Prisoners have sandwiches back in the van with the security guard watching – sandwiches which might have been made by Mikey. I chew around the crust, discard the rest.

'Nervous?' asks Mr Jones. 'Don't be.'

'I'm not,' I lie, and he says, 'Come on, then.'

Claire's gone. My stomach clenches in disappointment. But at least I know what I'm looking for now. And she'll be looking for me. I scan the crowd for her pink beret. I imagine her, anxious, searching, worrying she'll miss me. . .

'Twenty minutes,' he says. 'Come and start warming up.'

That's when I see her again – her pink beret, her grey scarf, black jacket, skinny jeans and boots.

Her big blue eyes, her pink lips, her heart-shaped face.

She's not looking for me at all. She's not even going to watch my race. She's talking and laughing and walking towards the café. I know the guy she's with. He's called Max. He used to be a good friend of mine.

He's kind of short, Max, but he's taller than Claire, and they look just right together, his arm around her shoulders. Claire and I always look wrong. I'm too tall, she's too small.

He's stolen my girl. He's stolen my Claire. I want to kill him.

I stumble. My headache's back – worse than it's ever been. Big bass drums thunder inside my skull. White-hot needles stab my eyes.

'Are you all right?' says Mr Jones. 'You've gone very pale. Do you need some water?'

I shake my head. He offers me a glucose tablet and I take it, feeling it melt in my mouth, feeling the sweetness trickle down my throat. I wash it down with a gulp of water.

Claire came here to show me that she's moved on. That's OK (it's not). It's actually good (it's not). Max is a nice guy (traitor), and he's always fighting for the right stuff and I'm almost sure that no one's trying to kill him – apart from me, and I'm not sure I really would do it.

He's much better for Claire than I am (true. It's true).

'Time,' says Mr Jones, and I follow him. My legs are a bit shaky. I'm not sure if I can actually do this.

He's looking at me. 'Are you ill?'

'No . . . just a bit . . . I feel a bit. . .'

'The best athletes can focus themselves to overcome any pain,' he says. 'The will to win is the most important thing. They learn to endure anything, until they reach their goal.'

'I can do that,' I say, and he says, 'I know you can. Go and do it.'

It's tempting to give up – forget running, forget living. What's my life going to be without Claire?

But there's a race to win, and somehow that still matters to me. I've lost everything else, but I can still have this.

So I line up with the other finalists. I give them the look which will transmit defeat to their hearts. I bounce on the balls of my feet. I turn my body into a running machine, built for speed, unable to feel pain, or fear, or anything apart from the hunger to reach the end.

We'll all die, I tell myself, *a horrible death – ripped to shreds by dogs, flung into an acid bath – all except the winner. I have to be the winner.*

And I am. And the pain in my legs and my lungs and my abdominal muscles tears me apart, but it chases away the clattering noise in my head.

People are shouting and clapping and it's all aimed at me. I am the centre of the crowd. Everyone is looking at me, seeing me, trying to talk to me.

And maybe the glucose wears off or something, because I'm sweating and shivering and my legs are too wobbly to hold me, and everything's gone blurry and I'm kneeling on the grass, which is wet, and coughing up the crusts from my lunch.

'Get up,' says a gruff voice, and I struggle to sit up.

'You OK?' says Steve.

'No,' I say, and then I see Mr Jones. He's talking to a group of three or four guys. He's grinning, gesticulating, saying, 'I consider myself a real force for rehabilitation. The Home Secretary should come and visit our gym, see what can be achieved.'

All the people he's with have notebooks or mini tape recorders. Jesus. He's giving a press conference.

'Luke's our star, but we've got other boys doing as well,' he's saying. 'Come over here, Luke. Come and talk to the reporters.'

'No,' I say.

'Just a picture,' says one of the journalists, and he pulls out a camera and starts snapping.

'No!' I say, but no one listens to me.

'You've just broken the UK record time for junior boys in the 1500 metres,' says one of them. 'How does it feel?'

I've got my arm up hiding my face, but they're taking my picture anyway.

'You've come out of nowhere, now you're about to take the athletics world by storm,' says another. 'Can you tell us how you've done it?'

'What's it like, training for stardom in a prison?'

'I can't say anything . . . go away. . .' I gasp, but Mr Jones says, 'It's OK, Luke. It's all good publicity. This'll get you training and maybe even sponsorship when you get out.'

'His name's not Luke,' says someone on the outside of the crowd that's gathered, and I look up and catch her eye. Zoe. Claire's friend, Zoe. She's a good runner, I remember, and she trains with Claire's sister Ellie, and she was always banging on about how male athletes got more fuss and attention than girls, which is bollocks, if you ask me.

No one seems to hear her, anyway, and they keep on with their questions, until I find my voice.

'I'm not talking! Go away!'

Other people are pressing in on me, and I'm finding it hard to breath. I try and speak to Zoe, but she's too far away and it's too noisy and anyway how do I start a conversation with someone who's going to call me Joe?

'Get me out of here,' I say to Mr Jones, and he tuts and says, 'It's all for your own good,' but he waves away the reporters and says, 'We'd better go back. We're on a tight schedule.'

Back at the van – record-breaker or not, I still get cuffed and stuck in the cell at the back – I try and keep my voice steady.

'What were you doing? Why were you talking to them?'

'Luke,' he says, 'you just took half a second off the UK record. Do you know how extraordinary that is? If you can get proper training, proper sponsorship, the world's your oyster. You could go the whole way, Luke. Olympic gold. And you'd have me to thank for it.'

I want to hit him. I would, if my arms weren't cuffed together.

'I can't be in a newspaper! I can't have my photo taken! I'm meant to be in witness protection! I've got a false identity. What were you thinking?'

He looks at me, so puzzled, so blank, that I think that's it's me who's got it wrong – just for a second.

Then he says, 'What do you mean, you're in witness protection?'

CHAPTER 12
Visit

Danny picks me up at 7 am from my auntie Marina and uncle George's house. Mum's in Frankfurt, Dad's in Newcastle. I've been trying to persuade them that they can leave me on my own, but they're not having it.

'It's not that we think you'd come to any harm,' said Dad, 'but we're quite fond of our house.'

It's fair enough, really, because if I was home alone I'd be obliged to have a party, and I've been to enough parties in the last few weeks to know that they can go out of control if you don't have loads of bouncers.

It's actually quite fun to have a week off from socialising and spend time with my little cousins Ludo and Atticus who think I'm a total hero, just because I'm loads older than they are.

They're not meant to know that Ty's in prison, but I tell them, anyway. Ludo's eyes are round and worried, but Atticus thinks it's great and draws him a card with arrows on the front ('Because that's what they wear on their prison suits') and 'Have a nice time! With best wishes from your cousin Atticus Tyler-Bennett!' inside, in his best joined-up handwriting.

I ask Danny loads of questions in the car, about what celebrities he's been taking pictures of, and what it was like playing Glastonbury and stuff, but I only get growly short answers and after a bit I shut up.

I don't know why he doesn't seem to like me. I think we could have a lot in common, if only he'd talk to me. But he doesn't seem really interested. I'm going to have to up my game a bit.

There's a big wire fence around the Young Offender Institution – well, I suppose there would be – and you can't drive in, you have to park outside and then walk. We all go in one by one, and they do a pat-down search of my body. I wonder how it felt when Ty came here for the first time. Was it like this?

And then you have to go through loads of signing things and waiting around until they show you into a room full of tables and chairs. There are other people waiting, but we get whisked away from them, taken to a separate place.

'Why aren't we with everyone else?' I ask, and Danny says, 'Security. Just in case anyone's out to get Ty. He's here under another name – they can't risk anyone finding out where he is.'

Ty's life is like something out of a Mafia film, except that in those films the Mafia guys always get their prey. And obviously that's not going to happen to Ty. It can't.

There's a whole load of waiting around in a room that's clearly a classroom – tables, chairs, a whiteboard with stuff written on it, pretty basic maths stuff (times tables, that kind of thing). They must have some really young kids here. It kind of cheers me up that Ty isn't the youngest. I mean, it can't be that bad, if they're teaching people who must be about nine years old. Maybe he can help out with them sometimes, teach them about running, that kind of thing. I think he'd like that.

And then he's here. He's really pale, and a little bit stubbly round the chin – I'm jealous – and he smells a bit off. Stale sweat. Maybe they don't get deodorant in here. He's wearing grey trackies, a bright orange T-shirt and some really naff trainers.

I try not to stare, but it's weird seeing him like this.

I feel a bit self-conscious in my sharp new skinny jeans, my dazzling white T, my Superdry plaid shirt, my aftershave (OK, I don't actually need to shave much, but at least I smell nice). I'm pretty cool. It looks like I belong with Danny (labels everywhere, but in a more subtle way) more than his own son.

How would I feel about me if I were Ty? I'd hate me, that's how I'd feel.

And that's before I've told him about Claire.

'Hey,' says Danny. 'How's it going? I told you I got them to give us extra visits – compassionate, because of . . . well . . . anyway, Archie's come along today.'

Talk about stating the obvious. Ty doesn't say anything, but his look flickers contempt. I'd been having difficulties imagining him as some drug-dealing criminal mastermind, but I'm swiftly revising my views.

'Hey, Ty,' I say. My voice sounds chirpy and childish.

'Hey, Archie,' he growls.

'How's it going?' says Danny.

'It wasn't my fault,' he says. 'They didn't tell the whole staff, only those who need to know. They reckon it's safer that way. Mr Jones, he didn't know.'

'Who?'

'In the papers.' He presses his forehead with his fingers, like he's trying to widen his skull. 'The papers. About the race.'

'What papers? What race?'

Ty just shrugs.

'Tell me,' says Danny, just the slightest edge of irritation in his voice.

Ty's instantly furious. 'I thought you knew! I thought that's why you were here! I thought maybe . . . maybe. . .'

'What?'

He shakes his head. 'Never mind.'

'Tell me,' says Danny, through gritted teeth. 'We haven't got long.'

'Mr Jones, he runs the gym here. And he organised for me to do training at a local club. And he put me into a sports competition at some place just outside Northampton.'

'Oh!' I say. 'Zoe mentioned she was going to that. It's really near where she lives, and loads of people go from her school, apparently.'

He's glaring at me. 'Yeah, and so I went and I won and some reporters wanted to interview me. . .'

'You what?' says Danny.

'. . . because I broke the record for UK junior boys 1500 metres. And Mr Jones was telling them all about me being in here, and it turned out he never even knew that I wasn't really called Luke Smith or about witness protection or anything.'

'What?'

'They have a need-to-know policy, and the governor was at some conference when Mr Jones asked permission, it was the assistant governor and she didn't remember who I was. . .'

'So are you in the papers?'

'. . . and I thought maybe you'd worked something out with them and I could go. . .'

'Have they shown you the reports?'

'. . . they might let me out a bit early. . .'

'Ty, what actually appeared in the paper?'

'. . . I thought *you'd* know. But you don't. They don't actually give us papers in here. I don't sit around with a sodding cappuccino and a copy of the *Independent*.'

They glower at each other.

'Jesus, Ty,' says Danny. 'You should have known better.'

'I broke a UK record,' says Ty, clearly bragging and you can tell – well, I can – that he's desperate for a fight.

'Yeah, well, that wasn't worth risking your life for,' says Danny.

'How many records have *you* broken?'

'That is so not the point.'

'It is to me.'

'I'll talk to the lawyer, see if we can use this to leverage an earlier release date,'

'Well done,' says Ty, his voice full of contempt and hate.

I'm really not looking forward to telling him that Claire wants a break. I'll have to start off by saying something like, 'Don't shoot the messenger.' *Don't shoot the messenger, but your girlfriend, who you adore, who makes your miserable life worth living – she wants to chuck you.*

OK, it's not going to happen.

'You're probably wondering where your mum is . . . why she hasn't been. . .'

Ty rolls his eyes.

'Well . . . she's not really up to it. She's not great, Ty. She's very sad about your gran, obviously and she's having to cope with Alyssa on her own.'

Ty's hands are balled into fists.

'I've suggested that she goes and stays with Emma for a bit in Spain – to get some sunshine, moral support.

What do you think?'

Ty shrugs again. It's as though he doesn't trust himself to speak.

Danny tries again. 'Do you think it's a good idea?'

'My picture's been in the paper,' says Ty. 'I think it's slightly essential.'

'Well . . . have you actually seen your picture in the paper? It was probably just someone from the local rag.'

'They were taking pictures!' He's almost screaming.

'Calm down,' says the prison officer.

'You know that money?' says Ty.

'What money?'

'You said you had money for me – for when I'm eighteen.'

'I have put aside some money, yes,' says Danny, very slowly and carefully.

'Give it to Mum – for Alyssa, tell her. And Spain's no good. Can't you send them to America?'

'I'm not sure.'

'Florida. We always wanted to go to Florida. Disney. Alyssa would like it.'

'I'll talk to her. . .'

'Yeah.' Ty yawns. 'You talk to her. Tell her that Alyssa needs to be safe. Florida should be OK.

Maybe Emma can go too.'

'Emma's pretty settled in Spain. She seems to be happy with Carlos.'

'She shouldn't trust him,' says Ty. 'Get her away from him.'

'Ty, I don't think. . .'

Ty waves his hand to shut his dad up.

'Don't think. I done all the thinking. I get a lot of time to think in here.'

His voice has changed, I realise. He's more east London. He's got that Jamaican rhythm, his words are all vowels, it's 'dis' and 'dat' and 'fink' and 'fings', and 'wha'eva'. And 'fu'' and 'fu'ing', every other word.

I sometimes put on that voice as a joke – a joke about chavs and being street, a charm against getting mugged or worse. That's the voice of the people who scare the rest of us. And Ty does it so naturally that it's as if it reveals the real him.

The drug-dealing him. The secret him.

'The rest of the money, I want it – ready for when I come out, in cash. You can give it to me when I get out of here.'

'I don't think. . .'

Ty narrows his eyes. 'I told you. I done all the thinking.'

'Finkin'.' If I listen hard enough, then I'm sure I can do this voice too.

'You don't have to worry about me.'

'Ty, stop it. You're only just sixteen, for God's sake.'

'I'm all grown-up.'

'Ty,' I say, 'I talked to Claire.'

I'm kind of hoping he'll have come to the same conclusion as her, i.e. they have no future, no chance, no hope and he's not right for her, anyway.

He drops his eyes to the table. 'What did she say?'

'She was . . . she was upset . . . she wasn't sure. . .'

'Yeah.' His voice roughens. 'Thanks for telling her. She's better off without me.'

Danny says, 'You'll be out of here soon. We'll sort everything out. You'll be fine.'

Ty shrugs. 'I can look after myself.'

'Oh yeah,' says Danny. He's got this talent for keeping his voice really smooth and even, although I can see he's upset. His hand is trembling. 'You can look after yourself with my money. Just like you did when you got your picture in the paper? Jesus, Ty.'

'I can look after myself whatever.'

Wha'eva. I so could do this voice. I almost open my mouth and join in.

'Where are you going to go? They'll want to keep

an eye on you when you come out, you know? Make sure you don't do anything that means you have to come back and serve the rest of your sentence. That's assuming you manage to behave yourself for six weeks. Think you can do that? You've not got a great track record, have you, Ty?'

'Better than yours.'

I'm getting a bit embarrassed now. It seems to me they'd be better doing this in private. Ty seems to be enjoying slagging his dad off in front of me. There's a dangerous smile on his face.

'Whatever I've done, that's gotta be better than abandoning your kid and spending a fortune on coke,' he says.

Danny winces.

'I've told you, tried to explain – addiction is an illness, not a lifestyle choice.'

'Yeah, right.' Ty's voice is thick with bitterness. 'My gran said you were a waste of space, said you were no good.'

Danny's calm voice wavers just a little bit. 'Yeah, well, maybe your gran didn't always know what was best.'

'Oh yeah?' Ty's voice is taunting now, twisting, setting traps, laying mines. I'm amazed that Danny can't see it. But he goes blundering in.

'She could have made sure that I was part of your life, Ty – not just me, my parents, Archie here, your whole family. But no, she didn't do that. She told lies, she hid you away. She wasn't perfect, any more than I am.'

Ty's lip curls. 'She didn't take drugs.'

She didn't sell drugs, either, I think. I don't say it, though. The atmosphere is explosive enough.

'I'm sorry. I did a lot of things I shouldn't have done. But I wasn't the only one at fault.'

'You saying it was all my gran's fault?'

'No, obviously not.'

'You saying she was a bad person?'

'No, Ty, that's not what I was saying.'

'Sounds like it to me. What about you, Archie? Doesn't it sound like he was disrespecting my gran?'

Oh shit. What do I say now?

'Err . . . not really completely. . .'

They contemplate me with identically hostile faces.

Danny takes a deep breath. 'Look, Ty, you're obviously angry. It's fair enough. Try not to blame people, though. We just want to help you.'

'You can help me by doing what I told you – my money, in cash. And then leave me alone.'

'I'm not going to do that.'

'Fine.' He stands up. 'Don't bother coming back. I'll manage on my own. Bye, Archie, nice knowing you.'

'Come on, Ty, sit down again,' says Danny, but the prison guard guy (he's the spitting image of that gardening bloke on the telly – you know, Alan Titchmarch) says, 'Time's up,' and Ty walks towards the door without looking back.

'Ty,' I say, as he's about to walk out, 'what shall I say to Claire?'

He glances back. There's no warmth in his face.

'Tell her what you want,' he says. 'Tell her goodbye, good luck with the rest of her life.'

CHAPTER 13
Kyle

Danny doesn't really want to talk on the way back to London but I go for it, anyway.

'He didn't mean it,' I say. 'He's just angry, you know, generally angry, and he let it out at you.'

Danny is furiously chewing gum. 'I know that,' he says.

'He's probably feeling really guilty about his gran dying.'

'Yes, I'm aware of that.' He pulls out into the fast lane, cutting up a Mazda6.

'He's scared that someone might see him in the paper. But he wasn't definitely in the paper. And he's a bit worried about Alyssa.'

'No, you don't say?'

He swerves in front of a Ford Mondeo. The driver honks him.

'He's probably missing his mum,' I say, and Danny says, 'You remind me of *your* mum, Archie – always dissecting other people's lives. Can you leave it out right now?'

I don't say another word all the way back to Islington.

When he drops me off, the house is quiet and empty. Ludo and Atticus are still at school, their parents are out. I think about ringing Paige, seeing what I missed in English, but I can't be bothered. I text Oscar and Lily, but they don't reply.

I'm like a spare part, an intruder. I don't belong in London like they do. I don't really belong anywhere.

I feel like a smoke, but I left my weed in Fulham. I'm running out, anyway. Oscar passed some on to me and I gave him money for more, but I really need to get my own supply.

I'm wandering around the house, like a burglar, picking up books which I might read one day, switching the television on and then off again. I can't really concentrate.

I get out my phone and I google the name of the Young Offender Institution, along with 1500 metres record. And there he is – Luke Smith. The amazing story of the prisoner who beat the country's leading young athletes, exclusive to the *Daily Mirror*.

I don't even hear my uncle George come back into the house.

'Woah!' I say, when he coughs and says, 'Hey Archie. Hard at work? How was your visit?'

'Rubbish,' I say, and I fill him in. I show him the screen. 'Look. He was right. He's in a national paper.'

George whistles. 'That's bad. Grounds to move him immediately, I'd say. What a screw-up.'

'I thought they were all in prison, the people out to get him.'

'The main ones are – Tommy White and his henchmen – but they've got people working for them all over the place. Come and have a look. I've been doing some research.'

'Have you? Why?'

'Well, it's a good story, isn't it?' he says. 'That's what I do, find good stories, dig around a bit, write them up. I thought, with the family connection and everything, that this might even make a book.'

Uncle George is a freelance journalist who does a lot for the BBC and for papers like the *Guardian* and the *Observer*. He's not a tabloid hack or anything like that. But even so.

'Ty would hate that,' I point out.

'Hmmm. Well. It's a bigger story than just Ty. Tommy White's going to come to trial next year sometime and the BBC have already said they're interested in a backgrounder. Could make a *Panorama*. And maybe one day I can tell Ty's story for him.'

Ty would never want that. So it'd only be possible if he were dead. I'm tempted to ask if Uncle George thinks that's likely. I don't.

'Here you go,' he says, handing over a file. 'You two are good friends, aren't you? Tell me if you think there's stuff I've left out.'

What the hell? I'm not going to be anyone's spy. If anyone's writing Ty's story, it's going to be me.

'Thanks,' I say, but his phone rings. 'Ah. Yes. We'd better go through his statement,' he says. 'Just put it all back when you've had a look, Archie. I might be some time.' And he heads off to his study.

I sift though the file.

There are cuttings from newspapers – the *Mail*, the *Sun*, the *Telegraph* – of the trial where Ty had to give evidence. Some bits are underlined. There's a police mugshot photo of a young guy with angry eyes and dark hair. There's a page where Uncle George has drawn a diagram – like a family tree, but instead of births, marriages and deaths, it's linking weird names and numbers together. Hacknee Boyz. Ruby's, The Nitebox, Ray's Boxing Club, E5.

Ray's Boxing Club. I'm sure Ty mentioned a boxing club once. I was impressed. It sounded dead hard and kind of Hollywood.

That's the first bit. Then there's a rubber-banded wodge of paper that's all about Ty. Photocopied school reports from St Saviour's ('Quiet in class . . . needs to speak up more.' 'More effort needed.' 'Tyler has a natural flair for languages, and has worked well in French this year').

There's a photo of Ty and the boy in the other picture – the police picture. They're in school uniform, and they're just walking down a road – I mean, it doesn't look like a posed picture, they're not grinning for the camera or anything. Ty's slightly behind the boy, head down. They look happy enough. You can see they're friends.

Looking at the newspaper cuttings, I can identify this boy. He's called Arron Mackenzie and he's the one who did the stabbing – the stabbing that Ty witnessed. According to the newspapers, Arron Mackenzie ran a gang in Hackney. He was supplying drugs to boys at his school – St Saviour's. He was mugging and stealing and dealing and all sorts.

And Ty was his best friend, had been forever.

I haven't got a best friend like that. Oscar and Lily, they're mates, but I always have this uneasy feeling that they're more important to me than I am to them. I kind of imagine it'd be great to have a close friend, someone to share stuff with, someone you can trust.

If your best friend was a drug-dealing mugger, then you'd be one too, wouldn't you?

It's three o'clock, so the twins will be home soon. They get picked up from school by a guy named Ferdy, who's studying Taxidermy and funds it by babysitting. He's OK, Ferdy, actually very interesting on the subject of skinning weasels, but the twins are noisy and I can't be bothered with them right now. And Uncle George is busy, so I can't ask him what it all means.

So I put everything back in the file, grab my jacket and my Oyster card and head out. It's a five minute walk to Upper Street, which is like the main road through Islington. There are loads of shops and cafes and things, including a massive Jack Wills (which, in case you're not cool enough to know, is a shop which not only has really good clothes, but they all have JACK or WILLS or JW on them so everyone knows they're really good).

But I ignore all the interesting places. They make me feel soft and spoiled and ashamed. Ty didn't grow up with a Jack Wills on every corner. Ty never had any money for this kind of stuff. And then I see a bus coming along and it says Hackney on the front and without really thinking about it, I grab my Oyster card from my pocket and I swing onto the bus.

Islington isn't really very far from Hackney (although it's much, much nicer) so it only takes half an hour before I'm standing on the street where they had Ty's gran's funeral.

There's no Jack Wills here, no Next or Gap or Paperchase or Starbucks – nothing that you'd see in a normal shopping street. It's African and Polish and Turkish and Cypriot, all jumbled together – weird vegetables that I've never seen before, greasy shish kebab going round and round, Afro hair specialists, halal butchers.

I can smell spice and blood and rubbish bins. What am I doing? Why am I here?

And then I see it – Ray's Boxing Club, a flyer on the church noticeboard. There's an address – 43 Rodney Road – it can't be far from here. How can I find out where it is? Obviously in an area like this I can't flash my iPhone around to use the GPS.

I spot a newsagent's a few shops along the row. Patel's, it's called, like 90 per cent of corner shops in London. I push the jangling door open. The blood and rubbish smell disappears. In its place is a strange mixture of old chocolate and bleach. There's a rack of magazines, and then the rest of the shop is food – Pot Noodles, Custard Creams, cheese and onion crisps. It's like an oasis of Englishness in a multicultural world.

'Can I help you?' says the Asian man behind the counter. He's looking at me very intently, almost staring.

'Errr . . . no, I don't think so.' I feel a bit awkward. Maybe he thinks I'm a shoplifter. 'I'm looking for Rodney Road. I think it's around here.'

He blinks. 'It's not far. . .' He counts on his fingers. 'Sixth on the left, other side of the road. Just past the Duke of York.'

'Oh right, ' I say.

'Why do you want Rodney Road?'

'Oh, err . . . there's a boxing club there. Thought I might check it out.'

He looks at me hard, one more time. What's going on with this guy? Does he fancy me or something? Is he a raving paedo? I glance sideways and he says,

'Watch out for yourself. There can be trouble at that club.'

'Oh right? Trouble?'

'Yes . . . I knew a boy, about your age—'

And then his wife bustles out of the back of the shop with a question about someone's *Women's Weekly* and I seize my chance to escape.

The door jangles behind me, and I'm walking past the kebab shop, along to a big, dark pub (Happy Hour! Karaoke! Cocktail Nite!) and here we are. Rodney Road. And number 43 is a big box of a building, metal shutters on the windows, a black side door and a buzzer marked 'Ray'.

Nothing ventured, nothing gained. I hit the buzzer.

There's a pause, then a woman's voice crackles through. 'Yes?'

'It's . . . my name's . . . err . . . Kyle. I wanted to know about lessons.' I make my voice as like Ty's in the prison as I can. I sound ridiculous, sure, but she lets me in, anyway.

There's a flight of stairs, walls painted black, and then another door. I push on it and it opens into an enormous space. Wow. Two boxing rings, circled by mats and those huge punchbags that hang from the ceiling, a free weights area, some bikes and things. The sound of thwack, thwack, thwack as fists hit the bags. And the smell of stale sweat and beer.

'Hello, dearie,' says a lady, who's got her own little office just to the right of the door. 'Want to join?' She looks me up and down. 'Complete beginner, I take it?'

I nod. 'Yeah.'

Up close I realise that she's quite old, but she's made an effort by dyeing her hair and wearing false eyelashes and really tight jeans.

'I'm Sylvia,' she says. 'What do you want, group or individual? Most of the beginners are younger than you, so you might want to start off with some one-to-one.'

'Um, yeah, right, OK.'

She passes me a form. 'Fill that in for me, dearie. You're not from round here, are you?'

'Just moved here,' I say.

'But I've met you before, haven't I? Now let me see. . .' She shakes her head. 'I can't remember when it was. But I've definitely seen you here before.'

'Not me,' I say, trying to sound confident. She must be thinking of Ty. Whoops.

I fill in her form, inventing an address for Kyle,

but giving my own mobile number and my surname. Minimise the lies.

I dig out twenty-five pounds from my wallet. 'Is that enough for a lesson?'

'It is, but you don't have to pay now, darling. Wait until the lesson. Sunday suit you? At 10 am?'

I've never actually got up before 12 on a Sunday (at home, that is, one of the inhumane things about boarding school is that they wake you up at 8 am at the weekend – even earlier at Allingham Priory, because we had to go to Mass).

But I can make an exception for this.

'Do I need to get any equipment?' I ask, and she says, 'You are flush, aren't you, dear? No, don't worry, we've got everything here.'

That seems to be it. She gives me another searching look up and down, and then snaps her fingers and says, 'Ty! Little Ty Lewis! That's who you remind me of.'

I try to look as blank as possible.

'Oh yeah, never heard of him.'

She's beaming. 'Knew it'd come to me. Little Ty. You don't know him? What a coincidence, you boys are like two peas in a pod.'

Not any more, I think, remembering how thin

145

Ty looked this morning, the dark shadows under his eyes, the short hair. I probably look more like Ty used to than he does himself.

I look round the room. 'He comes here a lot?'

She shakes her head. 'Not any more. They moved away, the whole family. Terrible thing. His gran . . . well, I heard she died. Not surprised.'

'Oh, right. Never heard of him.'

She cackles. 'Well, Kyle Stone, we'll see you Sunday. And we'll find out if you're a better fighter than Ty Lewis.'

CHAPTER 14
Alarm

Stark raving mad,' says Oscar.

'Impressive,' says Lily.

It's Saturday night and we couldn't be arsed to go to a party (although we had, between us, invites to three) so we're lying on the floor of my bedroom, getting stoned. Mum's still away and Dad's at the office.

'I'll be late,' he said. 'Don't wait up for me.'

It's never struck me before, but it's a bit odd, working late on a Saturday. Could my dad have a secret life – a lover, maybe?

I wonder how upset my mum would be if she found out. And how would I feel if they broke up?

'Run it past me one more time,' says Oscar. 'Why are you doing this?'

'Well, y'know, it seemed like a good idea, to find out more about Ty, sort of immerse myself in his life – his life before all the prison and stuff. And I'm exploring my roots as well. My dad's from round there, but he never tells me anything about it.'

'You've got your own life, Archie. Why'd you want to go and get beaten up by a load of East End boys?'

'I dunno.' I exhale and watch the smoke curl up toward the sloping ceiling. I'm laughing. 'Maybe I'll beat them up.'

'Awesome,' says Lily. She leans towards Oscar, tickles his cheek. 'You'd do the same if you were a real man. Why don't you go along with Archie?'

Lily thinks I'm a real man! Wow!

'Nah,' says Oscar, and I shake my head.

'I've gotta do this on my own,' I say. 'I'm going undercover.'

'I've got better things to do with my time,' says Oscar. 'Unlike you and Archie, I'm not being spoon-fed through my GCSEs.' He closes his eyes. Oscar never gets giggly and silly when stoned, like Lily and me. He aims more at a zen-like serenity.

Lily stretches her arms over her head. She's wearing a skimpy vest and I can see her whole midriff when she does that. She's absolutely gorgeous, but – luckily, I think – the weed knocks out the need for a preventative run down the Bakerloo line.

'I'm sooo happy. I'm leaving those bitches behind me!' Lily sings. She flings her arms around me. 'I'm going to be with my lovely Archie-bear, all day and all night.'

'Woo . . . steady on, Lil,' I say. I might be stoned, but I'm not *that* stoned.

Oscar sighs. 'Cop out,' he says.

'You're just jealous,' she sings.

Oscar raises an eyebrow.

'How did you persuade your mum again?' I ask.

'A little bit of this, a little bit of that. Skipping breakfast, throwing up after supper, refusing to talk to her, failing three mocks. . .'

'Tut, tut,' says Oscar.

'And then I left my diary lying around, and it was all about the pressure at that school, the bitchy girls, the competition to get ten A*s and how I couldn't bear it, I couldn't bear it, I couldn't *bear* it. . .'

'And she gave you a free pass to Butler's.'

'Whee! Whoo! Lucky, lucky me!'

Lucky me, I think. Having Lily there at Butler's will be fantastic. I'll be instantly Mr Super-popular.

'I can't wait,' I say.

Lily pins me to the floor. It's the nicest feeling ever. She stares into my eyes. 'Archie, you are so sweet,

I might have to eat you all up.'

Oh Jesus. *Lambeth North.* I'm not as stoned as I thought I was.

Go away, Oscar.

'I love you, Archie.'

She kisses me right on the mouth, taking me by surprise. Her mouth is soft – so soft – and wet and our teeth clash.

'Waterloo.' Oh God! I said it out loud!

'You want the loo?' Lily's laughing too much to go on kissing me.

'For God's sake,' says Oscar. 'I'm going.'

I don't know why he's so cross. Nor does Lily.

'Hey, Oscar,' she says. 'Group hug!'

'I'm going,' says Oscar again, 'and so should you, Lily. Archie, you need your sleep if you're really getting up to go boxing tomorrow morning. You'll want to be reasonably sharp.'

'Maybe I won't bother,' I say. My hand's on the smooth skin of Lily's back and it feels like heaven.

But Lily says, 'Oh yes you are. . .' and Oscar grabs her arm and yanks her to her feet.

'C'mon, Lil,' he says, and she smiles up at him and says, 'I love you both so much.'

It's only 11 pm, and Dad's not back yet. They

disappear down the stairs – Lily staggering and giggling and Oscar propping her up. I log onto Skype. Zoe's online, so I call her. I've kind of neglected her recently.

She fills up the screen, all dark hair and toffee skin and a red vest. She's so attractive that I wish I could just transport myself to her room. I wonder if one day that'll be possible through the internet? It'd be so cool – also good for the environment – but much harder to avoid people. And stuff like chatroulette would be really disgusting.

'Hey, stranger,' she says.

'Hey, Zoe,'

'How's it going? Are you home for half term?'

I feel bad. I haven't been in touch at all since I left school. Claire's not told her a thing, it's clear. Briefly, I fill her in – except I leave out the drugs, Ty's trial and the whole prison stuff, so it's a short enough story. I left boarding school because my parents were missing me, I tell her. I'm working really hard at my new school. Maybe I can come and see her some weekend soon.

And then she tells me about her school and her life and athletics and stuff, and I let my eyes glaze over and start thinking that Claire and I have loads more in common than Zoe and I do, but Ty and Zoe have athletics to talk about and maybe we could all just swap and they could go running together.

I have my hand down my trousers, I admit. Surely that's the whole point of Skype?

'I actually won the 1500 metres,' said Zoe, 'which was pretty amazing. Will you tell Joe?'

'Yeah, right,' I say,

'I saw him, you know. He broke a UK record.'

'You saw him?'

'Yeah, it was definitely him. But he looked really different, and they were calling him Luke something.'

'Mmm, Zoe . . . actually . . . about that. . .'

And then someone's hands are over my eyes.

'Argh! What the—'

Lily is laughing her head off.

'What's going on?' says Zoe.

Lily leans forward to the keyboard. 'Hello!' she says, waving like mad.

Zoe's head is doing that slow jerky Skypey thing, and Lily starts imitating her.

'Who's that?' says Zoe.

'I'm Lily and he's mine, all mine! Bye-bye, bumpkin!'

'Lily . . . Zoe . . . you can't—'

Lily switches off Zoe's outraged face. Oh bum.

'Go away, Lily! I thought you went ages ago.'

'Well, we went downstairs and then I was hungry, so we decided to make you a snack, Archie, wasn't that nice of us? And then Oscar's mum rang and there's some crisis with Marcus, so he had to go and I thought I'd come and find you again, because we don't want boring old girly girl on the Skype keeping my Archie from me, do we?'

'That was Zoe! My sort-of girlfriend!'

I ought to be cross with her, but my head's all muzzy and she's messing my hair and nuzzling my neck. And let's face it, I haven't been exactly thinking of Zoe much myself recently, what with Paige and Lily and the whole tricky question of Claire, which I'm not thinking about either.

'Forget it, Archie, forget her. How can you have a relationship with someone who doesn't even live in London? What about that girl Paige, who seems to be stalking you on Facebook?' She's discovered my flies. 'Oh! Naughty Archie!'

OK, this is what I've dreamed of, but still. . .

Lily's taken her top off, so I can see her bra. This is brilliant, but there's something bothering me . . . I can't quite work out what. . .

'Come on, Lil,' I say. 'You're stoned.' She's

pulling my T-shirt up and over my head.

'Leave it out, Lily,' I say. I have no idea at all where I'm getting my self-control from. Maybe it's performance anxiety.

She launches herself at me – 'Archieeee!' – and we sprawl onto the floor with a massive crash.

'Ugh . . . owww. . .' My head bangs against the side of the desk. But still, it's a good feeling, lying here with Lily writhing against me. It's just that . . . there's something. . .

No! The loudest, highest, most awful noise in the world suddenly goes off in my ear. What the hell? Have my parents fixed up some sort of naked girl alarm in my room?

'What's that?' quavers Lily.

I'm wriggling back into my clothes. I'm just hopping around with two legs squashed into the same sleeve – yes, I've got my T-shirt mixed up with my jeans – when my dad erupts into my room, yelling his head off.

'You stupid idiot! You could've set the house on fire!'

'What?'

'The smoke alarm! Can't you hear it? Jesus, Archie!'

'I was just coming. . .'

'You could've burned the house down! What do you think happens if you leave a piece of bread under the grill on full blast?'

'Uh . . . I dunno. . .'

'It bursts into flames, you moron! It turns into a blackened bit of charcoal and smoke pours from it and—' someone is bashing at the front door '—then the fire brigade turns up.'

He turns and crashes down the stairs again. Lily is laughing her head off and I'm trying not to laugh . . . but. . .

'Come on,' I tell her, 'get up. Get dressed. You've got to go.'

'Oh, Archie. . .'

'You nearly burned the house down!' Why does this seem hilarious? 'Imagine if we'd had to jump out the window!' I say, and we're both shrieking with laughter.

'I was making you a snack!'

'And now my dad thinks we were. . .'

'Oh, come on, Archie. . .'

We've just about got dressed, when Dad marches up the stairs again.

'Right, Lily, down the stairs,' he orders.

'Aaaw, Dad. . .' I plead.

Dad's forehead is wrinkled into a perma-frown and if I had any sense I'd shut up right now.

'Can't Lily stay over?'

'Come on, Lily,' says Dad. 'I'd better give you a lift home.'

Lily gets up. She's a bit shaky on her feet, and Dad barks, 'Give her a hand, Archie. We don't want her falling down the stairs.'

Lily can't stop laughing, and that makes me laugh, despite Dad's silent fury beaming into the back of my head.

Downstairs is freezing – all the doors and windows wide open – and still pretty smoky. The smell is disgusting.

'I'll walk Lily home,' I tell Dad. 'Maybe I should stay there tonight while you decontaminate this place.'

He points to the living room. He's got his grimmest face on.

'You're staying here.'

And he bundles Lily outside and into the Prius. Huh.

By the time he comes back I've started watching his box set of *The Wire*. Maybe we can bond over it. I might need to find some subtitles, though – no one seems to be speaking English.

Dad glides into the room, picks up the remote and freezes the screen – probably a good thing, because apart from a vague idea that it was about drugs, criminals, cops and lawyers, I had no idea what was going on.

And then he starts.

I am a loser. I am a waste of space. I am pissing away his money. This is exactly why he and Mum sent me to boarding school. What the hell do I think I am doing? Am I going to screw up this chance, like I've messed up everything else?

There's no point saying anything. I actually had no idea that this was how he felt about me.

The way I'm sitting there, trying not to laugh, seems to make him even angrier. And the angrier he gets, the more I want to laugh. And when I do, he gets even louder.

Haven't I got anything to say for myself? Why am I giggling like an idiot? What stunt am I going to pull next? Don't I realise that life is hard and there's lots of competition out there and you can't just dick around?

My eyes are stinging. It's probably the smoke.

Do I understand? Do I get it? It's not all about getting stoned and sleeping around and going to parties. It's about hard work. It's about making your fortune.

It's about taking on the world and winning.

'I don't need to make my fortune,' I say. 'You've already done that for me.'

It's meant to be a joke – because I'm good at them – but he doesn't get it. That's *exactly* what pisses him off. My sense of *entitlement*. I'm so *spoilt*. I've been spoon-fed all my bleeding life. I have no idea at all how it is in the real world.

'It's not my fault if you spoiled me,' I point out.

He shakes his head. 'You don't even understand what I'm talking about, do you?'

Actually I do. I get it completely. And I'm angry.

'If you wanted me to be just like you, then you should've brought me up like you were,' I say, 'instead of pushing me off to boarding school, and buying me off with tennis camp and PlayStation and all that, so that you could go away all the time and leave me with an au pair.'

He doesn't say anything, just starts opening more windows. I spy a colossal gap in his armour.

'Why did you both have to work, anyway? Haven't you got enough money? You care about your work and your bonuses more than you care about me! You and Mum, you're both as bad as each other! I don't know why you bothered to have me!'

'You have no bloody clue what you're talking about,' he says, but I have the advantage.

'You care more about money than you do about me! If you don't like me, then it's all your own fault!'

His mouth is open, but he has nothing to say, which means it's true. I take the opportunity to escape, and I have the satisfaction of having won. He booms after me, 'We've got more to discuss in the morning!' but he doesn't try to follow me.

We've got nothing to discuss. I lie in bed, full of fury and hurt and determined to show him that he's wrong, he's unfair, he's stupid and everything is his fault.

Boxing lessons seem like a good place to start.

CHAPTER 15
Shannon

My alarm goes off 8 am the next morning. I stare at it for a bit . . . WTF? 8 am? And then I remember where I'm going and just about why, and I drag myself out of bed. I choose my clothes with care: trackie bottoms – I never wear them, but we had to have them at school for PE – a plain white T, a black hoodie.

It's OK, but not nearly chavvy enough. I'm going to have to visit somewhere like JD Sports to put the Kyle Stone look together if I'm going on with this.

My dad's in the kitchen when I go downstairs, wearing shorts and a T-shirt which reads 'New York Marathon 2009'. He's wet with sweat and a bit red in the face. He's making himself an energy shake.

He puts on his friendliest face. Clearly we're meant to forget last night. What a fake.

'Want some?' he asks as I lace up my trainers.

'You must be joking,' I say in my iciest voice. Those shakes are made with soy milk, peanut butter and protein powder. They smell like cat vomit.

'Going out for a run?' he asks. 'Shame, you could've come with me. I've done ten miles already. I'm going for a bike ride later. You can come with, if you want.'

When I was about ten my dad and I used to go on bike rides together. In fact, the best holiday I ever had was in the Netherlands, when we took the bikes over on the ferry and did miles every day, counting windmills and cows as we whizzed past on wide, flat bike lanes. Dad and I got on really well.

But then he started pressurising me to go faster and further, and I went away to school and lost the cycling habit, and I used to come home for the holidays and just want to chill, not struggle up hills and get either a) wet, cold and muddy or b) hot, sweaty and dusty.

So I stopped, although Dad tried to tempt me back last birthday by buying me an amazing mountain bike with twenty-seven gears – awesome in theory, exhausting in practice. I've hardly touched it.

'No thanks,' I say, with (hopefully) biting sarcasm.

'Look, Archie,' he says, 'I'm sorry I went over the top yesterday. I'm pitching for a big deal. It's very stressful.'

'Oh, right.'

My dad is always either pitching for deals – 'Very stressful, don't talk to me, Archie, I'm busy. How dare those bastards offer that price,' etc. Or he's working on deals – 'Every bloody detail has to be absolutely right, I'm not letting those bastards on the other team take us apart because of a stupid error,' etc. Or he's trapped in meetings where the deal actually happens, which can go on and on for days and nights and more days. Very occasionally he's between deals, when he mostly sleeps. The rest of the time he keeps himself going with an insane amount of exercise.

I have occasionally wondered if it's all a big con and actually he spends half the time with a lover or two, but I've never found any real proof to back that theory.

He takes a big gulp of his shake and makes a face.

'Tastes like hell, but it's great for performance. Sure you won't have any?'

'You can keep it.'

'You should use the new bike for college,' he says. 'My commute's much easier by bike.'

'Sure, can you ask Jeff to take my books and stuff as well as yours?'

Jeff is Dad's personal driver. When Dad cycles to

work, Jeff comes and picks up his briefcase and suit and delivers them to the office for him. Then Dad has a shower and gets changed, and quite often Jeff drives him to an appointment at a client's office. That's how people cycle to work in London.

'You can manage,' he says. 'Archie, about last night. . .'

'I've got to go,' I say. 'I'm meeting someone.'

'We'll talk later,' he says, and I vow silently that we won't.

And then he stomps off to get changed into his cycling gear, and I crash out of the front door.

I've worked it all out – Tube and bus. I'm at Rodney Road just before 10 am. I'm shivering, but that's probably because it's icy cold and spitting with rain.

Obviously I'm not scared. Ty grew up round here. So did my dad. They walked these streets every day. Only a complete soft wuss would be scared. I just keep alert, that's all, and try and look well hard. I'm not sure my face can do it, but I've got a good swagger.

The gym's much fuller than it was the other day. The punchbags are swinging wildly, the air's full of bangs and thwacks and grunts. Sylvia takes my money – 'Hello, dearie! Wasn't sure you'd actually turn up!' – and introduces me to a grizzled old guy with a nose that goes in two directions at once.

'This is Benny,' she says. 'He's going to be teaching you. Kyle Stone, Benny.'

'Kyle Stone, eh?' says Benny. 'Any relation?'

'To what?' I say, and he says, 'Obviously not. Let's see what you're made of, young Kyle.'

Benny's about ninety, as far as I can tell, and he's shorter than me, and I'm sure that if I punched him he'd just fall over. He's not all that impressed with me, either. He gets me to hold my arms out in front of me.

'Weak,' he says, poking at my muscles. 'Ever done any upper body work? You're going to have to get your act together.'

I feel a bit sick. 'OK,' I say, 'tell me what to do.'

Benny cackles, hands me some gloves. 'Put these on,' he says, 'and we'll see how you go.'

Oh my God. This has to be the most humiliating experience of my life. I'm trying to land a punch on a midget pensioner, and he keeps dodging out of my way, and I'm like those Dutch windmills, arms flailing everywhere. By the time he stops – it feels like hours, but it's only twenty minutes – I'm red in the face, breathless and (secretly) close to tears. It doesn't help that two or three people – young guys, a bit older than me – are watching. They're smiling. I'm a laughing stock.

'Ha', he says, 'not so easy, eh? Let's see how you get on with someone younger.'

The boy he pulls over to fight with me is only about eleven, but he's built like a small tank and he's clearly been doing this for ages. I chew on the mouthguard, prance around on the balls of my feet, and swing wildly at him. By sheer fluke I make contact – thwack, on his jaw.

The old man cackles and says, 'Well done,' and the boy narrows his eyes and puts up his fists.

We dance around each other for a bit. He attacks my body with short, stabbing punches. I jump and dance, step backwards, right, to the side and . . . wham! I've got him! He goes staggering backwards, glove to his face, and spits out the mouthguard, swearing at me, saying I cheated.

I feel triumphant – *Ha, Dad, you should have seen that!* – and then the old guy says, 'You've got a long way to go, but I think we'll make a fighter of you. Maybe next time you can try one of the twelve-year-olds.'

And I remember that people are watching, and I go all hot, but pleased with myself, all the same.

So I pull out my mouthguard and say, 'Bring 'em

on,' and he shows me a punchbag and says, 'Give it a good forty minutes. You need to build up your upper body strength.'

When I leave – I have a shower, get changed into jeans and a black T-shirt, make sure my hair is just right – the boy is standing outside. He's with two girls, one about my age, one much younger. They've got one of those scary dogs – the ones with big teeth and ugly faces – and they're eating Cornettos . . . in November. Bizarre.

He glowers at me. 'You think you're so cool. But you ain't nothing.'

'Nuffink,' I say, genuinely trying to work out what he's saying, and the older girl says, 'You taking the piss?'

'No . . . nah . . . sorry. . .'

'That's OK. He's gotta learn to lose. Hear that, Billy? You can't win all the time.'

'It was just beginner's luck,' I say, and Billy scowls.

'Bye, then,' I say, and the girl says, 'Hang on. We're taking Stan for a walk. You wanna come?'

Who's Stan?' I say, playing for time, and she nods her head towards the dog and says, 'Stan's our Staffie. He's gentle as a lamb, really – as long as you're nice to us.'

This is easy. She's so flirting with me. She's true chav – huge gold hoop earrings, tight ponytail, fine-plucked eyebrows, fake tan and pale pink trackies – but she's really attractive too.

'I'll be nice to *you*,' I say, and we walk along Rodney Road, along the High Street, down a side road and past a block of grotty council flats.

'Here we go,' she says, and lets the dog off its lead, even though there's a big sign up which says 'KEEP DOGS ON LEAD'.

'Go on, Billy, Marie . . . run with him. Give Stan a good run.'

'Run yourself,' says Billy, and he turns back towards the flats.

But Marie says, 'Come on, Stan,' and they run down the path together.

'So,' says my new friend. 'Got rid of them. I've not seen you around before. What's your name?'

'I'm Kyle,' I say. 'I don't live so far away – down Islington.'

'Oh yeah, whereabouts?'

My mind goes blank. I'm scanning the streets near where my uncle and aunt live, the expensive Georgian squares, trying to think of somewhere horrible. . .

'Down the Caledonian Road,' I say, and she says, 'All the way over here from the Cally? You'd best keep that quiet.'

'Oh, right,' I say, wanting to kick myself. Of course people call it the Cally. I knew that. Even my aunt calls it the Cally.

We're walking towards a little playground. There's a wooden fort, some swings and a slide. Marie's trying to haul Stan up the stairs to the slide, but he's barking in angry protest.

'What's your name, anyway?' I ask.

'I'm Shannon,' she says.

'That's a pretty name,' I say, and she slides her eyes over to me. Her lips sparkle with gloss, and her lashes have little beads of mascara at the ends.

'Why, thank you, Kyle,' she says.

Marie's got Stan up to the top of the slide, and now they're flying down the other side.

'Quit that, Marie!' yells Shannon. 'He'll turn and then you'll be sorry!'

She turns to me, 'That's the thing about Staffies. One minute they're lovely, the next they're chewing your leg off. You never know when they're going to turn.'

Stan the Staffie reminds me of Ty. Ty's better looking, obviously.

There's a tree at the end of the playground area which has a load of flowers around it – dead flowers, brown and smelly. Some are in jam jars, some mouldering in cellophane. There's a girl too, a black girl. She's kneeling among the flowers, her face in her hands.

'What's that, then?' I ask Shannon, trying my best to slur the words together, lose my consonants.

Shannon's eyes are wide. 'There was a murder in this park, don't you know that?'

'A murder? When?'

'Over a year now.' She jerks her head at the black girl. 'That's his sister. She's here all the time. Everyone just leaves her alone. They know she's not going to make trouble.'

Oh my God. This must be it. This is the park where Ty saw someone killed, and the person who got stabbed, he was that girl's brother.

On the other hand, maybe they have loads of murders around here. Just walking along the High Street I saw another pile of dead flowers, just like these.

'What actually happened?' I ask. 'Did they catch the people who did it?'

'Oh they caught them all right,' she says. 'Put them

away. Put them in prison and threw away the key.'

'Do you know any details?' I ask. Get me, the big detective!

But Marie's calling her. 'Shannon! Stan's run off! He's chasing a little puppy! Shannon!'

'Sorry,' says Shannon, 'I'd better go. See you around, Kyle from the Cally.'

'See you,' I say.

She chases off up the hill, and I stroll on down towards the flowers, towards the girl. I'm annoyed with myself for not doing my research. All I know is the name of Ty's friend Arron, the one who's doing time for the murder. I can't even remember the victim's name.

I stand respectfully to the side of the girl, and look at the flowers. 'To Rio,' they say. 'To our baby, our son, our darling.' 'To a souljah.' 'To our brother.'

The girl looks up at me. 'Did you know him?' she asks, 'Or are you one of them? I don't want no trouble. Show some respect, eh? Let me have this time with my brother.'

I hold my hands up. 'I'm not here to make trouble,' I say. 'I'm very sorry for your loss. I'm not from round here. Can you tell me what happened?'

She shrugs. 'What happened to Rio happens to a lot

of lads around here. Wrong place, wrong time. Some idiot with a knife. You watch out, boy, it could happen to you.'

I have no idea what to say.

'What was he like, Rio?'

She smiles. 'He was my brother, my twin brother. We was together for our whole lives, until some white boy with a knife cut him down – took his life away. My mummy says it was meant to be, that Rio's in the arms of Jesus. I try and believe her, but – ' she shakes her head, 'I'm having trouble believing. You get that? They took away my Rio and they took away my belief, all at the same time. That's a lot to lose.'

'I'm really sorry,' I say.

'Not your fault,' she says. 'Just promise me you won't run around with a knife, attacking young innocent boys, you promise me that.'

'Umm, OK, I promise,' I say. I'm sweating. I feel like a fraud.

'Who were they, the boys who did this?' I ask. 'The ones in prison – who were they?'

'They were cowards. They attacked him, three or four on one. One of them got away with it, that's all. My mummy thinks he was a hero, because he gave evidence against his friends, but me, I think different. I think he ratted on his mates and he got away with it.'

She's talking about Ty. I know it. She hates Ty, even after all he went through to bring justice for her brother. Can she be right? Is he a traitor, a liar, a murderer?

She must've seen something in my face. She says, 'You know something, don't you? You're not just asking. You know something. What you bothering me for? You connected with them?'

I say, 'No, no, I don't know anything. I'm really sorry about your brother. I wish it could be different.'

I can see from her face – from the suspicion and anger written all over her – that she doesn't believe me. And she's right. But I do wish it could be different. I wish her brother could still be alive.

And I don't like what I'm finding out about Ty one little bit.

CHAPTER 16
Free

No more trips out for training. No more visits to the gym, even.

When the governor gets me into his office to talk about the 'regrettable incident – why on earth did you allow them to take your picture?' – I say to him that I think I know one of the kitchen trainees and I think I'm in danger all the time.

And he says, 'Good God, boy, why did you not tell someone before?'

And I say, 'Because I wasn't 100 per cent sure and I thought someone would have checked.'

He asks which kitchen trainee and I tell him Mikey's name and he checks his computer and then he says, 'But there's no one here called Michael Gregory.'

And I realise that he's lying like all the rest of them.

Then I have a long sweaty journey to another Young Offender Institution, two days in a room, all on my own. And now I'm free. It's six in the morning – dark and cold and silence all around.

Patrick is here to pick me up. I'm pleased, but I wish he'd never seen me here in this place. I wish he wasn't looking so carefully unconcerned. I wish I wasn't wearing my smart clothes for court.

'Your mum would have come,' he says, opening the door to his car. Immediately, I forget the prison, the clothes, the awkwardness. Meg is barking excitement at me, and I bury my face in her fur. I can't believe I used to be nervous around dogs. Meg's one of my favourite people on earth – at least, she would be, if she was a person, and right now I think dogs are a bit more evolved than most people, anyway.

'What's wrong with my mum?' I ask, instantly tense, and he says, 'Nothing at all. She's absolutely fine. Staying with us for the moment. She would've come, but the baby's got a cold, and I thought it'd be a good idea if you had a chance to draw breath, as it were, before you see her.'

'Is Alyssa OK?'

'She's fine. Babies get colds all the time. Don't worry about them, Ty. They're fine. Helen went to see them in Birmingham, and she invited them to come and stay for a bit . . . and then there was the fuss over your photo in the paper. We've been thinking about what to do.'

I'm sitting in the back of the car, my hand resting on Meg's back. She's curled up, her chin on my thigh. All I can see of Patrick is the back of his head, his broad shoulders, but already I feel safe and calm and really OK.

I can move and breathe and I'm a little bit chilly. It's the opposite of being in a sweatbox.

'Ty, you remember Alyssa's christening?'

I remember little flashes of Alyssa's christening, which feels like a hundred years ago, not three months. Gran, cradling Alyssa in her arms. Gran, watching the priest with a strange look on her face – happy, yes, but also kind of disappointed. My mum and dad hugging each other, too long for just friends. Alyssa's angry wail as the holy water splashed her head. Gran. Gran. Gran.

'Yeah.'

'You remember Mr and Mrs Webster?'

Alistair's parents. I've been very careful not to remember them. If I thought much about their old faces, the way Mrs Webster's mouth twitched and her eyes shone, I'd feel so guilty that I don't think I could live any more.

Because it was my fault that Alistair was shot. Their only son, shot instead of me, killed because of me.

I'll remember Mr and Mrs Webster all my life.

'Yeah,' I say warily. If he's going to start going on about them, I'm actually better off back in my prison cell.

'Helen's kept in touch with them. Nice people. They're very keen to play a role in Alyssa's life. She's all they've got now.'

'Oh, right.'

'They've been in touch with your mum too, encouraging her to carry on with her open university studies. As I say, nice people. She likes them.'

'Oh. Good.' I don't know what he wants me to say. Am I going to have to apologise to them?

'They have a business; they own holiday cottages in the Highlands, and some rental property in Aberdeen.'

'Oh right.'

'It's top end, for the oil industry executives that come from abroad. Short lets, mostly.'

'Oh, mmm, right.'

'So, they've been talking to Nicki about letting her

stay in one of their flats – so she's got somewhere to live, and they can help her out with Alyssa as she grows up.'

I freeze. What the hell?

'She's been saying no, she felt you needed to stay at the school in Birmingham. You've been doing well there.'

Meg nudges me with her nose. She doesn't like it when I stop stroking.

'But now, with the photo and everything – you can't stay in England, Ty. Scotland might be just the place for a few years.'

I'm trying to find words.

'What do you think?'

I find them. 'I can't. They'd blame me . . . for Alistair.'

'How could they blame you? Was it your fault that these criminals sent men to execute you? No. Was it your fault that the police were employing someone who fed information about protected witnesses to the people trying to hunt them down? You shouldn't feel guilty—'

'But I do! I do!'

Meg gives a little growl. She doesn't like me shouting either.

Patrick sighs. 'I'm sorry, Ty, but you're just

going to have to get over it.'

I stare out of the window, watch the world flying away.

'You agree it's best for Alyssa?'

There's a very tiny little bit of me which wants to suggest that Mum should give Alyssa to these Webster people, to keep them happy. She'd be safe and we could go and stay in Florida. But I love Alyssa. I miss her. I love her gummy smile, her sticky little hands, the way she does something new and different every day and it's so funny seeing her finding out stuff like looking in a mirror or clapping her hands.

I'd just like to be able to love her without feeling scared all the time that something terrible is going to happen.

'We could go and live abroad and they could visit us,' I say. My voice sounds lame and tinny and weak. 'Maybe with Emma in Spain,' I add. Perhaps Florida is unrealistic.

'I don't think so,' he says. 'First, Emma and Carlos live in a one bedroom flat. Second, Carlos is not at all keen on anything which might threaten his life, Emma's life or his business – not necessarily in that order, but you get my drift.'

I do.

'We could stay with Lou in Tashkent,' I say. 'No one would ever find us there.'

'Louise has given in her notice,' says Patrick. 'She's got a new boyfriend, the head of History. They're going to go travelling for a year, then apply for jobs at some other international school.'

Huh. Basically he's saying that my aunts are completely selfish and they don't care about me or my mum or Alyssa. It was just Gran who was holding us together and now we're not a family any more.

Patrick sighs and says, 'Don't take it too hard, Ty. They've been through a lot as well. Louise has been on her own for a long time. I think she carried a torch for Danny for years, to be honest. They were good friends and she was shocked when he and Nicki . . . well, it's all in the past now. . .'

I have no idea what carrying a torch is meant to mean and I have no intention of making myself look stupid by asking. If he's suggesting that my aunt ever fancied my dad then he's completely mad and wrong.

'We can go back to Birmingham,' I say. 'No one will know.'

'Even the police think that's too risky,' he says.

'We've been talking to Doug, and—'

'Doug? He's useless!'

It's not that I mind Doug, our old witness protection officer. He used to annoy me, but in the end we got on OK. It's just that he's all tangled up in my mind with Alistair and the blood and the splattered brains and the . . . and the. . .

'I think I'm going to throw up.'

'Didn't know you got car sick,' Patrick grumbles, but he indicates to pull in at a service station. 'Don't know about you, but I could do with some coffee.'

BANG! The car behind us shunts into us, bashing and crashing, rocking and rolling us. Our car lurches forward, stops, engine revving like crazy. Meg's barking, I'm shouting, Patrick . . . Patrick's quiet and still and. . .

CRASH! Again . . . again? He must have reversed, come back, smashed into us on purpose. . .

'Patrick! Patrick!'

There's a squeal of tyres, an engine roaring. The other car – grey, long, fast – skids past us and away, past the Little Chef, past the petrol station. . .

I'm shaking all over. Meg is barking frantically, growling, trying to jump over the seat. . .

'Patrick! Patrick!' I'm shaking his arm, trying to wake him, using my sleeve to wipe the blood from his face. . .

But there's no response.

CHAPTER 17
Chips

Ty's out! Free! But nothing ever goes simply for him. Apparently on the way back from prison he and Grandpa were in some minor car accident. Some moron bumped into them as they came off the motorway and then drove off without leaving his insurance details.

Mum's on the phone to Grandma for what seems like hours.

'Awful for them,' she says when she gets off the phone. 'Just terrible. Poor Ty. Dad knocked his head and blacked out and Ty had to run to the café and get help.'

'Is Grandpa OK?' I ask, while Dad takes a deep breath and says, 'Nothing but trouble, I told you so.'

'Oh, shush, David,' she says and he says, 'Don't shush me, you know I'm right. I take it they're both all right, or you'd be a lot more upset.'

'Dad's fine, but he had concussion so they're keeping him in overnight. Mum's with him . . . and Ty. . . She doesn't know what to do with Ty, he's physically OK, but quite traumatised by the whole thing. And there's the car to sort out – and the dog – I think I'd better go over there. It's just that I've got some crucial meetings today – I'm already late—'

'I'll come with you,' I offer, but Dad says, 'I'm not paying a fortune in school fees to have you bunk off every day.'

'It's the holidays!'

'What about your revision?'

'I don't need to revise, I've only just started there. . .'

'What are you doing today, David?' says Mum. 'Didn't you say you'd finished the Poseidon proposal?'

'Well, yes, but—'

'So things are quiet for you at the moment?'

'Well, yes, but I'm working on another pitch and you know how it is. . .'

'David?'

'Oh all right,' he says. 'Don't ask me to deal with Ty, though. He's Danny's responsibility.'

'Danny's in New York,'

'Oh, typical.'

'He's got to earn a living,' says Mum, and he says, 'Why? He made a fortune with his so-called band. Archie, you'd better come with me after all. I can't cope on my own with a dog and a delinquent as well as your grandparents and a smashed-up car.'

I'm still not really speaking to my dad after the whole Lily blow-up, and I'm not that keen on spending any time at all with him, but at the same time I do want to see Ty and Meg and check if Grandpa's OK. So I suppose I'll have to put up with his company.

It's awkward in the car, though, especially as he acts like nothing's wrong.

'Archie,' he says, as we hit the M25, 'I know you like Ty, but I'm not all that happy about you two being close friends.'

'Why not?' Damn. I forgot I'm not talking to him.

'He attracts trouble. Bad people are after him. I don't expect him to stick around in our lives.'

'What do you mean? You think they're going to kill him?'

He sighs. 'Don't blame me. It's not me that wants to kill him. But he's annoyed someone with a lot of power and no morals. Ty will disappear, one way or another. Hopefully on his own terms and still alive.'

'But you don't really care either way, do you?'

'It's not that I don't care, Archie. It's just that I can't do anything. Ty made bad choices and he's suffering the consequences. But he's not my responsibility. You are. I'm trying to make sure that you don't get mixed up in something you don't understand. You have to distance yourself from dangerous people, dangerous situations. Believe me.'

Oh right. He just assumes that Ty's the leader and I'm going to follow. Great. Thanks for the vote of confidence, Dad. He's obviously never thought for a second that I might be a good influence on Ty.

I don't say one word for the rest of the journey, which almost kills me.

When we get there, Ty's the first person we see. He's sitting outside the hospital, huddled on a bench, Meg at his feet. She's trembling, he's stroking her fur. Normally Meg greets me with a full-on, tail-wagging, leaping, barking round of applause. Today she looks at me mournfully and wags her tail only once.

'Aah, Meg, what happened? What happened, girl? Aah . . . Archie's here! I'm here! Everything's OK!'

'She was OK with me,' says Ty.

'I never said she wasn't.'

'She's worried about Patrick. I couldn't go in the ambulance with him, because of Meg. The police . . .

the police. . .' He can't even finish the sentence.

My dad's voice is actually quite kind. 'Has anyone checked you over, Ty? Or have you been here with the dog all morning?'

Ty shrugs. 'Helen came and she said she'd stay with Meg so I could see someone, but you have to wait for hours in casualty and I'm . . . I'm fine. And I thought she should see if Grandpa was all right because I didn't . . . I didn't know . . . he wasn't moving at all and there was loads of . . . of blood.'

'I think the best thing we can do to help is to take you and the dog back home,' says Dad, briskly. 'I'll just go and find Helen and talk to her, see how long Patrick will be in and then we'll get off. You'll be OK. Don't worry, he only has concussion.'

Ty's eyes are blank and scary and staring at nothing. 'There was blood. . .'

'Yes, I'm sure there was,' says Dad. 'Tell you what, why don't you two give Meg a bit of a walk before we get her in the car – give her a chance to do her business before she messes up the Prius? I wonder if Helen's got a blanket in her car?' He looks at his Rolex. 'See you back here in an hour, that should do it. Any idea which ward I want, Ty?'

Ty stares at him blankly.

'Never mind, I'll find out,' says Dad, and he's gone.

'Come on,' I say. 'We can get some chips or something. You must be hungry.'

'He's dead,' he says, in the same flat tone. 'He's dead. They're all lying.'

'He's not dead! They said concussion. Not even concussion. Suspected concussion.'

'Huh,' says Ty. 'They're all liars.'

'Come on, let's go.' I'm actually a bit worried about him. He seems super-freaked. Maybe I can cheer him up by telling him all about the Lily incident, otherwise known (by Mum) as the Cheese-on-Toast Inferno.

'I'm totally grounded,' I finish, 'and it's so unfair because Lily came and apologised and said it was her fault.'

Lily's official explanation was that she'd been feeling really ill and fluey, and had taken Night Nurse which made her forget all about the cheese on toast she'd left under our grill. She was really embarrassed, couldn't say sorry enough, and hoped that Mr and Mrs Stone would blame her and not Archie, who was completely innocent and actually slightly the injured party.

Mr Stone and Ms Tyler weren't buying any of it. They'd rung up Lily's mum to tip her off that Lil was drinking or stoned or both.

'Well, I'm very sorry about the burning cheese. . .' said Lily's mum – she's a former supermodel who's always known in our house as Mad Frieda – 'but what can you do? They are wild, these children. We must let them find their own way, make their own mistakes.'

'I don't think so,' said Mum. 'Frieda, Lily could've set our house on fire.'

'Yes, she is a very, very naughty girl. She reminds me of myself as a young girl in Stockholm. How I drove my mother crazy! But it all worked out in the end.'

'Frieda, I'm pretty sure she was stoned.'

'Well, I am certain you are correct, Penelope, but how can I stop her? She is nearly grown-up, she lives her own life. Ah, we parents, we just have to hope for the best. But you know, a little cannabis never hurt anyone, in fact these children are so stressed, so many of these stupid exams, it is good they know how to relax. . .'

And so on – I was listening on the landline – until Mum put down the phone and said, 'No wonder Lily's in such a state. You have to feel sorry for her.'

Then Dad said, 'We can ban Archie from seeing her,' and Mum said, 'That's so Victorian, David, and anyway, now they're going to be at the same school.

We'll just have to trust Archie.'

Dad grunted and said, 'We're all doomed,' and I decided that the most sensible thing to do for a week or so was lots of highly-visible homework, no mention of Lily or Oscar, and numerous demonstrations of what they call common sense, which mostly means using a plate when I'm eating biscuits so I don't get crumbs everywhere, and remembering to put stuff in the dishwasher.

I've even got my new bike out, and I've been experimenting with riding it to college. It only takes fifteen minutes – that's half the time of the Tube. And there's something about cycling in London that I love – the thrill of danger in the bus lane, the joy of whizzing past BMWs and Range Rovers as they sit emasculated in traffic jams. I might even consider going out with my dad one weekend, except officially I'm not speaking to him.

Anyway, I'm getting so into the boxing. I'm getting fitter and stronger and Kyle is developing a whole alternative life for himself.

Shannon, for example. She waits for me every week (that's three times so far) and we go and eat a kebab in the park, and she asks me questions about myself, which I expertly dodge, and she tells me about her mum and dad and brothers and sisters, and how she's doing a BTEC in Health Studies at a school called Tollington ('It's a dump and everyone knows it,') and one day she might be a nurse. ('That's my dream, Kyle, but I don't know if I can ever get the qualifications.')

Spending time with Shannon and hanging out at the club has also got me some attention from the guys there. Shannon's advice was to keep quiet about (supposedly) coming from the Cally, so I try and not say much, just echo things that they say, even if they don't make much sense to me. Mostly they leave me alone, but one guy – big, black, scary – came up and asked me who I was and where I was from.

'You're not from round here, are you?'

'Yeah, I am,' I said. 'I used to go to Tollington til I got excluded.'

'Oh yeah,' he said. 'Yeah, right.'

'Yeah.'

He looked at me through his tiny eyes and then he said, 'Sylvia reckons you look a bit like Ty. Ty Lewis. You know him? Related?'

Shit.

'Who? Nah,' I say.

'Good,' he says. 'Keep it that way.' And he walked away.

This is the moment when I decide that I'm not telling Ty about my adventures at the boxing club, but the silence is getting awkward. Then I see a fish and chip shop.

'What do you fancy?' I say, digging a twenty pound note out of my pocket.

He looks confused.

'Chips? Saveloy?'

'Oh . . . I don't know. . .'

'I'll chose,' I say. 'You stay here with Meg. I bet she'd like some yummy saveloy, wouldn't you, Meg?'

It takes a bit of time in the shop, and when I come out Ty's gone, disappeared. Jesus! Where is he?

I sprint up the street, around the corner, and there he is – walking fast, Meg jogging at his side. What the hell?

'Oi!' I yell.

He walks faster. I run after him. Meg pulls him back, whines for me.

'What the hell? What about me? Where are you going?'

He's got that blank stare again. He's twitching his head as though he's trying to look over his shulder.

'I . . . I thought . . . I could find him. . .' he says.

'Find who?'

191

'I don't know.' He shakes his head, fast and violent, like a dog that's come out of a lake. 'I thought. . .'

'Stop thinking and eat,' I say, shoving a bag of chips at him. 'You're probably hungry. When did you have breakfast?'

He thinks about it. 'Last night.'

'Last night?'

'They bring it . . . with supper, at five.'

'And you're meant to wait until the morning to eat it?'

'I suppose.'

I wave a chip at him. 'Bet this is better than prison food. Was it disgusting? Can't be worse than my last school. They made custard by squeezing the sixth-formers' spots.'

I think he's going to laugh, but he just stares over my shoulder and says, 'Oh yeah, right.'

'Ty, you are being weird,' I say. 'Stop it. And don't wander off again.'

His eyes focus. For a moment he's looking at me properly. 'No. Sorry.'

'Look, I know you've been through a lot, but it'll be OK. Are you still thinking of going to Florida?'

He looks over his shoulder again. It's like he thinks someone's listening to us.

'Maybe.'

'Oh. That'd be great, wouldn't it? Like a really new start.'

He jerks his head around again. 'It's best if I just disappear.'

'You could go anywhere. Any country in the world. And you really like languages, don't you?'

'I dunno,' he says. 'I've kind of lost it, Archie. I can't keep the words in my head any more.'

I don't know what to say. Ty was always trying to talk in other languages, coming out with bits of Portuguese and Polish and whatever, all the time. He was dead keen to try and speak French with Grandpa, which I found kind of embarrassing, as Ty had a really weird accent.

'My teacher at school comes from *Cote d'Ivoire*,' he said one day, which kind of explained it. Grandpa's normally really strict about French pronunciation with me – he's always correcting my verbs and stuff – but he'd just sit and listen to Ty mangle complete sentences into Afro-French with a dopey, proud look on his face.

I tell you, Ty's totally his favourite. It's odd, considering that he's only known him two minutes.

'Go somewhere hot, and it'd be like being on

holiday all the time and you can forget all about, you know, all the stuff that's gone on.'

And Claire, I think, *you can forget about Claire*, but I'm not brave enough to say it.

'I can't forget anything,' he says. He's constantly twitching – turning his head to look over his shoulder. I start timing the twitches – once, twice, three times a minute. Then nothing, a pause, then twitch, twitch again. It's really annoying.

'You should try,' I say, 'because it's all over now, isn't it? You've been to . . . you know . . . and the police have got those bad guys. I know their trial is coming up, but even so. You're free. You can leave it behind you.'

He's staring at the pavement, then – twitch, twitch – turns to me. 'Archie, if someone hurt you really badly, you wouldn't forget, would you?'

Uh-oh. What's this about? Is he trying to get revenge for his gran dying? Who does he blame for that? Or has Claire been in touch?

'I might,' I say. 'I wouldn't want to spend ages obsessing about stuff I can't change.'

'Yeah, but that's you. Some people wouldn't forget ever, would they? They'd just go on and on, hating that person and wanting to hurt them like they'd been hurt.'

'I suppose. . .' I say cautiously.

'And hating them and hating everything about them and wanting to hurt them like they'd hurt you?'

'Well, I wouldn't. . .'

'And it goes on and on until you've made sure they'll never hurt you again?'

I don't like this. I really don't like this. I don't know what he's getting at, but I don't like the way his eyes are hard and glittery, and the set of his jaw, and the way his hands have curled into fists, triceps bulging, body tensed.

I'm thinking about what Rio's sister said. I'm thinking about Kenny Pritchard. I'm thinking that I don't really know my cousin Ty very well at all.

So I say cautiously, 'Look, Ty, this isn't a good way to be feeling,' and he twitches again – is he even aware he's doing it? – and says, 'You're right, that's it. But what can I do?'

I shrug and say, 'Just get on with it. Try and forget it,' and he gives me a look like I'm the mad one.

Then I hear some music, and I smell the beautiful smell of frying onions and I see a fair. It's just getting started for the afternoon.

And I have a brilliant idea.

CHAPTER 18
Freak Out

'Come on, Ty, ' I say, 'this'll be great – just what you need. You can celebrate getting out.'

'I don't know. . .'

'We can take turns on things,' I say. 'The other one can stand with Meg.'

'I'm not . . . I don't. . .'

'It'll be a blast.'

There's a rickety-looking mini-rollercoaster, which could be fun. There's something massively tall and fast called a Freak Out – we can hear distant screams coming from the riders as they're flung around in the air. Teacups and roundabouts, obviously, a ghost train and dodgems. I'm not too keen on the really fast fling-you-around rides because I once threw up a little bit after I'd been on one. Mind you, I was only eleven and I'd eaten two hot dogs and some candy floss. So I'll probably be OK.

'What do you fancy?' I say. I nod at the Freak Out. 'How about this one?'

I'm kind of surprised when he says yes. The guy who runs it looks at Meg when we say only one of us is going to ride.

'It's OK,' he says. 'I'll watch the dog. I've not got many people yet. Both of you have a go.'

Oh well. I suppose statistically not many people actually die on these things. The iron bar comes over my head. I hope Ty won't notice if I close my eyes. I'm slightly regretting eating the whole saveloy.

And then we're slowly going up . . . and up . . . and it's fine, actually fun to be so high up, until it gets fast and faster and I start thinking about nuts unscrewing (not those sort of nuts, although now you mention it. . .) and machinery failing, and bodies flying through the air . . . not bodies . . . limbs . . . arms and legs torn off and flying through the air . . . and headlines screaming, 'Fair Disaster!' and 'Carnage!' I screw my eyes shut, although I'm sure my eyeballs have slipped from their sockets and are bouncing on the ground like slimy tennis balls. . . It's slowing . . . it's stopping. . . I'm still alive.

'You can open your eyes now,' says Ty. He's laughing. Maniac. 'That was OK. Shall we do it again?'

He's got to be joking. 'No thanks,' I say. 'Meg will be missing us. You can if you want. Have some tokens.'

He has two more goes. I have to mooch around, chatting to Meg, eating candyfloss morosely while he spins and flies and whoops.

Oh well. At least I've cheered him up.

Eventually he staggers off. 'Brilliant,' he says. He's breathing fast. 'Jesus. I wish I could do that all night.'

'Why?'

'It's just so safe,' he says, 'and like you're flying and no one can get you.'

What kind of person feels safe on a Freak Out? He's twitching again, scanning the crowd.

'What next?'

Neither of us fancy the ghost train. The roundabout is for babies. We try dart-throwing and duck-hooking, and Ty wins a fluffy troll for Alyssa. He seems quite relaxed. He's even laughing at my jokes.

And then we see the dodgems. I love dodgems.

'Want a go?' I ask him, but he shakes his head. Ah. Stupid me. Not the best thing when you've had a car crash. 'Hold Meg,' I say.

I'm spinning around, pretending I'm in a Ferrari, making kiddish Formula One noises in my head – *Brrrrrrrrrrrrrrrrrrrrrrrrrrrrrrrr* – when I spot Ty.

He's not looking too happy. He's sweating, twitching, eyes wide and alarmed.

I expertly pull my car over to his side. 'You OK?' I yell, over the blaring music.

Some guy slams his car into mine. He laughs, as I rock and shake. I forget Ty as I wheel the car around and pursue him.

It's only when the car glides to a halt that I put my hand to my face and realise there's a trickle of blood coming from my nose. It does that sometimes, nothing to worry about. Pity I don't have a tissue. I pinch my nostrils tight, look around for Ty.

And he's staring at me, white-faced and shocked, like I'm a ghost or something.

'Ty!' I say, but he's running. Meg's running with him. I run after them, but it's uphill and moving makes my nosebleed worse.

I think I spot his white shirt by the candyfloss stall, but when I grab his arm it's some other guy, and I step back. 'Sorry. . .'

And I spot Ty, running past the ghost train, past the helter-skelter, past the Freak Out.

I follow him. 'Ty . . . Ty . . . it's OK . . . stop. . .'

We've reached the edge of the fair. I can't tell if this is the street where we came in or not – same old bookies, same old halal kebabs. I manage to grab his arm.

'Go away!' he shouts. 'Leave me alone!' He pushes me away, and I'm so surprised that I fall to the ground.

'Ty, you nutter,' I say, but he's backing away from me, turning. And he's running along the dusty street – away from me, away from the hospital, as far as I can work out. Meg leaps and barks, but she stays with me.

We run after him, I try my best. But my nose is still bleeding and Ty's so fast – such a good runner – and his legs are longer and his stride's so wide and he twists round a corner and then another, and then I'm standing in a road with no sign of him, an alleyway to my right and a shopping precinct to the left.

He could be anywhere.

I have no idea where I am, and I'm not sure how to get back to the hospital. My iPhone won't pick up GPS. I'm lost.

What can I do? I say, 'Search!' to Meg, but she just waves her tail and looks at me with trusting eyes.

I call my dad, but it goes straight to voicemail.

'I'm lost,' I say. 'And Ty's run off. It wasn't my fault, honest, Dad.'

Then I start walking back, trying to work out which betting shop shows me the way back. I have a horrible feeling in my guts that I let Ty down.

But I have no idea how I did it.

CHAPTER 19
Fight

I've been lost for what feels like hours, when I see him. He's walking towards me. I blink, and then realise. We're near the hospital. We went past those flats. He just retraced his steps.

I've been wandering around for ages, anxious and panicking, covered in blood, looking like a fool, looking like a loser, wondering how I would explain to my dad what had happened, feeling humiliated and inexperienced and not streetwise or cool or clever at all.

And it was all his fault. And now he's sauntering towards me like he's not got a care in the world.

I was scared, I admit it. And now I'm angry. Disloyal Meg rushes up to him, licks his hand, jumping up with excitement.

'Are you OK?' he asks. 'I'm sorry. I just lost it there for a bit.'

'I'm fine,' I snarl. 'Don't worry about me. Oh, hang on, you don't, do you? You never worry about anyone apart from yourself.'

He doesn't say anything. He takes a step back.

'Claire, for example. You never worry about her, do you? Ever think what it's like for her, waiting to hear from you, not knowing what's going on?'

'I – I asked *you*—'

'Got me to do your dirty work? Yeah, and I did it. But I don't know what to tell her. Because I really don't know you very well, do I?'

He's silent again. His mouth opens and closes. If I wanted to hit him – and I do, to show him that he can't just dump me – then now would be a good time. I've been learning about timing, about watching, waiting, until your opponent weakens, leaves himself vulnerable. This is the time. He's open to attack. But I don't really need to use my fists.

'And Claire doesn't really know you all that well either, does she?'

'She knows I'd tell her anything – but anyway, Claire, Claire, she's—'

'Oh really?' I can't stop myself. 'Tell her everything? Oh really?'

'Yeah, I—'

'Tell her about your drug-dealing?'

He's silent. His big eyes stare at me.

'I met a guy, he told me you were his supplier.'

'You . . . who. . .?'

That wasn't a denial.

'I think more than that,' I say. 'I think you were the boss of your friend Arron. You were getting him to do your dirty work.'

He laughs. He actually laughs. I clench my fist, eye his jaw.

'What are you talking about?' he says.

'I think you got him to mug that boy Rio,' I say. 'You've got away with murder, haven't you, got away with murder and pinned the blame on your friend? Nice work, blud.'

'*Blud*?' he says. His voice is back in the boxing club. His voice betrays him. He pretends to be my friend, my cousin, part of my family, but actually he's as wild and unpredictable as one of them. Chavs. Scum. Gangsters.

'I know a lot more than you think I do. And I'm going to tell Claire. I'm going to tell her that you were dealing drugs and stabbing people and . . . and . . . she'll never want to see you again. . .'

He shrugs. I can't believe it. There's Claire breaking

her heart over him, and he doesn't give a shit.

'Claire,' I say, 'is a very nice girl.'

'I know,' he says.

'She deserves better than someone like you.'

'I know.'

'You ought to let her go free, let her stop feeling loyal to someone who's not good enough for her, who only gets into trouble, who everyone thinks is going to be in and out of jail for the rest of his life, probably.'

'Who . . . who said that?'

'Grandpa,' I say, and I have a really nasty feeling of triumph.

Wham! His fist comes out of nowhere, an explosion of pain, a burst of blood. I stagger backwards, hand to my face – my nose is broken, I swear – and my dad – my dad! – grabs my arm.

'What are you doing? What's going on?' he yells at Ty. 'Archie . . . Jesus . . . are you all right?' He digs a handkerchief out of his pocket, applies it to my nose – *ow!* – and pinches hard. 'Keep pinching,' he says.

Ty's just standing there, breathing hard, not moving.

Then my dad punches him so hard that he falls on the pavement.

'You little toerag,' he says. 'You leave my son alone. I didn't want him to have anything to do with you. You stick to your own kind, do you hear me? Don't mix him up in your troubles. Don't take it out on him.'

Ty's sprawled on the ground. Meg's barking like crazy.

Dad grabs him, yanks him up.

'Don't make out you're the victim here. You're just a thug, and I'm not having you bully my son. I don't want you having anything to do with him.'

'He wasn't bullying me,' I say, furious, but my words are muffled by the handkerchief and I don't dare drop it, because I can still feel blood trickling from my nose.

Dad looks me up and down. 'You've got no idea about the world Ty's grown up in. We know, don't we, Ty? Archie's like a little lamb, compared to you. Well, I'm not having him dragged into your life. Piss off and leave us alone.'

Ty's eye is red and swollen. He ignores my dad. 'He hit you like that?' he asks me.

'Umm, no,' I say.

'I'm sorry I hit you,' says Dad, not sounding sorry at all. 'I was defending my son.'

'Oh right.'

'Patrick's asking for you. I don't think we need to mention this to him, do we?' He holds his hand out to Ty, who ignores it.

'Can you lend me some money?'

'I beg your pardon?' says Dad.

'Can you give me some money?'

Dad doesn't say anything

Ty says it again. 'Can you give me some money? Maybe a hundred quid?'

'I can lend you fifty pounds,' I say, because I can't bear how they're looking at each other.

'I want his money,' says Ty. 'What've you got for me?'

Dad's furious – you can tell by the way his mouth is clamped together – but he pulls out his wallet and extracts a wodge of notes, counts them slowly.

'Two hundred pounds. Enough for you?'

I'm amazed.

Ty takes the money, folds it, sticks it in his back pocket.

'Thanks a lot,' he says.

'We understand each other?' asks Dad, and Ty nods.

'Then you'd better go and find your grandparents, and I'll take Meg home with us. We can bring her over in a few days.'

Ty turns towards the hospital. Meg whines at my side.

And I remember how scared Ty was – of what, though? – at the fair, and how much he loves Claire (if there's one thing I know that's true about Ty, it's that) and how he's Grandpa's favourite, and how I haven't really got any proof for anything I've said to him, it's just that. . .

'No . . . Dad . . . wait – Ty, I didn't mean. . .'

But Ty's walking away. And my dad says, 'You're better off without him, Archie.'

'You hit him! You shouldn't have done that! He's younger than you!'

'Bigger,' says Dad, 'and stronger. And he'd just slammed you in the face.'

'I'm fine,' I say, though it really, really hurts. It hurts more than anything in my life before. It hurts so much that I want to sob out loud.

'Why did you hit him? Why? I was OK! I was dealing with it.'

'I hit him because you didn't,' says Dad, 'and because sometimes that's what you have to do. You have to stand up to the bullies, the bad people. You can't let them get away with it.'

'Yes but—'

'Obviously hitting isn't the best way,' he says, 'but sometimes it's the only language they understand.'

'Well, how about the money? You were buying him off, weren't you?'

'Yes, well, that's another language they understand as well.'

'I could've hit him if I wanted to,' I protest, and he laughs, and says, 'Yes, Archie, but I don't think you'd have made much impact. Ty's had another sort of life – so did I – and thank God, you've not had that sort of life, and I hope you never will.'

I almost tell him about the boxing club, but my nose is still hurting and I know he'd ban me from ever going there again, and I can't be bothered arguing and lying to get my own way, when I can probably go on doing what I want, anyway.

So I say, 'Next time, leave me alone. I can fight my own battles. You shouldn't have done that.'

He pats my shoulder. 'Hopefully you won't have any more battles to fight.'

CHAPTER 20
Fire

I wake in the dark night, choking, coughing, wet with sweat. It's hot as hell, my nose and lungs are full of thick smoke. There's a strange, soft, crackling noise . . . it's fire! We're on fire! The house is on fire!

I leap out of bed, heart pounding, hit the floor, where the smoke's not so thick. And I'm crawling along, heading for the door, mind in a whirl. I have to save them! I have to get them out!

Flames leap up around me, the heat is blistering. I burst into the room where Mum and Alyssa are sleeping. For a moment my heart stops – can I find them in the smoke? How can they survive this? I run to Alyssa's cot – she's so still, too still. I grab her, hug her warm body to mine. She wails, but I ignore her.

'Mum! Mum!' I yell. 'Wake up! Wake up!' I'm coughing. I'm choking. The smoke is everywhere, stinging my eyes, drying my mouth. 'Wake up!'

She stirs. 'What—' she starts. 'Follow me!' I shout, and I lead the way through the flames, trying to run with Alyssa heavy in my arms. I give her a little shake. 'Wake up! Stay awake!' I scream.

And Alyssa cries. She cries and cries and the noise is all I can hear and it goes through my head like a siren, like an alarm, so I can't think, so I can't run and the flames are getting higher and higher and licking at my pyjamas.

'Ty! Stop it! Stop it! What are you doing to her?'

It's my mum's voice. She's out of bed at last, shaking my arm.

'We have to escape!' I hiss, grabbing her elbow. It's hard to hold Alyssa with one arm, so I tighten my grip. She screams even louder.

'What's going on?' Patrick's voice. He's alive. He's not burnt. I look around for him in the billowing smoke. He's there in the doorway, silhouetted against the flames – I stumble towards him.

'Get Meg! Get Helen! We can still get out!'

'Ty! Calm down! Everyone is fine. Nothing is happening!'

I stare at him. What does he mean? All around me the flames crackle and dance. But the heat – it's dying down. The smoke is clearing. I'm not hot any more. I'm as cold as ice, shaking, confused.

Mum grabs Alyssa. 'Come on, darling, it's OK. He didn't mean to hurt you.'

'I was . . . I was saving her.'

Mum just says, 'From what, Ty?' and Patrick switches on the light. I look around, puzzled – no smouldering blankets, no lingering smoke.

'Where did it go?'

Mum goes bonkers. 'Where did what go, Ty? What are you talking about? Every night you're waking us up, trying to evacuate us, and I can't take it any more! I can't! It took me an hour to settle Alyssa this evening! You've got to stop! You've got to get a grip!'

Patrick's hand is on my shoulder. 'Come on, Ty. Let's go downstairs, let Nicki and Alyssa get back to sleep.'

I'm still confused. 'There was a fire . . . there was—'

'All gone now,' says Patrick, and he manoeuvres me out of the room. I look back and I see my mum sitting on the side of her bed, rocking Alyssa. They're both crying. I look away quickly.

We go downstairs. Meg raises her head and wags her tail at me. There's no fire. There never was a fire. Everything's OK.

It's just that I feel as shaken and shattered as though the fire had eaten up every inch of the house and every person in it, and I'd been left staring at a blackened heap of ashes.

'Cocoa,' says Patrick, steering me towards the kitchen table. 'And I think we've got some biscuits somewhere.'

I'm not a big fan of cocoa, but the biscuits he finds are stem ginger covered with dark chocolate, and I eat four to help the cocoa go down. I feel a lot better afterwards.

Patrick's poured himself a whisky. 'This can't go on,' he says.

'I can't help it.' Now I've woken up properly I remember that this has happened every night this week. Once there was a gunman taking pot-shots at the windows. The house has been on fire twice. Once – most terrifyingly – the house was filled with a toxic gas that would kill you after ten minutes. It took ages for Patrick to persuade me that it was fine – about two hours, with me out in the front drive in the pouring rain, shouting at them to come out, watching Patrick through the window, dying of gas . . . dying . . . not dying. . .

'Something has to change. We have to get you some

help, and take you somewhere you feel safer.'

How can I explain to him that I'm never going to feel safe?

'Aberdeen—' he says, but I shake my head, and he says, 'Well, OK, how about France, then? We have our house in Provence. It's very quiet, very beautiful. You'd like it.'

I've seen pictures of this house. The walls are honey-coloured, there are rusty red floors and white-painted furniture. It's peaceful and soothing and beautiful.

Every time I look at it I see bloody corpses sprawled by the Aga, blood pooled on the floor tiles. And not just any bodies – people I care about, people I love, even Meg.

'There's nowhere,' I say, hopelessly, and he says, 'We need to take you to a doctor. You need something to help you sleep.'

I shake my head.

'I'd like you to see a psychiatrist.'

I freeze.

'You're displaying signs of paranoia. You're hallucinating. When we talked to a psychiatrist before we got a tentative diagnosis of post-traumatic stress disorder. . .'

When my mum and dad lived together, when he was nineteen and she was seventeen and I was just over one, she stopped eating. He talked to a psychiatrist. He got her sectioned, got her taken to a loony bin. He thinks he saved her life. She's never forgiven him.

No one's doing that to me.

I like Patrick a lot. I feel safe with him, I trust him, I'm glad he's in my life. But I'm seeing more clearly than he is at the moment. The car accident – that was no accident, that was a warning.

They're going to kill me. They're going to play with me first. I don't want drugs. I don't want to talk to a psychiatrist. I have to stay alert and ready for the next real attack.

It'd help if I stopped imagining other stuff as well.

I finish the cocoa. My eyes are blinking. I can hardly keep them open. For a moment I wonder if he's slipped in some sort of a sleeping pill. I thought I could trust Patrick. But what if . . . what if he's really not my grandad, after all? What if this whole Tyler family stuff is all a big charade . . . a trick . . . a set-up? Look at Archie's dad. When the mask slipped, he turned into a street fighter, just like Chris, the guy who used to hit me, hit my mum – Chris, whose brother is Tommy White, head of the gangster clan.

What if he's one of them? What if they all are? What if they're going to kill me when I'm . . . when I'm. . .

'Back to bed,' says Patrick, and when I shake my head, he says, 'OK, just come and sit in the living room, in the armchair. Stretch your legs out . . . that's good. I'll sit over here. Nothing's going to happen. It's fine. I'll put on a DVD.'

I'm not going to sleep. I'm concentrating on the French film he chooses, keeping my eye on him . . . but it's slow and the sound's on low and my eyes are hurting and. . .

I only realise that he tricked me into sleeping when Meg nudges my hand to wake me up in the morning.

Nicki's sitting next to me. She's looking tired and a lot older.

'Ty,' she says – kind and sweet, but not to be argued with – 'Ty, things can't go on like this.'

'I can't help it.'

'I know,' she says. 'It's not good for anyone. That's why I've made a decision. We can't stay here. We're going to Aberdeen.'

CHAPTER 21
Kissing Claire

If there's anything more humiliating than getting punched, it's telling people about it. The whole family knows. So do all my friends. They're OK – I just told them I was mugged. They were awed, sympathetic, caring.

My mum and aunts can't be fobbed off with that story, though. They're horrified. They think Ty and I had a big fight because Ty told his mum that I gave him the black eye. She told his dad in New York, he told my mum, chat, chat, worry, worry.

My dad flew off to Brazil to pitch for a contract. He left me with the lies and stories, the swollen nose and the purple and black bruises.

My grandpa – completely fine, just a cut on his head and a night under observation in the hospital – isn't sympathetic.

'Let them fight things out between them,' he told my mum. 'Danny and you worrying about it won't help either of them. I gather Archie punched Ty. Good for him – becoming a man at last. We shouldn't interfere in their fights. It's normal.'

'He's a dinosaur,' says my mum on the phone to Danny. 'You can't blame him for that, Dan, he's from a different generation. Archie won't talk about it to me. Can you find out any more from Ty? No? Maybe when you're home. Another fortnight? That's a shame.'

Now – my face still bruised, faded to green and yellow – I'm at the station in Claire's home town, looking around for her as I go through the ticket barrier. She said she'd be here to meet me. Please don't let her pull a stunt and send Zoe in her place.

'Archie!' Thank God, it's Claire. No sign of an angry ex-girlfriend. 'Oh my God! What happened to your face?'

I've spent the entire journey thinking about what to say. Do you tell a girl – a nice, sweet girl like Claire – that her boyfriend has an uncontrollable temper, can be goaded to violence, just like that? Or do you spare her? What if he got angry with her? Isn't it kinder in the long run – safer – to tell her the truth?

'I got mugged,' I say. 'It's OK, really.'

'Oh Archie. That's awful.' She's inspecting the bruises, really concerned, really caring. 'Poor you. And what on earth happened with Zoe?'

'Oh, it was just a mistake . . . a friend mucking around . . . Zoe got the wrong idea. But maybe it was for the best, anyway.'

'Maybe,' she says. 'I think there's another guy that Zoe's got her eye on. She did like you, though.'

'I don't think we've got loads in common,' I say. 'Did you tell her I was coming?'

'I thought I'd leave that up to you.'

'Oh, thanks. I can't quite face her right now – too awkward.'

'You're safe,' she says. 'She's at an athletics training thing today. She's very into her running – like Joe.'

'Who?'

'Joe – Ty. . .'

'Oh, Ty,' I say. 'Right. I always forget he was called Joe here.'

I wonder what it was like for Ty, having a new name and being a different person. I wonder if he felt free of the bad stuff he'd done – might have done – in London. Maybe he felt like he'd got a second chance, a new start, a clean slate. Now he knows that wasn't true. His past has caught up with him, trapped him, branded him. It can't be a good feeling.

How can I tell Claire what I've found out? How can I take her away from him? Will she hate me if I do?

We're walking down the High Street, past charity shops and WH Smith, a Starbucks, an estate agent.

'It's not very exciting here,' says Claire, 'there's a shopping mall – that's where the good shops are – but my whole school will be there. And it's a bit cold for the park. But we could have a coffee, if you want. I really want to hear about how you're doing at your new school – is it as good as you thought? – and anything you can tell me about Ty, of course.'

It's only the way her voice shakes when she says his name that makes me realise that Claire's actually a really good actress. I thought she was really interested in me there, just for a minute.

She points out a health food café. 'Let's go in there. It's quiet, and I won't see many people I know. They all hang out at the mall and in Starbucks.'

She's right, it is quiet. We're the only people there. She orders fruit tea and I dither a bit (no Frappuccino on the menu) and then ask for orange juice – which I hate. What's wrong with me?

Claire's wearing a blue top, exactly the colour of her eyes. She's got a cute denim skirt, black tights, lace-up boots. She's grown her hair a bit, pulled it back from her face with a flowery clip. There's something very clean about Claire. She's not like Lily, wild and brave. She's not like Shannon, sharp, hard and bright. Claire kind of reminds me of the old-fashioned toys my grandma has in her house. They always seemed so strange compared to the plastics and electronics I was used to, but you know what? I liked them better. I think I liked them best.

Claire asks me all about Butler's. She tells me about her drama club.

'Do they have after school clubs and things at your school?' she asks. 'I think you'd really enjoy something like that.'

'Not really – it's not really a school like that. Maybe I can find something.'

There's loads of stuff for kids to do where we live. And there's something called the National Youth Theatre – I googled it the other day. I'm thinking of auditioning. Even Lily and Oscar would be impressed by that, wouldn't they?

Funnily enough, I don't really care.

'So, what do you do when you're not at school?' She smiles, 'I bet you're not doing homework all the time.'

I grin back – God, I love her smile – 'I've been to a few parties. I hang out with my friends. And I've actually been working out a bit, learning to box.'

'You've been learning to box? Like Joe?'

Oh bum. I'd almost forgotten that I was here to talk about him.

'Yeah. I found the place where he learned – thought I could maybe find out a bit more about him.'

'Isn't it horrible learning to box? Do people hit you?'

Huh. She thinks I'm a wimp.

'It's fine – quite fun, actually. I'm getting a lot better at it. The coach says I might be naturally talented.'

That's not quite what he said. 'We'll make a fighter of you yet,' were the exact words. He seemed quite impressed by my bruises. 'Been practising?' he asked, with a wink.

'It'd be good if you were acting a fight scene. You'd look the part,' she says. 'Did you meet anyone who knew Ty?'

'Only the admin lady. Sylvia. She thought I looked like him.'

'You do sort of. You're a bit shorter, and your eyes are a different colour. Mind you, when I first knew Ty, his hair was really dark and his eyes were dark brown. It was really a shock to find out that he doesn't really look like that. Actually, your hair is more like his was then . . . when he was Joe, you know. . .'

When I first met Ty, his hair was dyed black, but you could really easily see his mousey roots. It looked completely rubbish. His new look works much better. I don't tell her that.

She swallows. 'Archie, it was the weirdest thing. Zoe asked me to go and watch her compete in this race. . .'

Oh yeah. She asked me too.

'And there was this boy who broke a UK record. She thought it was Joe. But they'd never have let him out of prison, would they? I said it couldn't be him.'

'It was him,' I say. 'They let him out for a day.'

'Oh my God!'

'I'm sorry.'

Stupid Ty, I think. *If you'd just write to Claire, or ring her, you could have told her yourself you were going to be there.*

'He did write me this letter,' she says, 'but he didn't say anything . . . it was all a bit vague . . . and so cold. . .'

'Oh right.'

'I showed it to Max and he thought maybe it was heavily censored.'

'Who's Max?' I ask, and she says, 'Just a mate. He's

great. Very into politics and human rights stuff. He's just set up a branch of Amnesty at school. He's brave as well.'

'Oh really?' I say, jealous as hell, and she says, 'He's the only openly gay person in our school. He came out last year, said he was fed up with lying all the time, pretending to be interested in girls when he wasn't. He's got a boyfriend at the boy's grammar and they're going to come to our prom at the end of year eleven as a couple.'

'Oh, cool.' I'm wondering who she's planning to take.

'Oh, I wish I'd seen Joe. I missed it all because we were having lunch. Athletics is really boring to watch if you don't know the people.'

'Even if you do, it's a bit tedious.'

'Did they cut off all his hair in prison? Does he look really different?'

'He'd cut it all off before,' I say, quickly readjusting my fringe. 'He looks really different now – older, stronger, a bit thin, but lots of muscles.'

'I can't imagine that. Archie, when did you see him? Was he . . . was he OK?

'He's OK,' I say. And then I just can't lie to her big, blue eyes. 'No, actually Claire, he's not OK.' And I describe the twitching, the fear, the staring into space.

'But he really liked the fairground rides. The faster and higher, the better.'

'I like those,' she says.

'So do I,' I lie.

She sighs. 'Oh, poor Ty. I wish I could see him. I was stupid to talk about a break. I've tried ringing, emailing. He's not been in touch.'

Probably best not to admit that I never actually broke the news to Ty that Claire wanted a break. 'He seemed really worried about his safety. Maybe he's trying to protect you, make sure there's no way anyone can connect the two of you?'

'When's he going to feel safe, though, Archie? And how come he's OK to see you and not me?'

'I don't know. Claire, I don't know anything about Ty any more. I feel like the more I find out about him, the more doubts I have.'

'What do you mean?'

'Well . . . I met this guy. I think he thought I was Ty. And he thought . . . he kind of suggested. . .'

'What?'

'That Ty was his dealer. He's been supplying him with drugs.'

She's very still. 'I don't believe that,' she says.

'Joe, wouldn't do that.'

'I don't believe it either,' I say, quickly. 'It was probably a mistake, just a coincidence. It's just. . .'

'What?'

'Well, I went to the park where the murder was, you know, the one Ty witnessed – where it happened. It's more than a year now, but people are still leaving flowers. There are all these dead flowers in cellophane, Claire, just sitting in the mud. And there was a girl – his sister, Rio's sister. Rio was the boy—'

'I know who Rio was,' she says. 'I read the court reports. His twin sister – Keysha?'

'I don't know her name. She was so sad, Claire. I mean, of course she was sad, but she was so angry as well. She was angry with Ty. At least, I think she was. She said she thought he'd got away with murder. She thought he was the boss of them, the gang. . .'

Claire's staring at me.

Don't shoot the messenger, I think. *Don't shoot the messenger.*

'She was angry and I've probably got it wrong and I probably shouldn't have even told you about it.'

'I'm not going to believe any of this,' says Claire, 'until I get a chance to talk to Ty. Have you talked to him about it? Have you asked him?'

I just cannot lie to her. She's got this power in her eyes.

'Sort of. But he wasn't in a great state, Claire. It's really not a good idea.'

'What happened?' Her voice is firm.

'I . . . he. . .'

'He hit you, didn't he? That's how you got your bruises?'

'I . . . he was upset. . .'

'He hit Carl once – at school, in the swimming pool. He broke his nose.'

'Who's Carl?'

'Just a boy. He'd been kind of bullying Joe.'

'I wasn't bullying him.' Not at first, anyway. Not in a physical way. You couldn't really call it bullying at all. I was perfectly entitled to say whatever I wanted. And so am I now.

'I know, I can't imagine you. . .' Her voice trails off. She's got her hand over her mouth. A tear trickles down her cheek.

'Oh God, Claire, I'm sorry. I'm so sorry. I didn't mean to upset you.'

She doesn't say anything, just shakes her head fiercely, pulls a tissue out of her pocket and blows her nose.

'I'm fine!' she says, but her voice isn't fine at all.

I put my head in my hands. Never mind my fringe.

'Claire, I've cocked this up. I never meant to tell you half of this. I don't really know anything. I could have it all wrong. Ty – he's not himself. He's got this thing, post-traumatic stress thingy. He's had so much happen to him. I don't think you should judge him. I'll go on finding out more. I promise, it'll work out OK.'

Tears again. More tissues, more nose-blowing. Thank God this café's so unpopular.

'Archie, thank you so much,' she says. 'I don't know what I'd do without you. I feel so bad that you got hurt.'

'It wasn't your fault,' I say, horrified.

'It was.'

'It wasn't.'

Somehow I've put my arm around her. Somehow she's leaning against me. Somehow she's crying into my Jack Wills hoodie.

And somehow I'm kissing the top of her silky hair. And then her forehead. And then her lips. And she's kissing me back too.

And then – oh, Jesus – someone says, 'Claire? What's going on?'

CHAPTER 22
Kissing Shannon

My love life is in turmoil! Oh my God! There's Paige – still giving me the eye at school after our one-off party snog, still posting on my Facebook wall. There's Lily, starting at my college this week, who's mad, admittedly, but who seemed, well, not uninterested the other night.

I know she was stoned (and Paige was drunk) but that's not the point. Either they felt such a strong passion for me that it overcame natural fears (of rejection) and inhibitions, and the effect of vodka/ weed, or their feelings were enhanced by artificial means and then they realised how incredibly desirable and attractive I am. Either way, I'm pretty certain that both of them would be happy to carry on where we left off, in the right circumstances.

Yes, OK, I mean vodka/weed party circumstances.

There's Shannon – Shannon, who's bright and funny and knows so much more than me about the way the world is. Shannon with her tight ponytail, her pierced tongue, her shiny lips. Every Sunday I see Shannon, walk with her in the park, eat chips with her, get to know her just a little bit better. Every Sunday night I imagine letting her hair fall loose around her shoulders, letting that tongue-stud graze my lips. I can't imagine Shannon being part of my life. That's a huge part of the attraction.

And then there's Claire. Oh God, Claire. Claire, who blushed and cringed when the girl in the wheelchair challenged us in the café.

'Claire!' she said. 'Joe!'

'It's not . . . I didn't. . .' said Claire. And then, 'Go away, Ellie. It's none of your business.'

'Oh God – it's not even Joe, is it?' said the girl, who was a bit older than us and looked like a blonder, sleeker, disabled version of Claire. 'Who the hell are you?'

'I'm Archie,' I said, and she frowned for a minute and said, 'I've heard of you. Joe's cousin. You're meant to be going out with Zoe. Claire, what the hell?'

'Ellie, it wasn't like that!' said Claire. 'Archie, I'm

really sorry, you'd better go.'

'Yes, you'd better go,' ordered Ellie, 'so Claire can explain why she's snogging her best friend's boyfriend, who also happens to be her boyfriend's cousin. Oh my God, Claire! What are you up to?'

I tightened my arm around Claire, just to give her moral support, but she turned to me and said, 'I'm really, really sorry Archie, but I think you'd better go.'

So I did and now I'm home and in bed and thinking about all these girls and I'm a mixture of horrified and delighted and right off the end of the Bakerloo line (Harrow and Wealdstone – I'll never be able to go there in real life), not that I need it in the privacy of my own bedroom.

It's all very well, though, but it's just a distraction from my other problems – my Ty problem. What if I'm right about my suspicions? Should I tell someone? Can I find out for sure?

What about my uncle Danny? Shouldn't he know about his son? He got back from New York on Friday, he's back in his studio. I could go and talk to him there. I might meet some celebrities as a bonus. And he'd be the perfect person to ask about how to juggle women.

I wouldn't tell him that I kissed Ty's girlfriend,

though, and she kissed me back. That might not go down well.

My head's spinning with it all, and it's a real relief to have a couple of hours on Sunday morning where I don't have anything to think about except how to fight and defend myself. I can see why people join the army (although I never would, because I don't like getting up early, getting shouted at and wearing uniform).

Benny sets me to spar with someone about my own age and size – Lee, his name is, and his reactions are slower than mine. I begin to feel better about Ty smashing me. It was just the surprise element, that was all. I'm sure I could fight him, take him on, with a bit more warning.

Shannon's waiting for me as usual – no brother, sister or dog this time. We buy chips, we buy kebabs. We go into the park to eat them.

We've spent weeks circling round each other. A little bit of flirting, a little bit of banter. Today she leaves her food untouched on the bench next to her. She touches my face.

'It's getting better,' she says. 'What happened? You can tell me, you know.'

I can't tell her about Claire. But I can tell her about Ty. Shannon will understand these things better than

Oscar or Lily. I bet she's seen some fights in her time.

So I lean against her and say, 'Shannon, the guy who hit me, he's my cousin.'

'Oh, really?'

'He's . . . I thought he was my friend.'

'Funny sort of friend, smashing you in the face.'

'He's just come out of prison and he's a bit nervy, you know. Sort of paranoid.'

She nods. 'My brother was the same. They get used to watching their backs all the time in there. There's a lot of rumours flying around – this one's gonna get you, that one's got a knife – that sort of thing.'

'I didn't know your brother was in prison. Isn't he a bit young?'

She laughs. 'My older brother – well, half-brother. You don't know him. Don't want to, neither.'

She's so casual about it. It's so normal to her.

'What was he in for?' I ask.

'Oh, this and that. He was in with a bad crowd, you know. And he's not clever enough about not getting caught. How about your cousin?'

'Carrying a knife,' I say.

'Oh, well. That's just stupid,' she says. She nods at the flowers, the stinking dead flowers piled up in memory of someone who wouldn't be dead if he hadn't met a boy with a knife.

'What are you thinking?' asks Shannon. I can feel her arm against mine. Suddenly my whole body is on fire. Claire's face flashes into my head and I'm confused and guilty and full of desire, all at the same time.

Which is probably why I begin burbling.

'It's just . . . look, Shannon, you mustn't tell anyone . . . but my cousin was one of those boys – one of those boys involved with that murder over there. He was here, here in this park. He was here when Rio died.'

I'm expecting shock on her face. I'm expecting horror, revulsion, disgust. I don't see it. Her lips part – I can see that little lump of gold – and her eyes widen. But she's not half as shocked as I expected.

'Tell me,' she says.

So it all falls out – how I never really knew him, how I've heard the story in bits and pieces, how the police charged him and he ended up in prison.

'Jesus,' she says. She puts her hand on my thigh. It's like there's a button there which instantly turns me on. It's not really what I need right now, but even so.

Shannon kisses me, very gently. The tongue-stud is hard and cold in my mouth. She tastes of ketchup and vinegar, she smells of Turkish delight.

I'm just getting comfortable, hand on her thigh, but I suddenly think of Claire's face when the wheelchair girl challenged us. It's like an instant cold shower. I disengage my lips.

'It's good to talk about these things,' says Shannon. 'It was bothering you, wasn't it? I knew it. I knew you were carrying around some secret.'

'I shouldn't really—' I say, but she kisses me again, harder this time, and pushes her skinny body against mine. It's no good, though. It only makes me think of Claire.

'It's just that I'm not sure about what he's told me,' I say, partly to stop her kissing me. It'd be embarrassing if she found out that my train was back in the depot, as it were. 'I've talked to people, found out stuff. I think he might have been more involved than he lets on. I think he might have been up to other stuff.'

Shannon sighs. She gets out a cigarette, offers the box to me. We light up, inhale, sit and stare at the rotting bouquets.

'You're not really called Kyle, are you?' she says.

'No.' What's the point in pretending? I'll probably never come back here again.

'Did you just come here to spy on us, to find out stuff for your cousin?'

'No!' I say. And then, 'Well yes, but not for him – for me, to find out if he was telling the truth or not.'

She looks away. There's a suggestion of a tear in her eye.

'It's just that . . . I thought you liked me – really liked me, for myself. I kind of knew you weren't really from round here, that you're a posh boy, aren't you? But I never realised that you were just snooping around, trying to find out stuff from me.'

Eh? Hang on a minute.

'What do you mean? Shannon, I do like you. I like you a lot, actually.'

'I like you too,' she says.

Oh Jesus. I've made two girls cry in two days.

I put my arm around her, pull her towards me. 'Don't cry, Shannon, please, don't cry. I don't understand. I just joined the boxing club to try and get to know more about this area . . . this world . . . where my cousin comes from. My dad's from round here too. It's nothing to do with you.'

'Oh, really?' she says. 'Do you swear? Do you mean it?'

'Of course,' I say.

'It's just – I think I know who your cousin is.'

Oh my God. I quickly rewind what I've told her.

Could I have given any details, put Ty in danger?

'It's Ty, isn't it? Ty Lewis?'

'I . . . no . . . yes. . .'

She laughs. 'I never saw it before, but you look a bit like him – better-looking, though. I wouldn't have looked twice at him.'

I can't help it. I laugh.

'Do you . . . did you know him well?'

She shakes her head. 'Not really. He's a quiet one, isn't he? You never know what he's thinking. I don't trust those quiet ones. No offence, but you never know what they're up to.'

'That's it. That's right.'

'He had a big influence over his friend,' she says. 'Ty talked less, but he called the shots, you know.'

'Really?' I ask. I don't want to hear this at all. 'How do you know?'

She looks surprised. 'Oh God. You really don't know, do you?'

'Know what?'

'I thought you were spying on me, but you weren't . . . you didn't know. . .'

'Know what?'

'I didn't know Ty so well, but I did know his friend – his friend that's serving time for murder. Arron.

Arron Mackenzie. He's the one I knew.'

I can't speak. She knows Arron. She knows everything. She can tell me the truth about Ty.

'How well did you know Arron?' My voice is just a croak.

'Pretty well,' she says. 'Arron Mackenzie was my boyfriend.'

CHAPTER 23
Babe Magnet

I am gobsmacked. But luckily I'm not the sort of person whose gob stays smacked for long.

'Tell me about him,' I say. 'Tell me about Arron. Did you believe he'd kill anyone? '

'Arron – he's a laugh, you know? Never took anything seriously. Out to have fun and not do any harm. I can't believe what happened to him. I can't believe he's in prison.'

'Are you – have you been to see him?'

She shakes her head. 'I don't know if he'd want to see me. We split up. I might go one day. I babysit for his mum sometimes, she said she'd take me any time I want to go. But he's bitter, I think, from what she says, angry and upset. I don't want to upset him more. Poor Arron.'

I stare at the flowers. I chew a bit of cold chip.

'Shannon, will you take me to see him?'

'You? Why?'

'I want to ask him for myself – ask him about Ty, about what actually happened that day and whose fault it was and what Ty's really like. Arron – he can tell me about Ty. He can tell me about the murder. He can tell me everything I need to know.'

Why do I need to know it? Why does anyone need to know anything about anyone? I just do, that's why.

'Arron might see you,' says Shannon. 'His mum told me that he wanted to give Ty a message, but she didn't know how to contact him. They just disappeared into nowhere. You know his gran died recently and they had the funeral at five in the morning, so that no one would know about it. Arron's mum was devastated. She said, "That woman was like a mother to me, like a grandmother to my boys. And they never even told me that she was being put in the ground. My own church." She's quite religious, Arron's mum, although neither of the boys are.'

'What do you mean, neither of the boys? Do you mean Ty?'

'Nah, Arron's brother Nathan. You must've seen him at the gym. Really tall – big, you know, big muscly arms. He's got much darker skin than Arron. They don't really look like brothers at all. I think they had different dads.'

'Oh right.'

'Arron's one of those guys who looks white but he's really black. It's not actually that easy for him.'

'Oh, OK.'

'Arron's really bright, you know. He and Ty went to that snobby school up west somewhere – Catholic school. Arron knew loads of posh boys, fitted in OK. He's really confident – he was, anyway. I can't believe he's locked up with a load of scum. I can't believe he's been done for murder.'

He's been done for murder because Ty told a court that he was guilty. I know it, even though she doesn't say it.

'I'm really sorry, Shannon,' I say. 'I would like to talk to Arron, but only if you think he would, only if you think it might help him.'

'I'll ask him,' she says. 'I should go and see him, anyway. I can't get my head around it. Arron was the most free person I ever met. He was going to go to Australia, Kyle, imagine that. He was going to leave school and go to Australia and work on one of those big cattle farms.'

'Really?' I look around the muddy park. I can't

imagine anywhere less like a vast, dusty Australian wilderness.

'He said he was fed up with living with loads of people and he wanted space and he couldn't think of a better way of getting it.' Tears are blurring her eyeliner. 'And now he's locked up for years and I bet that Australia won't take you if you've been convicted of murder.'

I bet she's right too.

'Look, ask him, will you? Shannon, do you think it's OK for me to come back next week?'

She sniffs, blows her nose, rubs her eyes.

'I'm not telling anyone anything. You keep on coming back, Kyle – I don't suppose you're going to tell me your real name.'

'It's Archie,' I say. 'Archie Stone.'

'Archie Stone, eh?' she says, thoughtfully. 'And your dad grew up around here?'

'Yeah, but he hasn't lived here for years.'

She laughs. 'Your secret is safe with me, Archie Stone. I don't suppose you come from the Cally, neither.'

'No,' I say. 'Fulham.'

'Oh, la-di-da.' She's laughing now. 'Can't say I'm surprised. Tell you what, take me clubbing in Fulham one day? That's where the royals go.'

'Oh, all right then,' I say, taken by surprise. 'I'm not sure I'd get in, though, you have to be eighteen.'

'You mean you're not eighteen yet – big, tall boy like you?'

She's teasing, I know, but actually, I have grown a bit recently, and I can't help smiling.

'OK, OK, I'll take you dancing with the Royal Family. Prince Harry comes round my house all the time. And Camilla walks the corgis past our door.'

'Oh, yeah, right, I believe you,' she says, and suddenly we're laughing, even though the jokes are really not up to my usual standard.

It's what she's told me that's on my mind as I wait for the bus – about Arron and her and Ty. In fact, I'm thinking so hard that I don't realise that I've got onto the wrong bus until I look out of the window and have a moment of panic because I have no idea at all where I am. So I get off, and onto the next one coming in the other direction and that's a bit of a strange route as well and here I am in Clerkenwell, which is full of really amazing clubs – Shannon has no idea – and people who live in converted factories, huge open spaces where they can hang out and be cool and it's definitely where I'd like to live when I'm older. And it's where my Uncle Danny has his studio. And we're actually going down the street where the studio is.

It's a sign, although I'm not sure who it's from, as God (if there is one, which I don't think there is) definitely doesn't have anything to do with Transport for London – not unless he's a complete joker. Mind you, that could make sense.

I get off the bus, walk down the street, work out which direction to go. I've never actually been to his studio. I've hinted enough times, but he's never seemed that interested in inviting me over.

But he's living there now, and he got back from New York yesterday and I'm sure he'd be happy to see me. And I'll kind of work out what to say when I get there.

There's no big sign or anything outside the building where the studio is, just a scribbled 'Tyler' next to a bell and it seems to be above an art gallery. I press the bell, but it takes quite a few times before a voice comes out of the intercom.

'Whoissit?' it slurs. 'Whassup?'

'It's me, Archie,'

'Who?'

'Archie. Your nephew.'

'Oh. OK.' There's a pause – quite a long pause – and then the door buzzes open. A stairwell, stairs, walls – everything painted dark grey. The only light comes from a dim overhead light. I climb and climb. It seems like an hour before I get to a door propped open with a camera bag, and push it open to find myself in a dazzling white space. I blink a few times. It's a bit disorientating.

Danny's sitting on a battered old leather sofa, looking crumpled and unshaven and baggy-eyed.

'What are you doing here?' he asks, but he doesn't put it as politely as that. 'I only got back from New York at seven this morning. I'm shattered.'

'Oh sorry,' I say, 'I'll go away,' and he shakes his head and says, 'Nah, it's OK.'

He's a bit out of it, if you ask me, a bit spacey. Must be jet lag.

'Nice place,' I say. 'Is this where you bring the celebrities?'

'Yeah,' he says. 'Actually, Beyoncé's here now – just preparing for her nude shot, up on the roof terrace.'

I'm halfway up the stairs leading to the roof when he laughs and says, 'Never seen anyone move so fast. Only joking.'

Oh. Ha ha. I'd have thought he was a bit old for pathetic jokes like that.

He's slumped against the sofa. His eyes are half

closed. I can smell coffee – there's a flash Italian coffee machine in the little kitchen that takes up the far wall – and smoke.

'Want some coffee?' he asks.

'Yes . . . please. . .'

'Smoke?'

'Yup.' My hand's on the cigarette, when I remember that Mum and Dad are really anti-smoking, in fact, Dad's a real health freak fascist about it, and I worry for a moment that Danny's going to inform on me. He sees my hand waver and he smiles and says, 'Don't worry. I'm not a snitch. Does your dad give you a hard time?'

'Well, you know – about smoking and homework and stuff.'

'Oh, I know, I know. Works twenty-four/seven, earns pots of money, has to win everything, and can't understand that not everyone's like that?'

'Umm, yes. . .'

'Makes you feel like you're not a real man unless you take him on and beat him?'

'Oh . . . well. . .'

'I knew it!' He pours two mugs of steaming coffee. 'Milk? Sugar? When you were born, I said, "Poor little sod, he'll be crushed by his alpha dad."'

'Oh . . . errr . . . I don't think I've really been crushed. . .'

'Good,' he says. 'Good. Glad to hear it. So you're on track for Oxbridge and the law and running marathons every weekend?'

'Oh, well, I don't know about that. . . I thought I could go on television . . . or maybe be a foreign correspondent . . . or a famous actor. . .'

He's laughing. 'That's not what your mum thinks. Last time I talked to her she told me that you were settling down nicely at this new school and she thought you might enjoy Philosophy A level.'

'Oh, right.' Actually, I do think I'd enjoy philosophy. It's all about questions and arguing. I've had quite a bit of philosophical experience in my life, plus it'd impress older women if I could drop names like Nietzsche and Sartre into casual conversation.

He's smoked his cigarette, and lights himself another. It's the last in the box, and the ashtray is pretty full. He only got back at 7 am, he must have been sleeping some of the time, so I reckon he's been smoking non-stop when awake. Either that, or his studio's been house-sat by a chain smoker.

He follows my gaze. 'I really shouldn't,' he says, 'but . . . you know. Life's kind of rubbish right now.'

The studio we're in is huge and light and has a vintage jukebox at one end, and a kitchen/bar at the other. It's all sleek and interior-designed. Celebrities come here all the time. Plus he's just got back from New York, which is one of my favourite places on the planet.

He yawns. 'I need a bit of a kip, really. Did you have any particular reason for coming to see me, or was it just a social call?'

He's going to chuck me out, I know. I need to come up with something.

'Oh, I just . . . I wanted to ask you something. I thought you might know.'

'Oh God.' He runs his hands through his hair, which is dark and thick and wild and on a good day makes him look a bit like Johnny Depp. Today is not a good day.

'It's not drugs, is it?'

'Drugs?'

'Pen's sent you, hasn't she? She reckoned I should talk to you about drugs, tell you to keep off them. From the horse's mouth, as it were.'

'The horse . . . oh . . . right. . .'

He narrows his eyes.

'Don't ever start, kid. Not worth it.'

'Start what?'

'Start with the drugs.'

'Oh. Umm.' I'm unusually tongue-tied.

He's getting agitated. 'I've spent thousands of pounds in rehab, and whenever there's a crisis – and my whole sodding life is a crisis right now – all I can think about is getting off my head.'

'Oh.'

'You know it all, don't you, about the health risks,' he says. 'No point telling you about my ex-friend who's in a wheelchair because he had a coke stroke, or my other mate who needs to pee every ten minutes because ketamine buggered his bladder. Ruins your social life, something like that.'

'Oh . . . err. . .'

'No point telling you about Angie, Angie, my assistant. When I met her, she was selling her body through an escort agency to get the money to buy heroin. And no, that's not how I met her.'

'Oh, well, I. . .'

'There's no point, really, because you'll be just like me and you'll think none of these things will ever happen to you.'

I don't say anything, but what I'm thinking is that

actually none of these things did ever happen to him.

He reads my mind. 'Horrible things did happen to me. But I'm your uncle, and you're friends with my son, and I'm going to preserve a little bit of dignity, if you don't mind.'

'Oh. Um. Sorry.'

'Anyway, the thing that might persuade you is that drugs make you boring – really, really boring. In the end, all you can think or talk about is what gear you're doing, and then, of course, how rehab is going. I've lost so many friends. . .'

He might have a point there. Marcus is pretty boring. He's asleep most of the time.

'Think about it,' he says.

'Oh, right, yes I will,' I say. 'Actually, I don't do drugs at all,' I add, just in case this is going back to my mum.

He raises an eyebrow. He's a lot more like my grandpa Patrick than you'd think.

Quick, quick, Archie, change the subject. I open my mouth and this is what comes out.

'Actually, I wanted some advice about women.'

It works. He laughs. He laughs a lot more than he needs to, in my opinion.

I tell him about Paige (he waves his hand

dismissively. 'Forget her. She'll be off with another guy, next party she goes to').

I tell him about Zoe ('I like sporty girls. You should make it up with her').

I tell him about Lily ('Way too much trouble. You need to cut her out of your life 100 per cent. Life's too short for crazy girls – that's actually the most important piece of advice you'll ever be given, Archie, so don't forget it. Crazy girls seem great, but they do your head in').

I'm feeling bolder. So I mention Claire. I don't say who she is, of course. I twist the facts. I pretend Oscar's got a girlfriend and we've got loads in common and I really like her. And I think she really likes me too.

'And what does Oscar think?' he asks. 'Does he know how you feel?'

'No . . . obviously . . . but he asked me to spend time with her . . . well, talk to her, anyway. . .'

'Why's he doing that? Is he trying to offload her?'

'Um. . . I don't think so. . .'

'It's easy. You have to work out which one means more to you, the friend or the girl.'

'Oh. Right.'

'Is he a pothead, your mate?'

'No.' I think of Ty's spaced expression at the fair.

'I'm not sure. Sort of.'

'He won't be that bothered, then,' he says. He sounds sad. 'He probably won't notice if you take her off him. Good for you. Is she nice?'

'She's great,' I say. It's really nice to be able to talk about Claire. 'She's really into drama and music and she reads good books and stuff.'

'Sounds like trouble to me,' he says. 'Arty girls are often mad pixies. Are you sure she isn't one?'

'Absolutely,' I say. 'Completely. Errr, what actually is a mad pixie?'

'Quirky,' he says gloomily. 'You get them in films a lot – funky hair, vintage clothes, they like odd music and old books and classic films, dance around screwing with people's hearts. You need to recognise them when you see them. Dangerous.'

'Oh! I've never heard of them before.'

'I wish someone had warned me,' he says. 'They never teach you the good stuff at school. Angie, for example. She's a total mad pixie. I just had to sack her – can't keep off the drugs.'

'Was . . . is Nicki a mad pixie?'

'Actually, no,' he says, with a big grin. 'Nicki was the ultimate sporty girl when I met her – confident and strong and cocky and funny. She was a champion runner, she was top of her class. So amazing. And she came from this different world, which meant she was tough and strong and street, in a way that I just wasn't.'

'Oh. God. I know a girl a bit like that. She likes me too.'

He raises an eyebrow. 'How long have you been back in London?'

'A few months.'

'Archie, you're a babe magnet,' he drawls.

I try to look modest.

'That's why you remind me of myself,' he says, and throws back his head and laughs.

And then the door buzzes again.

'Who's that?' he says. 'I've got nothing booked.'

He walks over to the door, presses the intercom.

'Yes?' he says, 'Who's there?'

Silence. He tries again. There's a burst of static, the noise of traffic rumbling down the road.

And then, 'It's me. It's Ty. Let me in, please. . .'

CHAPTER 24
Starbucks

I've always thought Ty was a lot fitter than me, but I revise that opinion when he reaches the top of the stairs and he's shaking and gulping for breath and virtually collapsing into the door.

'What the hell?' says Danny. He leaps towards Ty, almost carries him over to the sofa. 'Get him some water, Archie,' he orders.

Ty's hand is shaking as he drinks, and he spills as much as he swallows. It feels a bit much to stand over him, so I retreat to one of the window seats. Down below I can see people going in and out of Starbucks, people whose only problem is deciding whether to have a skinny latte or a soya Frappuccino. It's another world, and usually I'm in it.

'What's going on? What are you doing here? What's happened?' says Danny, sounding incredibly calm and gentle. He actually reminds me of my mum for a minute, her best 'talk-to-me' voice.

Ty can't speak. That's obvious. 'Mum—' he gasps.

'What? What's happened to Nicki?' Danny's lost his cool. He grabs Ty's shoulders. 'What's happened? Is she OK?'

'She's . . . she's OK now, but. . .'

'What? What?'

In my opinion, shaking someone is not the best way to get them to talk.

'Let go of him!' I shout and Danny loosens his grip on Ty's shoulders. He resumes calm, kind and gentle mode.

'What's going on, Ty? Tell me.'

'We were at the station and there was a man following us—'

'What station? Where? Why?'

'Euston. To go to Aberdeen. I didn't want to go, but Mum . . . it was safer for her and Alyssa and I thought I could go and then leave. . .'

'Ah,' says Danny. 'Aberdeen. OK, she did mention it to me. It's just – OK, I can see why she did it—'

'There was a man! He was following us!'

'Ty, my dad called me last week and he told me you've been. . .'

'He was following us!'

Danny sighs. I can see that Ty can see that he doesn't believe in the man.

'So what happened?'

'So we got onto the train and then I said, "Mum, there's a man following us, and I'm going to get off again." And she didn't want me to, but I did it, anyway. I did it really obviously, so the man would see, and he got off as well.'

'He got off as well? Are you sure?'

'Of course I'm sure! Do you think I'd have left them all alone on a train if there was a man . . . a man who was following them?'

'What if there were two men?' I ask, and Ty's face goes a strange greeny colour and he says, 'There weren't two men. There was one man. He got off the train.'

'Yes, but what if—' I start, and Danny says, 'Shut up, Archie. What happened then, Ty?'

'He followed me right out of the station and then I started running and I ran and ran, and I couldn't think where to go, but I knew you were here, so I thought maybe . . . maybe. . .'

'And was he still following you? Did he follow you here?'

'I don't think so.' He looks around, as though the man's going to materialise in a corner. 'I don't think so.'

'Will they know where Nicki's going,' I ask, helpfully, 'if they saw her getting on a train to Aberdeen?'

'They won't know she's going all the way there,' says Danny, 'and I imagine she has to change at – where, Ty? Edinburgh?'

'Yeah, I think. . .'

'Ty, I need to call her. I'll tell you you're OK. And maybe I'll suggest that she takes a different route to Aberdeen.'

I can see that he's just humouring Ty, and Ty can see that too.

'Will you really?' he says, and Danny nods.

'OK, I'll go downstairs where I get a better signal.' He glances at the coffee machine – it's empty. 'Fancy a coffee from Starbucks?'

We order Frappuccinos. We listen to him go down the stairs. We watch him cross the road and get his phone out.

'How did you know this particular man was following you?' I'm thinking there must have been loads of people getting on the train.

Ty rolls his eyes. 'I recognised him.'

'You recognised him?'

'He runs a boxing club I used to go to. Ray. He's married to Tommy White's sister. She's called Sylvia, she helps in the club. He's in it, they're all in it. . .'

'Ray? Ray was following you?'

Ty looks at me, eyes narrowed. 'How do you know Ray?'

'I don't. I just mean, you went to a boxing club run by a gangster?'

'I didn't know that. I was nine years old. Even when I was fourteen, I was too stupid to realise. There's lots of guys there that aren't involved in anything. But Ray and Tommy, they're into everything. And Tommy's son Jukes, he ran a gang, ran it for his dad, so his dad could get the drugs onto the street. Kids younger than you running around, mugging people on his orders, dealing drugs on street corners and at schools, at clubs, you name it. . .'

'Oh.'

Ty's rocking back and forward. 'Where is he? Maybe he can't get through. Maybe you were right, Archie. Maybe there was someone else on the train and they've shot them already. . .'

'They're probably just going through a tunnel.'

'Arron, my friend, he joined their gang,' says Ty. 'He was selling to rich kids like you. You ever bought weed, Archie, from someone like Arron?'

'No,' I say, but I wonder who Oscar buys from.

'Rich kids like you keep the gangsters rich. People like Arron, they think they're going to get rich too, but they end up in prison instead – in prison or dead.'

'They make loads of money out it it,' I say, 'people like your friend Arron. He just got greedy.'

Ty takes a deep breath, glares right at me.

'Archie, you have no frigging idea.'

Downstairs we hear the noise of the door slamming.

'Danny,' says Ty. 'Do you think he rang her? What am I going to do if he didn't?'

'It'll be OK,' I say. 'He's more sensible than he looks.'

I glance out of the window again. There's a guy coming out of Starbucks who looks familiar, in a speck-like fashion. He's got messy black hair. He's got long thin legs. He's carrying three cups in a holder . . . he's . . . he's Danny, that's who he is.

So who the hell's coming up the stairs?

'Ty . . .Ty. . .' I gesture him over to the window. We watch Danny cross the road. We hear the steps on the stairs.

'It's probably just his assist—' I start, but Ty's running to the stairs at the back of the studio.

'Quick. . .' he hisses. 'Come on. . .'

'But . . . but Danny. . .' I say, but I follow him. The steps are creaking closer.

The door is bolted and a bit stiff, but not locked. We're on a roof terrace, a little green space on the flat grey roof. We're breathing in the London fumes, high, high above the traffic.

'Woo,' I say. 'I never knew your dad liked gardening.'

It's a joke, really, because it's all a bit brown and bare – fair enough, I suppose, it is winter – but there are loads and loads of pots and some funky lime green bean bags. I'm all ready to flop down on one but Ty shakes his head and says, 'We gotta get help. What about Danny? Can you ring him?'

I feel for my phone. No signal.

'Jesus,' says Ty. 'Come on.' He climbs over the iron fence that surrounds the little terrace. We're on the flat roof, nothing between us and a three storey drop. It's not exactly narrow, but even so. . .

I don't look down.

We clamber over a sloping roof, dodge around a chimney, find ourselves on a long, thin bit of roof.

It's OK because there are walls at the edges of this bit, but I make the mistake of looking down as we walk across.

'Can't you go faster?' says Ty, as I fight to stay upright.

'I . . . no . . .Ty. . .'

From not so far away, we hear a crack, a popping noise. It could be a motorcycle backfiring far below us. It could be . . . it could be. . .

'Jesus!' yells Ty. 'Run! He's shooting at us!'

I don't dare look back. I don't dare look to the side. I fix my eyes on his back and I make my feet run. If I fall . . . if I trip. . .

Bang! It was louder this time. The roof is wider, flatter, greyer. Ty speeds up.

'Come on!' he hisses. 'We have to . . . we need to. . .'

I lift my eyes. Oh God. There's a gap in the buildings ahead – a narrow gap, sure, hardly a gap at all, the sort of gap you'd skip over on the ground, you wouldn't notice it, it wouldn't feel like any risk at all, but five floors up, we're five floors up and. . .

Ty jumps over the gap. I slither to a halt.

'For God's sake!' he screams at me. 'Jump, you moron! It's nothing!'

'I can't!'

He reaches out his arm. I grab it.

'You can . . . come on. . .'

Slowly, carefully, hating him, despising myself, hearing my heart thump, thump inside me, I step over the gap.

It's all silent.

'Come on,' he says, and we climb over another little wall – more roof ahead.

'Ty!' I say. 'The noise! It's stopped!' but he shakes his head.

'We need to get further . . . need to get away. . .'

'But your dad. . .' I'm imagining Danny coming up the stairs, coffees in hand, pushing open the door and then? What did he find? What happened to him?

He shakes his head. 'Too late,' he says. 'Too late.'

He starts to run. It's OK on this bit of the roof. It's wide, and flat and the wall's behind us . . . and I'm running with him, running forward . . . and then. . .

Oh Jesus.

A much wider gap.

I turn back. 'We can't. . .'

But he shakes his head. 'It's nothing. We can do it.' He looks wildly over one shoulder. 'We have to run . . . run Archie. . .'

I can't run this fast.

We're nearly there. He's way ahead of me now, faster and faster.

'I can't do it,' I gasp, 'I can't! Stop! Ty! Stop!'

He doesn't listen. He's there. He flings himself forward, He's flying through the air.

I can't look. I swerve sideways, slam into a wall that I didn't know was there.

And the wall gives way, and I'm falling. . .

CHAPTER 25
Falling

I'm falling . . . splat onto some concrete stairs, rolling over and over, fingers grabbing at the slippery walls, moving so fast that I can't stop myself, can't slow down, limbs crashing against the stairs, head bashing against the walls, until I reach the bottom, smash, crash, bash onto the floor.

I can't help it. I yell out loud. Who'd have thought it would be so painful, falling down a flight of stairs? James Bond does it all the time and he just gets up and starts running around and shooting people. I feel like I've been paralysed.

I move my foot carefully. It's a miracle! I must be bruised all over, but nothing seems to be broken. I scramble to my feet, rubbing my elbows, checking for bruises. There's a massive scrape along my left shin and a trickle of blood down my right knee. My hands are pink and raw with friction burns, but all in all, I got off quite easy. In fact, with a bit of practice, I bet I could do a James Bond finish. I'm OK. I'm really OK.

I can even work out what happened. I fell against a wall that was actually a door, and for some reason it was open and I fell right into a building.

I've feeling quite relieved and pleased with myself. Woo, Archie! With a leap he was free. . . And then I remember Ty flying through the air, trying to bridge that impossible gap, with a gunman chasing after him.

Oh Jesus. What can I do?

I look around. I'm in a stairwell, with more stairs leading down – thank God I didn't fall down those too, they look like they lead to the centre of the earth. There's a door, leading out onto a corridor. I push open the door – more doors. One has a bright pink sign on it – 'Blanchflower & Blannin, Branding.' There's a buzzer. I press it down. I keep it pressed down.

Nothing. No answer. Nothing.

And then I remember that it's Sunday and this is an office building and there probably won't be anyone here until the morning.

I search for my phone, but it must have fallen out of my pocket when I ran or when I fell.

OK, I have to escape from here. I have to find Danny

and tell him that his son's probably strawberry jam on the pavement, and the Following Man was real and even has a name and an address. . .

And a wife who had my mobile number and who instantly realised that I was connected to Ty. . .

And. . .

It's quite possible that Danny's been shot himself. I am the only one who knows who did it.

Oh Jesus. This is the scariest thing that's ever happened to me, including watching *The Human Centipede* (which was disgusting, rather than scary. Oscar almost threw up, although he blamed a dodgy batch of sushi) and having three teeth out without a general anaesthetic (not quite as bad as you'd imagine).

I stand up, then sit down again pretty quickly. I ache all over. My arm is killing me. But I can't be a wimp. Cautiously, I start slithering down the stairs, half sitting, half lying, wincing when I knock my arm against the wall.

It takes forever, but eventually I make it down to the ground floor. I crawl to the door. It's too heavy to open.

I struggle to my feet, throw myself against it. And I go sprawling into a shop – a shop selling office furniture for cool people. There are desks and chairs and filing cabinets – aubergine purples and glowing reds and a fabulous silver desk which looks like the command desk of a starship captain. I'd love a desk like that. I wonder if my parents . . . for my birthday. . .

Get a grip, Archie!

The security shutters are down and I can't even attract anyone's attention, although I can see feet passing on the pavement outside.

There must be a phone here somewhere. It takes some time to locate – you try finding the sales desk in a dark showroom full of office furniture. It's worse than a needle in a haystack. (I've always wondered what sort of idiot sits on a haystack to sew, anyway. They deserve to lose it.) But I make it eventually, grab the phone, stab randomly until I get an outside line.

My head is fuzzy and hurting so much, so when I call 999 and they ask me which emergency service I need, I can't think what to say.

'I'm trapped in a shop,' I say, 'but I don't know where. And my cousin might have fallen off a building. And my uncle might have been shot.'

And suddenly it's all too much and there are tears pouring down my face and I'm shaking and shaking, and thinking of Ty's body crumpled on the ground, smushed to strawberry jam. My mouth fills up with vomit. All I can do is groan, 'Help me,' into the phone and lean forward to throw up into a designer bin from Italy that costs £284.

And then the lights go out, which is weird, because they weren't on in the first place.

I wake up with someone yelling into my face, and I suppose I must be in an ambulance, because it's noisy and small and bumping around all over the place, and I'm sick again right away, which means I start choking and swallowing vomit, because some idiot has strapped me to a bed.

Then it all goes blurry again until we get to hospital, where I'm sick over and over – but at least there's a bowl this time, and a nurse holding my hair back and giving me sips of water and then they wheel me onto a ward – a children's ward, bloody hell – and stick me in a bed, with a drip in my arm.

It'd feel a bit more bloody dramatic if there wasn't a huge mural of Humpty-Dumpty on the wall and a bandaged eight-year-old in the bed opposite. His parents are looking at me like they think I'm going to explode.

'Here you go,' says the nurse. 'Your mum and dad have been contacted and they're on their way. We just want to keep you under observation, in case you've got concussion. That's a nasty bump on your head.'

'How did you know my who I am?' I ask.

'You had your wallet in your pocket,' she says. 'We just called your mum. She's very upset. On her way.'

Oh great.

'My cousin. . .' I say. 'Is he . . . do you know. . .?' I can't bear to say it.

'What is it?'

I catch the eye of the little kid in the opposite bed. He's listening to every word. His mum looks horrified. I try to whisper.

'We were on the roof together. I think . . . I think he fell. . .'

'I've not heard of anyone falling off a roof in central London,' she says, 'but mind you, I'm pretty busy when I'm on duty. Tell you what, I'll see if I can find out for you. Did you actually see him fall?'

'I saw him jump,' I say, completely without hope, and she looks a bit shocked, pats my hand and says, 'Don't give up. You do hear of miracles happening.'

I'm not very comforted. And I'm not very sure she knows anything about anything. And I really don't want to have to explain what's happened to Mum.

So as soon as she's gone I struggle to sit up and start examining the needle taped to my hand. Can I pull it out? Can I get out of here?

I can't. Or rather, I could, but I don't really want to. I prefer telling myself that I feel really ill, weak, dizzy and hot, that I can't walk – my legs are throbbing with pain – that I may have fractured my skull. If I pulled out the drip I'd probably bleed to death. The little boy's mum would stop me, anyway.

Besides, if Ty is dead, what can I do? I keep thinking about our last conversation. What if I led the gang to him? What if they got his number from my mobile somehow? What if they hacked into my messages? Did any come from him?

What if he didn't care any more? What if he thought he'd sacrifice himself for the safety of Claire and Nicki and Alyssa?

I could never do that in a hundred years.

The door bursts open and I'm expecting my mum. But it's Danny, unshot, as far as I can see, wild-eyed and raving at a nurse.

'Of course I'm allowed to see him! I'm his uncle! Jesus! Archie! What the hell happened? Where's Ty?'

'Ty . . .Ty. . .' OK, this is worse than I expected. Why

doesn't he know that Ty's dead on the pavement? Maybe he was unrecognisable? Maybe Danny didn't make the connection? And now I'm going to have to tell him.

'There was a man . . . someone chasing us . . . shooting at us. So we ran . . . up . . . on the roof. . .' I trail to a halt.

'Yes?'

'And we ran and ran. . .'

'Ty! What happened to Ty? Is he here? Penny rang me, told me that you were here, but Ty . . . why isn't he here? Where is he?'

'I . . . he . . . he jumped. . .'

'And then?'

'I don't know . . . I thought. . . I fell down some stairs. I might have concussion.'

'He jumped? Where did he jump? Jesus, Archie!'

'Do you mind?' says the little boy's mum. 'My son's getting over an operation and he needs peace and quiet.'

I can see Danny's about to be rude to her, so I say, 'Sorry,' for him and whisper, 'Between the roofs. From one roof to another. But I don't know if he made it – it looked really big—'

'He must have,' says Danny. 'I'd have known. . .'

'Yes, but what if he fell into a sort of alleyway or something and no one noticed?'

'Jesus,' says Danny again, and a whole lot more. Then he pulls out his mobile.

'You're not allowed to use that in a hospital,' says the boy's mum, 'and I'd appreciate it if you moderated your language.'

I brace myself for Danny's response, but he just collapses into a chair, puts his head in his hands and says, 'I can't face ringing them, anyway. What if you're right? What am I going to tell Nicki?'

I want to hit him, but luckily my mum arrives and takes over. She says very firmly that it's extremely unlikely that Ty could have fallen off a roof.

'I've just come in a taxi all the way from the City, I went straight past your studio, Danny, and believe me, if there'd been a major incident like that, I'd still be sitting at Old Street.'

'Yes, but what if he's lying in some alleyway somewhere and no one's seen him?'

'So unlikely,' she says.

The police come a bit later, and they ask loads of questions and tell us that a) they've checked every alleyway and there's no Ty-flavoured jam on the pavement, and b) there is evidence that a gun was shot on the roof.

So Ty was right.

And now he's disappeared.

CHAPTER 26
Disappearing

The only thought in my head is to get out of London. As soon as I'm sitting on a coach pulling out of Victoria bus station, I feel better.

I wasn't paranoid. I wasn't making it up. They were still after me.

I was getting a bit worried about my own sanity for a few minutes there.

But then the questions kick in. And there are always questions. What happened to my dad? Were my mum and Alyssa safe on the train? How about Archie – I don't think he fell, but what happened to him? Patrick and Helen – are they safe?

I can't call anyone because I dumped my phone at Victoria station. Phone in one bin, SIM card in another. I scratched the SIM card as much as I could, tried to destroy it so no one can trace it back to me.

I can see what I have to do now. I need to wipe myself out – start again.

Can you save yourself by starting another life? And is it worth it, if you have to lose everything you love?

It is, I decide, because I'm not doing it for me. I'm doing it to keep everyone else safe. I'm too dangerous. I'm bringing bad stuff to everyone's lives.

The coach rumbles into the night and I know that in the morning I'll be somewhere new where no one knows me and I can look for work and somewhere to stay. I'll put on an accent and all the people I've ever been will be washed away.

I'll buy a newspaper and I'll see if there's anything about a celebrity photographer being shot, about a woman and a baby being attacked on a train, about a teenage boy called Archie falling off a roof in central London, falling and falling and—

What will I do if they're all dead?

CHAPTER 27
Marcus

No one hears from Ty at Christmas, and no one hears from him at New Year – at least, as far as I know. The police found my phone on the roof and gave it back to me, so I keep on calling him. It never rings.

I think about contacting Claire – there's been radio silence since our snog – but I don't really want to tell her that Ty might have been shot, or captured, or possibly splatted in some place that the police haven't stumbled over yet.

I'm spending as much time as possible getting stoned with Oscar and Lily. We compared notes on Boxing Day, as to who'd had the most rubbish Christmas.

'Mine was awful,' I offered. 'Grandpa and Grandma were really down about my cousin who's kind of disappeared. And my parents argued all the way there and back – that's two lots of two hours.'

'Mine was crap,' said Lily. 'I hate Mum's new boyfriend and I hate his brats and we all went to some hotel where I couldn't even have wine. I lit up in the ladies and the smoke alarm went off.'

'Mine was worst,' said Oscar. 'My parents staged an intervention with Marcus. That's when you tell someone how much it's hurting you that he's addicted – except Marcus says he's not addicted. There was a huge fight, Marcus hit Dad, and they chucked him out and changed the locks at 10 pm on Christmas night.'

OK, that did sound like the crappest Christmas.

'Why did they pick Christmas Day to do this intervention thing?'

'They've been seeing this rubbish counsellor. She's from America and she's very into discipline and boundaries and getting your kids to do as they're told. She said it was a good idea to do it at Christmas, because it'd work on Marcus's happy memories of the past.

'Did you even get any dinner?'

'We were halfway through the turkey when they started. Never got as far as the pudding. Actually, it's still in the fridge if anyone fancies some.'

We did fancy some, even though it meant creeping past Oscar's mum to get to the fridge. She seems to spend all her time sitting at the kitchen table, weeping. I felt a bit awkward, but Oscar shrugged his shoulders.

'Serves her right if she's upset,' he said, once we got back upstairs. 'She was the one banging on about tough love and limits and stuff. Just because he borrowed a bit of cash from her purse. I think it's an abuse of his human rights. I mean, he's seventeen. Surely it's his choice if he wants to stay in full-time education and follow their agenda, or give it up to become a musician?'

'Of course it is,' said Lily. 'Poor Marcus. He's a misunderstood artist.'

'He's a misunderstood stoner,' I pointed out. I didn't like the admiring look in Lily's eyes.

Now it's New Year's Day, we go and see Marcus in the bedsit that his parents have arranged for him. I think it's going to be an exciting, grotty dive, but it's actually a large, light room in a house owned by some famous writer. Oscar's mum produced some of her plays.

'It's a pit,' says Marcus, sitting on his bed, plucking his acoustic guitar. His stuff is in black plastic bags all around him, although there's a chest of drawers and a wardrobe. There's a pizza box on the floor and five empty cans of Stella. At least, I think they're empty, but when I accidentally kick one over, it turns out to be half full.

'They're bourgeois bastards,' he adds. 'Don't worry, Archie, it'll make this place smell of something other than Mr Sheen.'

'All right,' I say dubiously. The room smells of beer, weed, Lynx and decaying pizza.

'Got any money for me, Ozzie?' he asks. Oscar shakes his head.

'I'm not doing your thieving for you.'

'Oscar!' Lily's eyes are wide. 'Poor Marcus! What's he meant to live on?'

'Don't make me laugh. Mum's been bringing him two bags of food from Waitrose every week.'

Lily glares at him and says, 'Poor Marcus. Do you get lonely?'

He strums a few chords. 'So lonely. . .' he sings. 'So . . . o . . . lonely. . .'

'That's beautiful,' breathes Lily.

'And I've got no money . . . my folks hate me. . .'

'That's so unfair!' says Lily, blowing smoke rings at his ceiling. 'So unfair! Poor Marcus. Do you want to come and live with me and my mum?'

'Are you sure?' he asks.

'Hadn't you better ask your mum?' says Oscar, but Lily laughs and says, 'She'll be pleased! She spends all her time at Peter's house, anyway.'

The next thing we know, Marcus has left a note at the playwright's house saying 'Moved out,' she's threatening to call the police about fifty pounds that seem to have gone with him, and Marcus and Lily are spending most of their time in Lily's bedroom.

Oscar and I are mutually furious.

'Typical Marcus,' he says. 'He always nicked my stuff, even when we were little kids. It's Armed Forces Action Man all over again.'

'I honestly thought I was in there,' I moan. 'Lily's been my personal choice for years, to be the first woman lucky enough to enjoy the pleasures of my body. I've been *grooming* her . . . I thought she was just ready. And it was all going my way, until your stupid brother stepped in.'

Oscar snorts. 'Grooming her, my arse.'

'I was! She fancied me too. Look at that night – you know, the Cheese-on-Toast Inferno—'

'Huh. First, she was stoned. Second, she was only trying to make me jealous. Lily's been crazy about me for years. Shacking up with Marcus is just a ploy to get my attention.'

'Yeah, right.'

'Yeah, right, actually.'

My phone rings. I fish it out. Ty? Could it be? But no it's. . . 'Shannon!'

'Hey, Kyle – Archie – hear the news?'

'What news?'

'The boxing club – it's closed down temporarily. Ray's been arrested. Firearms offences, that's what I heard.'

'Oh,' I say. I wonder what else Shannon heard.

'I wanted to make sure you knew. Didn't want you turning up, finding it closed.'

'Oh right.' How could I explain that was never going to happen?

'I'm dying to see you.'

I can't resist. Lily's rejected me, Claire's ignoring me, even Paige has stopped tagging me in Facebook statuses.

'Me too, Shannon,' I breathe in my sexiest voice. Oscar raises an eyebrow.

'I did what you wanted.'

This sounds like it could turn into genuine phone sex, and I gesture to Oscar to make himself scarce.

'You did?' I murmur into the phone. 'What was that?'

Annoyingly, Oscar stays put.

'I asked Arron if you could come and see him.'

'Oh! I . . . I . . . well, that's great,' I say lamely. Oscar sniggers.

'Tomorrow. You free?'

Tomorrow's meant to be first day back at Butler's. I suppose I could give it a miss.

'Meet you at Paddington? 10 am?'

'OK. See you then.'

I turn off the phone. Oscar's looking thoughtful.

'Who was that?'

'Oh, some girl.'

'Some girl, who?'

'She's – I met her at the boxing club.'

His eyes widen. 'A girl boxer? Wow, Archie, and you're worried about Lily? That is serious hard core fantasy stuff. Has she got any friends?'

I'm laughing. 'No, she was there with her brother. Is that your secret, Oscar? Want to find some woman to beat you up?'

'Very funny, Archie. God, I'm bored. Want to go down Westfield, look at the shops?'

'Umm . . . not sure,' I say. Shopping with Oscar is

hard work. He takes it dead seriously, tries on piles of stuff, and asks me to take his picture on my mobile at various angles before he'll make a decision. I tell him that's what girls do, and he just says something like, 'This is the twenty-first century, Archie, and I've got no time for your outdated gender stereotyping. Do you think the Superdry jeans would look good with the Jack Wills stripy jacket?'

'I'm not going as your personal photographer,' I say. Last time we went to Westfield, I bumped into two girls from college in Hollister. I was doing really well with the old banter when Oscar came out of the changing room and said, 'Let me see the picture of those skinny jeans. . .'

'OK, OK, if you're not going to be helpful.'

My phone buzzes with a text. Not Ty. Not Shannon. It's my dad, suggesting a bike ride. He's been coming on strong with the father-son suggestions ever since the roof incident. He looked genuinely upset when he finally turned up at the hospital five hours late.

'What took you so long?' snapped my mum.

Dad spread his hands, 'You know what it's like. We had to force through the deal before the deadline – we had a lot resting on it. . .'

'How come I manage to drop everything to find

out whether Archie's alive or not, and you don't?'

'Well you know, people make more allowances for women. . .'

I feel a bit bad texting back, 'No, busy, soz'. It's actually a really nice day for a bike ride – one of those bright winter days when the air bites at your skin. I can see he's making an effort. But I'm still not over the big cheese blow-up, and I can't forgive him for the time he hit Ty. And we're never going to talk about that.

• • •

I meet Shannon at the station. She's all dressed up – a mini skirt, low-cut top, massive earrings, five different gold necklaces. It wouldn't work on lots of girls, but Shannon looks great. We kiss – more of a kiss than I'd expected. She grins at me.

'You ready for this?'

'I suppose so.'

'Arron, he was a bit unsure about meeting you. Said he'd never heard of Ty having a cousin. I think he's curious, wants to find out who you are.'

'Yeah, because I never even knew Ty before last year. He just turned up at my grandparents.'

'Really? How come?'

She's got the tickets already – I give her some money

– and we get on the train. We manage to find two seats where we can sit together. I put my arm around her shoulders.

'There was some family quarrel. His mum didn't want him having anything to do with us.'

'So how come he just turned up?'

'Oh, well, he was living under witness protection. You know – like in American films. The police give you a new identity and everything. But then his mum's boyfriend got shot and they thought Ty wouldn't be safe, so his aunt took him to my grandparents, to hide out.'

'Oh my God! That was brave of them, to take him in.'

I'd never thought of that. 'Yeah, I suppose it was.'

'Anything could have happened. Especially if they were in London. Right near the gangsters. So brave.'

'Oh, they don't live in London. They're way out in the country. Cambridgeshire. Middle of nowhere.'

'Oh, but even so.'

'I know. They are brave. That's where I get it from.'

'Oh, well, I'd guessed that.'

I'm dying to tell her how I dodged a gunman by leaping over the rooftops, but as she potentially knows him, it's not such a great idea. So I tell her a bit about when I first got to know Ty, how screwed up he was, how he was hallucinating, would wake up in the night.

'It doesn't surprise me,' she says. 'Arron says he was always a bit of a nut-job.'

'Oh, really?'

'Flaky, you know – would lose his temper.'

'Oh yeah. He threw a book at me once.'

She sucks in her breath. 'Ouch.'

'Yeah, well, I gave back as good as I got.'

'I bet.'

She's kissing me, and I'm kissing her, and the rest of the journey we don't really talk, apart from when the ticket collector tells us to cool it, so we stop for about thirty seconds.

We get to the station and we get on a crowded bus and we get out by a massive wall. A load of people get off when we do, and they all head for the same door – the door to the prison.

It's all pretty similar to when I visited Ty, but this time we're taken to a room with lots of chairs and tables. I realise I'm feeling nervous. I wipe my lips, make sure that none of Shannon's gloss has lingered. Arron's her ex – how's he going to feel about me?

And then he's there, sitting opposite us – taller

than me, as tall as my uncle Danny. Short dark hair. Light brown skin. Dark brown eyes, staring at me. A wide mouth that smiles at Shannon. White teeth, long eyelashes.

I've got to admit it, I can kind of see that girls might fancy Arron. He can even pull off the orange T-shirt/ grey trackie trouser look.

'Hey Shan,' he says, and his soft voice isn't what I was expecting at all. How can this guy be a murderer? 'Aren't you going to introduce me?'

'Arron,' she says, and you can see – I can see – that she's forgotten me, that I don't exist any more, that she's just marking time until Arron's out of here.

'Arron, this is Archie. He's Ty's cousin.'

'I can see that,' he says. 'You guys – you kind of look alike. You're thinner than him, though – thinner and taller.'

Neither of those things is true, but I'm not going to correct him in front of Shannon.

'Hey,' I say. 'I'm here . . . I just. . .'

'I never knew Ty had a cousin,' he says. 'We were best friends for years and he never told me. I don't know why he'd keep that sort of secret.'

'He didn't know,' I say. 'I didn't know about him, either.'

Arron raises an eyebrow. I wish I could look that cool.

'I only met him last year,' I say. 'I'm his dad's nephew.'

'Oh yeah, his dad,' says Arron. 'He told me lies about him as well.'

'Arron, ' I say, 'I need your help. Ty, he's living in fear the whole time. The gangsters are trying to kill him. He only tried to tell the truth about the murder. He didn't mean to get you locked up, I'm sure of it. Can you . . . can you help him at all?'

Shannon lets out a hiss. 'Shit, Archie, what're you talking about? Why should he? Ty dropped him in it. I bet it was all down to Ty, anyway. Wasn't it, babe? Didn't Ty get you into that gang? Wasn't he lying to save his own skin?'

Arron shakes his head slowly. 'Nah,' he says. 'Shannon, you're wrong. Ty wasn't doing nothing but telling the truth. He was too dim to realise what trouble it'd get him into. My fault. I should've explained to him . . . how these things work. . .'

'He didn't know what would happen,' I say. I'm not certain about this, but right now I'm giving Ty the benefit of the doubt. 'I actually think he was trying to make sure that you didn't go down for murder all by yourself. He didn't want the other boys to get away with it.'

Arron laughs. He's the only person laughing in a room of whispered conversations, and heads turn towards us.

'Typical. Ty always made a mess of everything. If he'd kept out of it, I'd have done a few years for manslaughter and been a hero for not snitching on my mates.'

'Oh right.' I can't even begin to get my head around that. I remember Rio's sister sobbing over the dead flowers. How would she have felt? Would she have realised that people had got away with murder?

Does justice make anything better? Is it worth it?

'Ty was my friend,' says Arron, 'and he always will be. I'm loyal to my friends. You tell him that. And you tell him something else as well.'

'OK.'

The bell goes. People start standing up, leaving the room. Arron leans forward.

'Bring him here to see me.'

'I'll try, but—'

'I can call them off. Tell him that. '

'I'll try but—'

'I can set him free.'

CHAPTER 28
Adam

Where to start searching for Ty? Obviously I start with Claire.

'Hey, Claire,' I say. I've decided not to embarrass her by referring to our snog. Or, more accurately, I've decided not to embarrass myself.

'Archie,' she says. 'What do you want?'

'Well, I was wondering if you'd heard from Ty . . . errr . . . Joe. . . '

'No.'

'It's just that he's disappeared and I thought he might. . .'

'You thought wrong.' She rings off.

What? I shake the phone, try again. She doesn't pick up.

Hmmm. Some people might think, *OK, fair enough, she's answered my question.* Other people might think she's embarrassed about our kiss. But Archie Stone, otherwise known as Professor Stone, Master of Freudian psychoanalysis, mind reader and student of human nature, thinks differently.

I think that Claire's a lovely person who hates lying and would never be rude. Therefore, if she's being rude, it's likely she's feeling bad because she's lying. That, my friends, is what they call forensic psychology.

I call Zoe. It's only when she picks up that I realise that I haven't spoken to her since Cheese-on-Toast night.

'Hi Zoe,' I say.

'What do you want?'

'Well . . . I'm really sorry about the other day. . .'

'The other day was weeks ago.'

'I know, but a lot's been happening. That night, my house caught on fire. Three fire engines it took, to put it out, and they sprayed water on my laptop, so I couldn't communicate with the outside world. And then just before Christmas I fell off a roof and nearly got killed. I've been in a full body cast ever since. I'm speaking into a headset.'

'You are so full of it. Do you think I don't see all the pictures on Facebook – the ones with you tagged at parties with loads of different girls? Not to mention all your puerile comments when Chelsea are playing.'

Zoe supports Liverpool. Naturally she's a bit sensitive about really top clubs.

'I was scared you'd shout at me,' I say in my most winning voice.

'Luckily I know what you're like,' she says. 'Anyway, I have a new boyfriend, so you are off the hook. His name's Will and he's a hurdler.'

'Oh, well, that'll come in useful if you've got any gates you need someone to jump over.'

'He's got very long legs,' she says, 'and a spaniel called Bilbo.'

'No one could possibly compete with that, Zo. I hope you'll be very happy.'

'I will be,' she says. 'How about you, Archie? How's it going?'

'Oh well, it's a bit confusing, really.'

'You're not all loved up with that girl who was in your bedroom?'

'Who? Oh, her, no. She was just a friend who'd had a bit . . . got a bit . . . Anyway, she's shacked up with my friend's brother now.'

'Oh, nice one.'

It's clear to me that Zoe has no idea about my

little encounter with Claire. She'd be about a million times more angry. What a relief.

'Zoe, I'm ringing to ask you something.'

'Oh yeah? Hurry up, then, because I'm meeting Will. We're going to go for a run.'

'It's just, I was wondering if you'd seen Joe at all – my cousin. Maybe with Claire.'

'Oh yes, I've seen him.'

'You have?'

'He was running at the last athletics event that I went to. I won the girls' under sixteen 1500 metres and he won the boys' under eighteen. He broke the UK record, great run. But he wasn't calling himself Joe. They said he was Luke someone, but I recognised him immediately.'

'Have you seen him since? Maybe with Claire?'

'Oh no, not since then.'

'Oh right. Oh well—'

'Mind you, I've hardly seen Claire at all recently. She's doing some drama thing with the Youth Theatre in Milton Keynes – goes there every weekend. Loads of rehearsals.'

'Oh right.'

'And I think there's a new boyfriend too. Can't get many details out of her, but she seems quite keen. She met him there.'

'Oh, right.'

Great. Zoe's replaced me with a spaniel-owning hurdler. Now Claire's met some youth actor from nowhere.

'He's Polish, I think. Marek, or something like that. I don't know much about him.'

'Oh, OK. Thanks Zoe. Look – I'm really sorry it didn't work out. I like you a lot. It's just . . . distance and all that.'

'No hard feelings,' she says, not precisely accurately.

I lie on my bed and I think about Zoe and Will and Lily and Marcus and Claire and Marek. Claire and Marek. Marek the Pole.

I remember when Ty and I ran away, ran away to see Claire. And Ty's idea was that he'd pretend to be Polish and get a job as a cleaner, and he could do it because he knew a little bit of Polish.

I don't think Marek is a youth actor at all, at least, not with a theatre group. He's acting, all right, but not on stage.

There's no point calling Claire back. Which is why, three days later, I'm spending my Saturday sitting opposite the Youth Theatre in Milton Keynes, in a café, drinking coke and keeping the building under constant surveillance.

God, it's boring, plus awkward. I really need to pee. But I can't risk missing Claire.

Three long hours pass, and obviously I do have to go and pee (coke is not the drink for surveillance, be warned). So I'm not sure if I'm on a pointless mission. I'm about to give up when I see her. She's got a beret thing on her head and a pink scarf wrapped round her neck and she's standing right outside the café, putting on lipstick and looking into a mirror.

I dive under the table.

'Are you all right down there?' says the waitress, and I hastily shove a tenner at her ('Keep the change') and make off after Claire, who's striding along the street.

I dodge in and out of shops – I nearly fall over a toddler coming out of the pound store – and then I see her knock at a door next to a kebab place. And the door opens, I can't see who's there, and she's gone. Just like that.

I sprint across the road to do some more surveillance, but all I can see is a curtain being pulled closed.

I decide to buy a kebab and engage the owner in casual conversation.

'I'll have a chicken shashlik,' I say. 'I don't suppose you know a guy called Marek, do you? I think he's Polish. Lives round here.'

The guy behind the counter stares at me, suspiciously.

'Lots of Poles round here,' he says. 'Is all Poles. All called Marek or Tomek or Josef or whatever.'

'Oh, err, right.'

'All taking our jobs.'

'Err . . . OK. . .'

'All eating my kebabs. So I don't ask no questions, OK?'

'Oh, right, OK. It's just that I heard he lived upstairs here.'

He shakes his head. 'No Pole called Marek here.'

My heart sinks. All this way. . .

'Albanian called Adam. Young boy. Never talks. Has girlfriend, though.'

'Oh right.'

'Sometimes she stays whole weekend.' He laughs, spit coming out of his mouth, just missing the sizzling, revolving doner kebab. 'Looks very young! Too young! Good luck to him!'

I really don't like this guy.

'Thanks,' I say.

'No problem!'

Outside, chewing the kebab – surprisingly tasty – I consider my options. I could wait until Claire comes out, I suppose, but that might be some time.

Or I could write a note asking Ty to call me and put it though the post box – except there isn't one, so I'd have to leave it with kebab man.

Or I could knock at the door.

That's what I do.

Nothing happens. I knock again. Nothing. Then the door opens, just a crack.

'Who's there?' I'm thrown for a moment, because the voice is deep and hoarse and definitely foreign.

'Ty? Is that you?'

The door slams shut.

I thump again. I'm shouting. 'It's me, it's Archie. . .'

Open again. This time it's Ty's normal voice. 'Shut up, you tosser. Can't you just go away?'

'No I can't! I've got something important to tell you.'

He lets me in. He grabs me by the shoulders. 'What's happened? What's happened? Are they – is it Mum? Alyssa?'

'No, they're fine as far as I know.'

'Who then? Patrick?'

'Look, can't I come upstairs? I can tell you properly. Everyone's OK, though, just worrying about you.'

There's a dark flight of stairs, and then another door. He knocks gently, three distinct knocks.

'That means it's OK,' he says. 'She knows not to open the door otherwise.'

The door opens. Claire's not happy at all.

'What are you doing here? Did you follow me? You should keep your nose out!'

'I needed to see Ty! And you lied to me!'

'Of course I lied to you. What's more important, telling the truth or keeping him safe?'

I'm a bit hurt, to be honest. How come Claire gets to know where Ty is, and no one else does? They're meant to be on a break, not sharing nights of passion above a kebab shop.

'Claire, it's OK,' he says. 'I'm actually really glad. Archie, I kept on thinking about you on that roof. What if you'd tried to jump? I made it, but I know you're really scared of heights and you're not so good at running, are you? I thought you'd fallen.'

'I told him you hadn't,' said Claire. 'I said, "If Archie's dead then his ghost is on Facebook, bragging about Chelsea beating Arsenal."'

'Six-nil,' I say, and Ty says, 'Wait until Man United

play them. I bet we can score eight, at least.'

He's really normal, I realise. No twitching. No staring into space. No shaking.

'Are you OK?' I ask him.

'Yeah.' He sounds surprised. 'It's OK here. But I ought to move on, really. It's just . . . I didn't know what had happened, whether you were all OK. I thought maybe there'd been a news blackout or something. And I was . . . I couldn't stand it. . . So I got in contact with Claire. She saved me, basically. I found this room and she can come here sometimes, and I've got a job cleaning offices.'

'Oh, OK.' It's my idea of hell.

'I can't stay, though. I'm going to move around a bit, leave Ty behind. It's the only way I can feel safe.'

I look around the room. There's the battered brown sofa, with Ty sitting at one end and Claire lying against him. There's a black leather-look bean bag, which I'm finding less comfortable than it promised. There's a pine cupboard, a little formica-topped table, a dusty lampshade, a sink, a mini fridge, a microwave.

'It's a bit basic,' I say.

'It's very cheap.'

'Where do you sleep?'

'The sofa converts to a bed.'

'Where do you wash?'

'There's a shower upstairs.'

'What about a telly?'

He shrugs. 'There is life without telly.'

'Do you get free kebabs?'

'Wouldn't want them. There's rats in the bins.'

'We don't need food. We don't need a telly. We only need each other,' says Claire, 'and when I've finished with school at the end of next year, we will be together and then we'll go abroad or something.'

'So you're going to hide out for another year and a half?'

Ty nods.

'Do you really think you can do that?'

'Of course he can,' says Claire fiercely.

'It's a long time. Have you got a passport?'

'I did, but I don't know where it is now. My mum might have it.'

'I could find out. I could get it for you. Then you've got options.'

'He doesn't want options,' says Claire. 'Go away, Archie. He's fine as he is.'

Ty kisses the top of her head. His eyes are closed. It's as though he's breathing her in, trying to absorb her fight, her love, her soul before he has to say goodbye.

For a moment, telly or no telly, I envy him.

'You'll come here one day, Claire, and he'll be gone. He'll have seen something or heard something and he'll have to stop being Marek—'

'Adam.'

'OK, Adam, then. Adam will disappear. And you might hear from him again, or you might not. And then you'll be in the same position as the rest of us.'

'I won't.'

'You will. Just by being here, you're putting him in danger.'

'I'm not.'

'If I can find him by following you, so can other people.'

'No one knows about me and him.'

'Want to bet?'

'The thing is,' says Ty, 'that I'm putting her in danger.'

'I went to see Arron.'

Ty's mouth falls open.

'You what?'

'I went to see Arron – in prison.'

He doesn't ask me how. He's too shocked . . . scared . . . fascinated. . .

'How was he? Does he blame me . . . for everything?'

His voice is little more than a whisper.

'He said you were his friend, and you always would be. And he's loyal to his friends.'

Ty's shoulders sag. 'But I wasn't loyal to him.'

'You did the right thing,' says Claire. 'He's a murderer. You owe him nothing.'

'He said you told the truth.'

'I did tell the truth.'

'He wants to see you.'

'He wants to see me?'

'He says if you see him, he'll call them off. He'll call the gangsters off. You'll be free.'

'Why would he do that?' Claire's voice is loud and angry and scared.

'He might,' says Ty, slowly. 'He might. Arron always looked out for me. If he'd told me . . . told me what he was into, then I'd have kept away. Maybe he feels bad for getting me involved.'

'He said that. He said, "I should've explained how these things work."'

Ty looks exhausted.

'Can he really call them off?'

'Of course he can't,' says Claire. 'How can he?'

'That's what he said.'

'And you can arrange for me to see him?'

'I think so.'

Claire's shaking. Her voice is all wobbly. 'You're safe. Joe, you're safe. Why spoil it? Why take the risk?'

'Arron was my friend. I had Arron when I didn't have anyone else. I'm out here while he's locked up . . . I owe him. . .'

'You owe him nothing. Don't trust him. You need to stay here.' She hugs him tight.

He looks at me over her head.

'Archie, I'll do it. Just tell me where and when.'

CHAPTER 29
Lily's Party

I can hardly concentrate at college. I write essays, solve equations, sit mock exams. All the time I'm thinking about our meeting with Arron.

Shannon says it'll take a month before she can get us in to see him.

'Obviously he can only have so many visitors at a time,' she tells me. 'I have to wait until there's a week when his mum won't be going. Are you sure Ty's going to show?'

'I'm not certain,' I tell her, 'but I think so. Don't tell anyone, Shannon. This could be really dangerous.'

'Who'd I tell?' she says. 'Now, when are you taking me clubbing in Fulham?'

I can't take her clubbing. They've got really strict door rules. But when Lily says she's having a party, I invite Shannon along. I want to keep her sweet, so she

304

won't forget to sort out the visit that could set Ty free. I'm so proud of myself.

I've spoken to Ty a few times – he won't use a mobile, but he's called me from a payphone. He asked me how come I'd been to see Arron, how come I'd found out where he was being held.

'Research,' I told him. 'It's a little-known fact that I'm an undercover investigative reporter. I went underground and I tapped my criminal contacts and I found out exactly where he was.'

'Archie, stop talking bollocks and just tell me—'

'I found out where he was being held. Then I wrote him a letter, setting out the case for him to see me – I said I had essential information, could be life or death—'

'Didn't the prison read it?'

'I don't know, maybe.'

'Oh, OK, it just seems a bit. . .'

'A bit. . .?'

'I don't know . . . a bit . . . unlikely.'

The pips go. He needs more money. He doesn't seem to have any.

'Bye!' I shout, but the line's dead.

Claire's rung me too. Claire's furious with me. She thinks I'm putting Ty in incredible danger.

'I want to know, the minute you meet. You text me. You text me the minute you come out of that place. You text me when Joe gets on his bus.'

'Yes, Mum.'

'I can't believe you're making a joke about this! I can't believe you're suggesting this is a good idea!'

'Oh chillax, Claire. Has anyone else found a way of calling these people off? Trust me. It'll be fine.'

'Oh, well, if you say so.' She's even more sarcastic than my dad.

'Claire, about, you know, the other day. In the café.'

Annoyed silence down the phone.

'Let's not talk about that,' she says. 'It was a total mistake. I temporarily lost my senses.'

'Oh right, it's just that I thought you and Ty were on a break, and. . .'

'On a break? I don't know what you're talking about,' she says. 'If he gets hurt, if this goes wrong, I'll never forgive you, Archie.'

'Oh yeah, and when it goes well, what's the reward?' I ask, but she's already ended the call.

All in all, I'm ready for a party. Shannon looks great when she comes out of the Tube station. She's cut the Fake Bake and bling, she's let her hair out of its tight ponytail, so it ripples over her bare shoulders. She's wearing a simple black dress, very short, very tight. Her shoes are Beckhamesque – and I'm not talking football boots.

'Wow,' I say, 'you look fabulous.'

She's pleased, I can tell, but she just says, 'Shut up. Good enough to meet your posh friends?'

'Of course!' Huh. Anyone would think I was a snob.

Lily and her mum live on the top two floors of a big flat-fronted house in Parsons Green. You can see the river from their balcony. If you go up onto the roof – it's not an official roof terrace, but it's a nice flat space, and Lily's mum has a table and some loungers out there – you can see for miles, over the river, south to the rooftops of Putney.

When Lily and I were younger, we used to watch the boat race from her roof. I'd shout for Oxford because my dad went there, she'd shout for Cambridge just to make it more interesting. I used to imagine myself following in Dad's footsteps, riding a bicycle and wearing a gown and getting up at dawn to go rowing, talking in Latin about very clever stuff.

When I told Dad that I wanted to go to Oxford, he snorted and said, 'Well, with the expensive education you're getting, there's no reason why not.'

Dad went to some crappy school in Mile End, left at fifteen to work on his dad's market stall, then went back to night school when he was eighteen. He got a place at Oxford two years later. When I realised how amazing that was – and how I'd never be able to top it – I stopped imagining myself at Oxford. Who wants to wear a stupid gown, anyway? I'd rather sleep than go rowing.

Lily's flat is all white walls and white floorboards and fairy lights. She's cleared most of the furniture into her mum's bedroom, and the space looks massive. Oscar's DJing at a huge deck. Paige is right by his side – they met on my Facebook page and bonded during a thread on hair products. They've been together two weeks. I suspect that Oscar's trying to make Lily jealous – that's certainly my plan in bringing Shannon here tonight – but he won't admit it.

People are dancing. People are smoking. Shannon stands in the doorway, her eyes wide.

'Wow,' she says. 'This is amazing.'

We dance for a bit. We drink. We sit in a corner and kiss. I see loads of kids from college staring at me, staring at Shannon. The girls are curious, the guys are definitely impressed. It's not often that someone totally new turns up.

Then I see Kenny Pritchard coming towards me. I bet he's about to ask me if I've got any gear. I'm really not interested in talking to him right now.

'I'll show you the roof,' I say, heading for the stairs.

The cold air hits me as we step out into the night and I realise I've made a big mistake. This is the first roof I've been on since that day, and it's all coming back, except worse, because last time adrenaline pumped me up, but this time I'm feeling sick and giddy and nervous.

I clutch Shannon's arm, 'This is it . . . it's cold, though. Let's go back down.'

But she says, 'It's brilliant. Look at all them little candles.' The candlelight is reflected in her huge eyes. She lifts up her face to me, gives me a kiss—

'Archie!' It's Lily – hair in mad springy ringlets, dressed in a lime green catsuit. 'Ooh! Who's this?'

'I'm Shannon.'

Lily nods at her.

'Where's Marcus?'

Lily's shouting. 'Marcus is not here! Marcus is a selfish wanker! He couldn't be bothered with helping me get ready for the party. He couldn't be bothered to stay. I've had it with him! He's lovely-looking, OK, and he's a great musician, but he's a totally crap boyfriend – completely self-centred.'

No! Why did I bring Shannon?

'I'm going to chuck him out. In fact, let's do it now.'

I'm grateful to have an excuse to get off the roof. We follow Lily as she charges downstairs. I'm never ever going on a roof again. I'm quite pleased. I've got a really exciting reason for being scared of heights.

Lily ejects two couples from her bed and starts rushing round the room, stuffing Marcus's things into bin bags.

'I'll leave it outside the front door,' she says, 'or maybe I'll throw it out of the window, or off the roof. What do you think, Archie? Can I hit the river?'

'I doubt it, it's five streets away.'

'Really?' It looks closer. She heaves the first bag up to the window, struggles with the lock. 'There! That'll show him!'

'Where's it going to fall?' Shannon whispers in my ear. 'She's a bit mental, your friend. What's she on? She's totally hyper.'

Lily's holding Marcus's guitar. 'This is what he really loves! This and skunk. He'd rather play on his guitar than be with me! He'd rather smoke his skunk than spend time with me!' The guitar follows the bin bag out of the window. Far, far away we hear a noise that might be someone shouting.

'Stop her,' says Shannon. 'She's off her head.'

'Lily,' I say, 'Lil.'

She's screaming now. 'Leave me alone! This party was for him! He couldn't be arsed to turn up! What's wrong with him? What's wrong with me?'

Her face is bright red and her eyes are kind of bulging. There's white froth at the corner of her mouth.

Shannon says, 'Here, Lily, drink this.' She's found a bottle of water from somewhere. 'Archie, we need some help here. I don't like this.'

I go and find Oscar, swaying at his decks. I pull at his earphones.

'Oy! Leave them alone!'

'OSCAR!' I yell. 'Come and help me with Lily!'

'What about Lily?'

'I need help!'

Oscar hands the headphones over to Paige. 'Can you keep it going? Put on that one, it lasts forever. . .'

We get back to the bedroom just in time. Lily's fighting Shannon, holding her shoulders, shaking her back and forward, screaming, 'Leave me alone! Leave me alone!'

It takes Oscar and me together to drag her away. She's developed superhuman strength.

Shannon's remarkably calm. 'Stupid cow must've taken some sort of upper,' she says. 'She's off the planet. I had to tackle her, she was throwing books and all sorts out of the window – notebooks, a big metal box of papers.'

Oscar's shocked. 'She's thrown Marcus's poems out of the window? His music? He'll never forgive her!'

The music has stopped. I get the uncomfortable impression that everyone's listening to what's going on.

'Leave me alone!' screeches Lily. The door flies open. Jesus. It's Marcus. For the first time in years he looks completely awake and absolutely furious.

'What the hell? What are you doing? You stupid bitch!' Tears are pouring down his face. 'My guitar – smashed to bits. My music! My poems!' Now it's Lily who's being shaken back and forth. 'What have you done! What have you done?'

Shannon throws water over them, plus the bottle, so they're soaked, and Marcus gets bopped on the head. The bottle bounces towards Oscar and he expertly catches it.

Lily's sobbing and retching. The room is full of people. Some girls are taking pictures on their phones.

'Get out of here!' I yell. 'Leave her alone! She's not well.'

'Not well – she can't take it,' I hear one say. I go on shouting until they're all gone. They're all filing down the stairs. I'm standing in the doorway, yelling at their backs. 'Go away!' I shout. 'Leave her alone!'

I watch as Lily runs up the stairs on to the roof. I watch Shannon and Marcus and Oscar following her. I know I should go after them, but my legs won't let me.

I just hear the screams when she jumps.

CHAPTER 30
The meeting

I might be about to do the most stupid thing in my life. That's what Claire thinks. In fact, she thinks my life's going to end today.

'Why would he want to see you? And how can he call them off? And how did Archie set this up, anyway – Archie, of all people? Joe – please don't do this. Things are fine as they are right now.'

But things aren't fine. I mean, it's great that I can spend time with Claire – we talked all night, the weekend she was pretending to be at drama camp – but everything's still there. I'm looking over my shoulder all the time. In a way, I'm still in prison.

I've had enough of living like a rat in a hole – a scared rat, a guilty rat, a rat who doesn't know what's right any more.

And how can I explain to Claire that my bond with

Arron goes back so long and so deep that if I don't take this chance to put it right, then I might never be able to live my life again?

Friendship means trust, if it means anything at all.

But is Arron still my friend?

We've arranged to meet at the station and get the bus to the prison together.

Safety in numbers, I think, at least there will be lots of mums and families going on that bus together.

But when we meet, we're the only ones waiting at the bus stop.

'Archie,' I say, 'are you sure you've got the time right?'

He nods. There's something weird about Archie today. He's not his normal stupid self. He's not making jokes or showing off. His eyes look larger, somehow, his mouth more serious. There are dark shadows under his eyes.

'What's up?'

'It's nothing . . . my friend . . . she had an accident.'

'Oh, that's bad.'

'She might be paralysed. Her back is broken.'

'Oh, Jesus, that's really bad. How did it happen?'

'She fell off a roof. Or maybe she jumped.' He turns his head away, brushes at his eye. 'She'd been taking something . . . amphetamines. . . She was out of it.'

'She fell off a roof and she survived?'

'A tree broke her fall. I know, she's incredibly lucky. But it doesn't feel lucky.'

'Have you been to see her?'

He shakes his head. 'I want to. But I'm not – I can't do it.'

'Even if she is paralysed, she's not dead. There's stuff she can do.' And I tell him about Claire's sister Ellie and how amazing she is and how she competed in the Paralympics and won two silver medals and a gold. He's not really listening, though. He's chewing his thumbnail and trying not to cry.

'Lily wouldn't do stuff like that,' he says. 'I don't know what she's going to do.'

'You can cheer her up,' I say. 'Give her a bit of your banter. Go on, Archie, you know you're the man for the job.'

He smiles. 'Thanks,' he says.

Still no bus. Still no one else waiting.

'Archie,' I say, 'there's something wrong here. You've got the time wrong or the day or something.'

'I'm sure I didn't. She said Monday, 11 am. I'll find the text.'

'Who's *she*? Someone from the prison?'

He's scrolling through his texts. 'She's called Shannon Travis,' he says. 'She's Arron's ex and I met her at your boxing club.'

Kazam! The words Shannon Travis hit my brain like a grenade.

'Shannon? Shannon Travis set this up? Jesus, Archie! We've got to run! Get out of here!'

'You what?' he says.

And then the car swings round the corner – driving too fast, screeching and swerving. My legs scrabble to get away, but someone grabs me from behind. And I see Archie struggling in the arms of a masked man, and a gun is crashing onto Archie's skull, and I'm. . .

I don't wake up for hours and hours and when I do, we're lying side by side on a stinking, muddy floor, arms and legs bound with tight rope that rubs and bites into the flesh. There's a handkerchief in my mouth and I try and spit it out, but there must be tape over the cloth because all I do is retch. I'm wet with what could possibly be pee. Archie's completely still. I can only tell he's breathing because we're lying so close together.

I try and nudge him. It's not easy, but I've got some movement in my ankle, so I kick him gently.

His whole body jumps as he wakes up. He starts

coughing and choking on the gag right away. I try and get him to shut up, but when you can only communicate by eye movements and kicks, it's not easy to get the message across.

Slowly, painfully, I remember how we got here. I remember Archie saying that he'd been at the boxing club. He'd met Shannon Travis.

I bet he thought it was a big coincidence that he met a girl who just turned out to be Arron's ex. I bet he fancied her too, Shannon was always a looker, even when we were in primary school.

I bet the minute he walked into that boxing club, Sylvia got on the phone to Shannon and told her to be ready to make a new friend. I bet they'd worked out who Archie was within the hour.

How was he meant to know that Sylvia's brother is Tommy White, the biggest gangster in east London? How was he meant to know that Shannon's her daughter, that Shannon introduced Arron to her cousin Jukes, that she was the one who got him into the gang in the first place?

I can't really blame Archie. I've known these people all my life and I never worked it out myself until it was too late.

It's strange how you think you know people, and

they've got so much going on that's hidden away.

None of that matters now. I have to get us out of here.

What I can't understand is why we're still alive.

A guy comes into the room. He's old – he's got a white beard – and he's not too steady on his feet. He's got a foreign accent – I can't identify it. It's actually hard to understand him. He's laughing at us.

'Well!' he says. 'What have we here?'

He takes off the gags. Archie vomits as he does, and the guy steps back in a hurry. Now the room smells of sick and pee and something even worse – something ripe and shitty and old.

Archie starts yelling, 'Help! Help us!'

The guy just laughs. 'No one's going to hear you. What's your name?'

Luckily Archie's not completely stupid. He shuts right up. He's crying, though, sniffing and whimpering and trying to move his hand to wipe his eyes. He doesn't seem to realise he's tied up.

'Which one of you is Ty Lewis?'

Neither of us says anything.

'It won't make much difference. You might as well tell me.'

'I'm Ty Lewis,' I say.

'I'm Ty Lewis,' says Archie.

'Oh, very clever. Well, we'll find out soon enough.'

'What happens to the one who isn't Ty Lewis?' I ask.

The man shrugs. 'I know not. I care not.'

'Will he go free?'

He ignores me.

'He's going to go free, isn't he? Otherwise you'd just kill both of us.'

'I'm Ty Lewis,' says Archie. 'Let him go free.'

'You stay where you are. I don't kill people.'

Archie relaxes a fraction, but I don't. All he means is that someone else has that job.

He goes out and closes the door. We stare at each other.

'I'm sorry,' says Archie. 'This is all my fault.'

'What was all that about? "I'm Ty Lewis?" Are you trying to get yourself killed?'

'I saw it on a film. Grandpa's favourite. They want to kill Spartacus and they all get up and say, "I'm Spartacus," and then they can't.'

'Archie, this is not some stupid film. The question is whether they'll let you go if we can persuade them that you're nothing to do with any of this.'

'Why are you so calm? They're going to kill you!

They're going to kill both of us!'

I have no idea why I'm so calm. I suppose it's because I've dreaded this for so long, and now it's going to be over. At least being dead won't be so scary. I'm assuming that my gran had it wrong about the hellfire and demons.

Maybe it'll be peace and quiet and nothingness – not being scared, not looking over my shoulder all the time.

'You've given up, haven't you?' Archie's voice is furious. 'You've given up. What am I going to tell Claire? What am I going to tell Grandpa? Your mum? "Ty wanted to die, so he just gave up."'

'There's nothing we can do.'

'There bloody is. Look at that nail sticking out of the wall.'

I look. It's a rusty old nail. It's sticking out about an inch. There's nothing special about it.

'Yeah, and?'

'Rub the rope against it. That's what James Bond always does. It'll fray it.'

'In about a million years. And we don't have. . .'

Archie's wriggling like a maggot. 'Actually,' he gasps, 'I don't think these ropes are great. Mine are giving . . . just move around like I am. . .'

I give it a go. There's a minute amount of give.

'Hang on,' says Archie.

'What?'

'There's a lighter in my pocket. If you roll over here, maybe you can get it.'

'Even if I can, then what?'

'You can burn the ropes off.'

'Burn the place down, more like – with us trapped inside.'

It's a farm building, I realise now – wooden walls, hay stacked inside. It'd go up in flames in seconds.

'It's got to be worth trying.'

We inch towards each other until I can just about put my hand near his pocket. Then Archie attempts to turn himself upside down, to get the lighter to fall out. It's like playing the stupid game where you can't take your hands off the floor, and you tie yourself in knots. That usually ends in collapse and giggles. This is all sweat and swearing.

Ten minutes or so later, the lighter falls out of his pocket. I throw myself on the floor and roll around until I can feel it under my fingers. But I can't actually pick it up. I let out a groan of disappointment. He had me hoping there for a minute.

He's bum-shuffled over to the nail and is rubbing

his wrists against it. 'Ow . . . it looks really easy in the movies, but it's killing me. . . I'm going to get blood poisoning. . .'

'Shh,' I say. I can hear voices outside. They're not speaking English, though. It's a language I don't know . . . a bit like English . . . bit like German.

'Dutch. . .' Archie hisses. 'They must have brought us to Holland on the boat. Or Belgium.'

'What boat?'

'I woke up in the night. We were on a motor boat.'

A boat – I can't believe it! I've wanted to go abroad my whole life. I never thought it would be like this.

'I thought they were going to chuck us in the sea.'

Again the question – why didn't they?

I can't understand them at all. Stupid me. Why didn't I ever learn Dutch? I sift the words in my mind, trying to make sense of them. Something about a mobile – a mo-bee-ler tell-a-fon. Something about a fo-to-graff. And then someone says Archie's name. Stone. They say, 'Er-is-van-der-Stone fam-il-ee. Der Stone fam-il-ee.' And then, 'Dat-can-neet.'

'That means, "It's not possible,"' says Archie in my ear. 'Dad and I came here and that's what they said at the cycle shop when we asked about getting a new wheel. Dat-can-neet. They said it a lot.'

'It's not possible for them to kill you,' I say. 'Good news, Archie.'

'Why not?'

'No idea.'

'Good news for both of us, because they'll never work out which is which.'

Just for a split second I believe I'm going to see Claire again. But then, 'Fo-to-graff. Mo-bee-ler tell-a-fon.'

'They will, because someone's sending them a picture of you on their mobile.'

'Who?' he says, and then, 'Oh. Shannon. Bugger.'

'You know Jukes, the guy who stabbed me? Shannon's his cousin.'

'I'm really sorry.'

'It's OK.'

The door creaks open. Old Dutch Beardy has some food for us. Cheese rolls and cartons of milk.

'How're we meant to eat these with our hands tied up?' says Archie.

'I will untie . . . one at a time. No funny business.'

We've not got much time, I reckon. When they get this photo, they'll want to get rid of me as soon as they can. I'm not sure what will happen to Archie, but it'll involve getting him a long way away from here so he has no idea where he's been held.

He unties me first, holds the carton to my mouth. Out of the corner of my eye I see Archie's face. He's . . . he's winking at me. He's. . .

Wham! Archie launches himself at the old guy. Smash! I shove the milk carton in his face. Bam! Archie's got his hands free – that rusty old nail did the trick – and he's hit Old Beard with a great punch to the jaw.

I'm on him before he can cry out, stuffing the cheese roll, wrapping and all, into his mouth. We use the rope that was round my arms to tie him up, and sacrifice Archie's T-shirt to gag him properly. Archie's already got rid of the ropes round his legs – he unties me too.

Archie gets hold of the lighter, eyes the haystack.

'We can't, give it to me,' I say, pointing at Old Beard struggling on the floor. 'He'd be toast.'

'Serve him right.'

'We can't. Quick, before his mate comes back.'

I grope in the old man's pocket, take his phone, his keys, some money.

'*Auf wiedersehen*,' says Archie.

'That's German, fool,'

We lock the door behind us, chain it, padlock it. Then we look around.

In front of us it's nothing but flat fields. You'd spot someone running away miles off.

And behind us, farm buildings, machinery and more flat fields, as far as the eye can see.

CHAPTER 31
Gunfire

My plan is that we burn down the farm to create a diversion, then run away as fast as we can. Ty shakes his head.

'We could be miles from anywhere. There's no point.'

'What do you suggest, then?'

I'm going to be 100 per cent honest. There's this tiny, tiny bit of me which knows that if we get caught I can just say, 'I'm Archie Stone, let me go,' and they probably will. I don't know why they will, but they will. I'm not really in danger here – not like Ty is.

We sneak around one huge shed and into another one. It's full of rusting machinery – things that cut and bind. It'd make a good torture chamber.

'Where's his phone?'

Ty hands it to me.

'No GPS,' I whisper, 'but here's the photo.' I delete it. 'We were just in time.'

'I don't know why they're so bothered about you.'

'I don't know either.'

Maybe Shannon asked them to save me, I think, but then, why would she have set me up like this?

'Where's the other guy? What are we going to do about him?'

It's too quiet, too creepy. The sun's setting and soon it'll be dark. I wonder about setting out over the fields in the dark. But we'd have no idea where we're going.

Crack! We whip around and he's there – a younger, stronger, taller guy. He won't be so easy to overpower. Even with two of us, I'm not sure we can fight him.

Plus, he's holding a gun.

'How did you get free?' he demands. 'What have you done with Maarten?'

Ty narrows his eyes. 'You're not going to shoot us,' he says.

'Who says?'

'I say. Because we're under the protection of the Stone family, both of us. And you don't want to mess with them.'

What the hell?

The guy's still smiling, but his gun wavers for a split second.

'Only one of you, I think,' he says. 'This one.' He points at me. 'Mr Archie Stone.'

'Nah,' says Ty. 'You've got that wrong. We're both members of the family. You kill either of us and they'll take revenge. Don't worry, they'll find you.'

I think of my mum and dad tracking down this guy and shooting him, and a terrified giggle forms in my mouth. I swallow it down.

'Where's Maarten?' he says, and that's when Ty flings the lighter straight at his eye. He yells, steps back, slips in a puddle and the gun goes off, bang! It flies out of his hand, falls into the field. . .

Ty goes for his throat, I chase the gun, searching frantically among the green, down in the soil. . . Here it is! Shouldn't it have a safety catch or something? What if it explodes in my hand?

Obviously, I've shot hundreds of people in my time, but only on the Xbox.

Ty turns him over, grinds his face in the mud, I pick the gun up gingerly, try and work out how to . . . how to lock it? Shut it off? Use it?

I settle for pointing it at the guy in the mud and saying, 'Do what we want, or I'll kill you.'

Ty looks a bit alarmed, and I realise that the gun's pointing straight at him, too.

The guy stops thrashing around.

'You did it, didn't you?' says Ty. 'You killed Alistair.'

He says nothing. I move closer, hold the gun carefully, poised. . .

'Answer,' I say.

'We could kill you now, like you killed him,' says Ty.

The guy's almost crying. 'You got no proof,' he says. 'You got no proof.'

'Alistair never did anything,' Ty tells him. 'Come to that, nor did I.'

What am I going to do if Ty tells me to shoot him? I don't think I can do it. My hand is all sweaty and the gun's really heavy and my arm is shaking and. . .

The gun falls out of my hand.

It hits the ground, explodes with a massive bang.

The guy leaps up and runs over to a motorbike.

Ty falls back, into the mud.

The motorbike roars, runs over Ty's arm, disappears down a track. . .

And nothing. Silence. Nothing.

The sky is purple and the fields are grey and

I can only hear the sound of my breath, in and out, in and out.

Ty's just lying there, twisted and still, and his blood's as dark as the muddy puddles around him.

CHAPTER 32
Rehabilitation

If you're going to screw up your education, then getting kidnapped by a ruthless gang is a pretty good excuse. I never made it back to Butler's. Me and Lily, we sat out the rest of the year. She was in a rehabilitation hospital in Putney. I was just taking things quietly.

I was there when she started physiotherapy, crying with the frustration, angry with everyone, especially herself.

I was at the side of the pool when she started hydrotherapy.

I was there when they told her it was extremely unlikely that she'd ever recover the use of her legs. And I held her as she cried and cried, great silent gulps shaking her torso.

Claire's sister came to see her, gave her a pep talk

about doing as much as you can, even though you might be in a wheelchair. Lily made faces and didn't say much.

Claire didn't come. That was too much to ask – in the circumstances and all.

My job is to keep Lily going. Her job is to keep me going, but we never mention that. We watch telly together, DVDs, box sets. We listen to music. We read magazines and books. I tell her jokes. If I get a smile, then I've done really well.

Last week I made her laugh – best moment of a crappy year.

Lily and I talk all the time.

We talk about Marcus, how he's refused to go to the expensive clinic his parents picked out, how he's living in a squat now, some supposed dive in Dulwich. We talk about Lily's mum, how she was charged with possession of drugs, because the uppers Lil had taken, she'd found them in Frieda's bedroom. We talk about my dad and how he's decided to quit his job.

'I never thought he'd do that,' she says. 'Your dad! He lived for his job!'

'He said he was fed up spending his life in meetings and pitching for deals to clients he despised, and he'd made enough money for anyone and now he's going to get to know me better, be a proper dad. Blah, blah.'

He's said a load more than that – all about how he's been neglecting his family, and letting the stress of the job get to him, and how Mum and I are the most precious things in his life, and how, when I was missing, he couldn't sleep or eat and he realised that if he lost me, he'd hardly known me. It was all a bit cringey, like he'd suddenly woken up in some crappy American movie.

Lily's dad has only been to see her once since what everyone calls 'the accident', even though it wasn't. He flew in from Dubai, where he's living now, with a load of electronics for her – a cool camera, a new laptop, an iPad. And then he flew away again.

She shakes her head at me. 'You're lucky. Don't blow it.'

So when Dad suggests that we go for a bike ride, I agree. It's actually good to get out of that hospital for a while, although not fair on Lily, who can't escape.

We cycle for miles – out into Surrey – and then we get to a hill that's too steep for the bikes, so we chain them together at the bottom and climb up to the top, where there's a little café that serves fruit cake and orange squash. We sit and eat and I say, 'Dad, there's something I need to ask you.'

'What's that?' he mumbles, mouth full of cake.

'When we, Ty and me, when we were, you know, *there*. . .'

Dad knows where *there* is. He nods.

'They wouldn't kill me because they were scared of something called the Stone family. What did they mean?'

'All my adult life,' says Dad, 'I've been trying to get away from them, all *your* life trying to make sure you never got involved. I'm not quite sure how I failed, but I did. Maybe you can never really escape who you are, where you come from.'

'You what?'

'My father, my uncles, my brothers were all criminals. The market stall was just a cover. They fenced stolen goods, ran a protection racket. My brothers, they've stayed in the business. They're not as big as Tommy White but still, you don't cross the Stone family. It's a lifetime away.'

'Was that why you didn't want me to be friends with Ty?'

'Poor Ty,' he says, 'not his fault, but I just saw trouble. I tried, you know. I went to see my brother Gary. I hadn't seen him for fifteen years, but I went and asked him to see if he could get the Whites to leave Ty alone. I did it early on, when Ty first re-emerged, when he was staying with your grandparents. Gary said he didn't have any influence. But then I went to see him again – after that incident on the roof. He took it more seriously once he knew you were involved.'

'Oh right, yeah.' I think I'd rather not get to know my uncle Gary any better.

'Mind you, if I'd known you were stupid enough to be going to that boxing club, I'd have done something a lot earlier.'

It's kind of reassuring that my dad hasn't totally changed his entire personality.

'What did he say?'

'Said he'd do his best. Obviously his best wasn't good enough.'

I swallow. I can't talk about Ty. The memories are too horrible. I found out that day how easy it is to kill someone, and I don't think I'll ever get over it.

'Oh well, he's out of it now,' he says. 'Archie, your mum's going to her yoga retreat on Lesbos again. I know we're all going off to Barbados at Christmas, but before that, why don't we have a holiday together? Somewhere interesting? Get to know each other better. Make up for wasted time.'

'Yeah, we could, I suppose.'

He takes a gulp of orange squash. 'You know, Archie, I don't think London's right for us. How about we look at houses round here? Surrey. Nice small towns, good state schools. You can have a new start, and you're still near enough to see Lily and Oscar.'

'Oh, right,' I say, wondering what a small-town version of myself would be like. Different from London Archie, that's for sure. I suppose that's not all bad.

Then we eat some more fruit cake and we don't talk any more.

CHAPTER 33
Cambodia

We went to an amazing place yesterday – a temple, right in the jungle, the one where they filmed Lara Croft. The buildings are all tangled up with the tree roots. You can't tell which one came first. If you took away the roots, the buildings would fall down. Everything is connected to everything else. It was awesome.

We had a tour guide, he told us about when things were really bad in Cambodia, when everyone was being killed and they all had to go into work camps and they didn't have enough to eat. They used to pee on the ground and then sieve the dried mud to get salt. They used to make a hole in their soup dishes, so they'd get more meat and rice and less liquid. If you didn't do that you'd starve to death.

When you hear about stuff like that, it helps you realise that we didn't have it so bad. You can get over things. If our *guide can build a new life after everything that's happened to him, then anyone can.*

Anything's possible.

It's a bit weird travelling just me and my dad, but so far it's going OK. He's all right, really. We've had some good laughs.

I get bad nightmares, but it's getting better – being somewhere like this, where everything's different, everything's strange, it makes things easier. He said it would, and he's right.

I'm learning how to feel safe.

Today we're sailing on a lake called Tonlé Sap. There's water as far as I can see. It's silver and still and there are huge green leaves floating on the surface. It reminds me of a book I liked, that the teacher read to us in primary school, about a mouse who wanted to find the end of the world.

This feels like the end of the world.

There's a boy near our boat, a boy using a tin tray as a little circle of a boat. He's got a paddle, but only one arm. There were lots of landmines in Cambodia until really recently. You couldn't walk anywhere without the fear that the ground would explode. Can you imagine that?

I can.

These days, most of the mines have gone. There are loads of people without an arm or a leg. They're getting on with their lives. They're finding boats and paddles and moving through the water.

Now that I can use my arm again, I've sent emails to Mum, and to Patrick and Helen as well. I've told them that I'm OK, that I'm feeling better.

I've been in touch with Claire. And she says that when she's eighteen, she's going to come and find me. Wherever in the world I end up, she's saving her money for a ticket. She might meet someone else, I know that, but right now just the promise, just the hope, it's enough for me.

So, there's just you left. Thank you for calling the police and the ambulance. Thank you for saving my life. If you hadn't stopped the bleeding, I wouldn't have survived. You did everything right.

Dad says you blame yourself. I know that technically you shot me. But it was an accident, and accidents do happen and you never meant to. I know that. Do you?

I actually miss you and your stupid jokes a lot – more than I'd have thought. I started off hating you, but you're OK, really – immature, but OK.

After we've travelled for a bit, we're going to start again somewhere. I don't know where. I don't know how. I couldn't tell you even if I did know.

I'd just like you to be part of it.

What do you think?

Acknowledgments

My lovely husband read the first five chapters of this book and told me exactly what was wrong with it. It took me another 40,000 words (and much anguish) to see that he was correct. Thank you Laurence, for everything as always, and thanks too to our long-suffering (but never uncomplaining) children, Phoebe and Judah.

Thanks to all the readers who let me know that they enjoy my books. Your encouragement and emails are essential to my well-being. Special thanks to Matt Hearn, Joe Lucy, Claire Zamirski and Jacob Scarrow.

For help with research, many thanks to Catherine Johnson (prisons), Tony Metzer (law) and Emma Cravitz (corporate lawyers).

For lending me their home to help me finish this book, many thanks to the Rutnam/Longman family, and to Bilbo the spaniel, the perfect writing companion. Thanks also to Valerie Peake, an equally charming but slightly less ideal writing companion, because much more chatty.

Thanks to readers Tiger Bloggs, Jimmy Rice and Avital Nathan.

Thanks to writing friends Amanda Swift, Anna Longman, Becky Jones, Lydia Syson, Jennifer Grey, Fenella Fairburn, Keris Stainton, Luisa Plaja, Gillian Philip, Tamsyn Murray, Sophia Bennett, Kay Woodward, Susie Day, Candy Gourlay and Inbali Iserles. And especially the very wonderful Fiona Dunbar.

I am privileged to work with the fantastic team at Frances Lincoln Children's Books, in particular Emily Sharratt and Maurice Lyon. Many thanks as well to my agent, Jenny Savill, whose advice is invaluable, her assistant Ella Kahn and their colleagues at Andrew Nurnberg Associates.

Thanks to all my family, most of all Mum, who spoke up for Ty's legs.

Keren blogs about her life and books at
www.wheniwasjoe.blogspot.com

You can also follow her on Twitter
@kerensd

or find out more about *When I Was Joe,*
Almost True and *Another Life* on Facebook
on the **When I Was Joe** page

Growing up in a small town in Hertfordshire, **Keren David** had two ambitions: to write a book and to live in London. Several decades on, she has finally achieved both. She was distracted by journalism, starting out at eighteen as a messenger girl, then working as a reporter, news editor, features editor and feature writer for many and various newspapers and magazines. She has lived in Glasgow and Amsterdam, where, in eight years, she learnt enough Dutch to order coffee and buy vegetables. She is now back in London, and lives with her husband, two children and their insatiably hungry guinea pigs.

Keren's other novels for Frances Lincoln are the acclaimed *When I Was Joe, Almost True* and *Lia's Guide to Winning the Lottery*.

READ THE WHOLE TRILOGY!

WHEN I WAS JOE
Keren David

It's one things watching someone get killed.
It's quite another talking about it.
But Ty does talk about it. He names some ruthless
people and a petrol-bomb attack forces him and
his mum into hiding under police protection.
Shy loser Ty gets a new name, a new look and a cool
new image. Life as Joe is good. But the gangsters
will stop at nothing to silence him. And then he
meets a girl with a dangerous secret of her own.
A completely irresistible and award-winning thriller
by an exciting new writer.

ALMOST TRUE
Keren David

Ruthless killers are hunting Ty. The police move him
and his mum to a quiet seaside town.
But a horrific attack and a bullet meant for Ty
prove that he's not safe yet.

On the road again, Ty's in hiding with complete
strangers . . . who seem to know a lot about him.
Meanwhile he's desperate to see his girlfriend Claire,
and terrified that she may betray him. Ty can't trust
his own judgement and he's making dangerous
decisions that could deliver him straight to
the gangsters.

**A thrilling sequel to *When I Was Joe*, shot through
with drama and suspense.**